Reuchmaire:

Ju Ju and the Mammy Queen

by

E. Q. Rainey

PublishAmerica
Baltimore

First printing

ISBN: 1-4137-3615-7
PUBLISHED BY PUBLISHAMERICA, LLLP
www.publishamerica.com
Baltimore

Printed in the United States of America

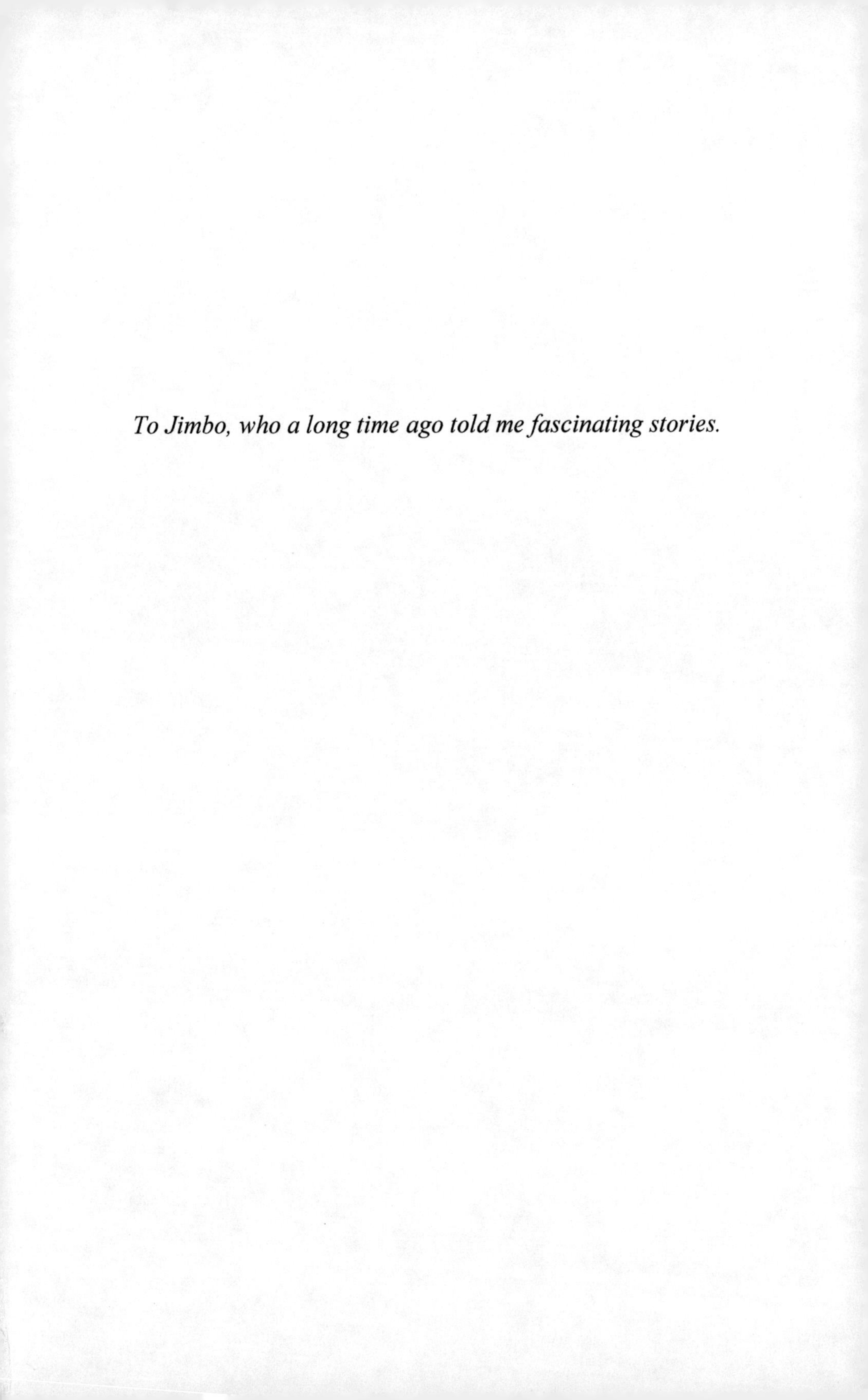

To Jimbo, who a long time ago told me fascinating stories.

Acknowledgements

Many thanks to Queen Quet Marquetta L. Goodwine, of the Gullah/ Geechie Sea Island Coalition on St. Helena Island, SC. Queen Quet, Chieftess of the Gullah/Geechie Nation, helped me name, and translated the dialect of, the Gullah characters in this story, and advised me on other aspects of Gullah society. Notably, the titular Mammy Queen. It is a name of great respect among Gullah (and among today's Sierra Leonians who speak Krio, a language derived from Gullah by repatriated former slaves returning home).

Also, I could not have gotten to Ms. Goodwine, and thence to Gullah, without the help of my good friend Sue Hutchings, of Kerrville, CA, who supplied the Krio, remembered from her Peace Corps years in Sierra Leone, for Ms. Goodwine to translate into Gullah.

This work would have not begun without the inspiration and assistance of my cousin, Jim Quattlebaum, of Beaufort, SC, who a long time ago introduced me to story telling with his own imaginative yarns. Jim even claims to have seen the fictitious J. Beauregard Reuchmaire, the protagonist of this story, strolling the streets of Beaufort accompanied by his Yorkie.

Foreword

The Sea Islands of South Carolina are ancient barrier islands, composed mostly of sedimentary shale and marine deposits covered with sand dunes, and called barrier for the protection they offer from the assault of the sea on the tidelands just inland. In South Carolina, these tidelands and the Sea Islands are known as the Lowcountry, or Low Country, as you may choose. It is a flowery, piquant, semi-tropical land of serpentine waterways and salt grass prairies bounded by and sprinkled with thick growths of oak, pine and palmetto. Here thrive feather, fur, fin, and shell nurtured by a rich brackish broth of seawater come inland to flush the land. The land abounds with life, and with death.

The people here speak a drawl easy on the ear, and despite its distinctly Southern terms is American English. Among the people are descendants of Africans imported as slaves. They are called Gullah, both the people and the language they speak. The language is an amalgamation of African tribal dialects and English, formed by strangers in a strange land forced to adapt to conditions they did not choose. This unwritten language, Gullah, survives today in the Lowcountry. I chose to leave it intact in the text rather than streamlining, or "Hollywoodizing" it. I think the reader can figure it out with little difficulty.

The Gullah in this story play pivotal roles, and their Gullah dialect is just as you would hear it if you were to travel to the Lowcountry and to Beaufort, South Carolina, where this mystery takes place.

I hope the residents of Beaufort will forgive me for slight variations and creations I made in the layout of their charming town. It was done solely for the purposes of this story, which is after all, fictional, as are the characters.

Chapter 1

The Queen sat on the porch of her house and smoked a corncob pipe of her own creation. Her ample body overflowed an old wooden rocker and she shifted occasionally to a more comfortable position. She wore a bright cotton dress, the kind she wore in summer when she made cordgrass baskets and sold them in Beaufort, down on Bay Street by the old Revolutionary War houses. The pipe was taken briefly from her mouth to spit onto the dirt of the yard. Several of her chickens scurried over to investigate then returned to their strutting and scratching. She was old, her hair a crown of gray wool, but her eyes were bright and shrewd. Her skin, wrinkled in many places, still held its dark luster. A breeze rustled pines and oaks around the house, tinkled her coquina earrings, and moved out over a vast salt meadow. She watched it press the cordgrass down in slow waves as it worked toward the bend of a tidal channel. To her people she was the Mammy Queen, *de Mamma ob dese islands*. She was sage of sages, arbitrator, judge and jury, and weaver of black magic, *de juju*. All respected her power and wisdom. She felt the Lowcountry in her bones, in her blood felt the creep of tides in their endless cycles, bringing life and taking it. In her breath the seasons came and went. Nothing in this land changed without her knowing.

The Queen was resting while she watched dark clouds build on the horizon. Collards picked, washed and chopped were in the pot with a slab of hog-jowl, corn bread in the oven. Yard swept, house cleaned, she took time to enjoy a day too temperate for December, but summer seemed to have forgotten fall. From beneath the porch came the contented sigh of a sleeping dog.

“Oona sleep, Old Bones,” she said. “Sleep good, caze deys a storm comin’. De change gwine come, and de rich mon be gwine die.”

A coal-black cat with yellow eyes hopped onto the porch and rubbed against the rocker. Mammy Queen reached down and stroked the silky fur, jingling seashell bracelets on her arms. "Ain' dat so, Amos? Oona know it be de true, caze oona tol it to me. And dat good doctah, Doctah ROCKmo', he be done fin out how. But he need hep. It be come time fo' de juju."

* * *

Not far across the salt marshes and waterways from the Queen's house lies the town of Beaufort, South Carolina. There talk and action are slow and smooth and nothing of any note has happened since the Civil War when the town was occupied by Yankees. Nothing unusual was ever expected to happen in Beaufort, discounting, that is, the schemes and illicit activities of Bull Goldfield, Beaufort's billionaire.

Along Bay Street, Beaufort's main drag, strolled Dr. J. Beauregard Reuchmaire. Beyond trim but short of portly, the good doctor of psychiatry stepped lightly and tapped cadence with a jade-handled umbrella. To heel trotted a bright-eyed Yorkie exuding an air of superiority.

The doctor was on his evening stroll. As usual he was lost in thought, tonight unpleasant thoughts about Bull Goldfield. Goldfield had a pair of antique dueling pistols the doctor wanted, and wanted badly. Earlier that day he went out to Goldfield's mansion and made a generous offer. Goldfield refused with an expletive and a guffaw that rattled every vertebra of Reuchmaire's spine. Reuchmaire refused to stoop to Goldfield's coarseness, repressed his anger, and left. Now he was mulling what he should have said but was glad he hadn't. A gust of wind and a roll of thunder startled him. "Well, General Stuart," he said to the Yorkie, "we had best beat a hasty retreat to the house."

The General agreed with a sharp yip.

"Just one thing I wish to attend to first." Reuchmaire stopped in front of a recently opened art gallery. A new gallery, perhaps new paintings. He loved marshscapes of the Lowcountry. On a business card, he wrote by his name, "pronounced ROCKmore," and inserted it in the door beside the CLOSED sign. “Now, General Stuart, let’s be off.”

Neon flashes lit the tidal marshes beyond the river followed by enormous peals of thunder. Dust swirled, trash flew, trees bent, and wires hummed along Bay Street. Merchants, customers, the few December tourists, and Dr. Reuchmaire with General Stuart, scurried to their cars and homes.

* * *

Windows rattled in the Goldfield mansion at the edge of town. Here the river, more of a wide tidal flow than an actual river, made the southward of two bends that embraced the mansion and Beaufort itself in a large U before it turned south again to flow past Port Royal down to the Sound. The only light in the main house shone from a second-story bedroom onto strands of moss swaying in old oaks. Silhouetted in a French window, one hand casually upon the border of velvet drapes, a stocky, middle-aged man watched the storm roil the normally placid river.

Bull Goldfield lit a cheroot and smiled. He stretched contentedly and ran a hand through gray hair scattered with dark strands. There’ll be storm enough in here shortly, he mused. Isadora was dressed finally and sat at the vanity repairing the dishevelment of illicit passion. Why was it that women were so slow to get dressed after sex? Of course, she was dragging this out, not wanting to leave. But she didn’t know the half of it. Too bad this was the last time. She had been fun.

Isadora pulled a brush through her dark hair with slow, even strokes and forced herself to remain calm. This was not going as planned. She had to keep Bull occupied until Fast Nickie got in and out, and she had told him to come after midnight. Keeping Bull occupied was not a problem. He really was an expert in bed, and she was startled when he finished and abruptly got up to get dressed. As she eyed him from the vanity she sensed an impatience foreign to their trysts. He had *that look.*

Putting on her best pout, she said, “I thought I could spend the night.”

Bull shook his head and answered in his gravelly Southern drawl, eh's and ah's and long i's thick as the nuts fallen from the hickories along the south wall. His speech was a raspy abomination of the smooth and pleasant Lowcountry brogue. "Too chancy. Annabell will be back tomorrow. She might show up early."

Hers, a Manhattan-flavored alto, was a crisp and sexy contrast. "My car's down at Pigeon Point. I'll go out the tunnel before daylight, just as I came in. Who'll see?"

"Nah. Anyhow, we need to end it."

The hairbrush stopped. She turned, eyes wide in a face draining of color. An upturned nose and pinched mouth, although not unattractive, gave a comic effect to her dismay. "What did you say?"

He took a drag, savored it, and let go the smoke while lightning rippled over the river. He felt the electricity in the air and he loved it.

Her voice rose an octave. "Bull, I asked—"

"I heard you." It was like playing a marlin. Ease the line until the pressure hits, then strain and reel for all you're worth. So, let's pull the line and let her fight. She could carry on all she wanted, but he had the gaff. He knew about her scam, and it burned deep that he had been taken in. But, had *he* taken *her* in. Oh, yes, *had* he. Just like all the rest, she ate up flattery and promises, flowers at the right time and maybe a necklace or two. He turned to face her. "I said, it's over."

She blinked. "Over?"

"You catch on quick."

Her mouth worked at the words while the hand with the hairbrush descended to her side. "But, what about us? You said—"

He laughed. They all said the same things, almost word for word. "I thought it over, decided it won't work. Divorce? Nah! Annabelle would make a stink, get the estate, half my money. I like you, baby, but I like money better."

She rose and moved toward him among ante-bellum pieces, mostly antique, some reproductions, all expensive. She tried to smile. "Bull, you said you loved me…said you'd marry me." The words sounded foolish, school-girlish, but she couldn't help it. She had really believed him, had actually fallen for him, as much as she could fall for any man.

His lips tightened into a thin amused line.

She stopped before him, an inch taller, control over him ebbing with each moment. She searched his eyes for some indication he was kidding. All she saw was ice. She felt sick. Her plans teetered on the brink of an abyss. He was her ticket out of the art scam she and Fast Nickie ran. He was a ticket to an easy life as a billionaire's wife, basking on a yacht instead of constantly looking over her shoulder for some P.I. or tec.

"Bull, talk to me! You can't mean this." Tears, at least partly sincere, welled in her eyes.

"Can't I? Listen, bitch, Goldfields have lived in this house for two hundred and fifty years, so I'm not about to risk losing it over some two-bit con artist."

"Two-bit con artist? You bastard!" She drew back a hand for a blow.

He grabbed her jaw with one powerful hand. "I said it's over. *Kaput. Finis*. I've had all of you I want in every way I want. You breathe one word of this to anyone and I'll have you put away for a long, long time. I know how you doctor paintings, make an expensive original look fake. Then you replace it with a copy, restore the original and sell it again and again. Real slick. But you shouldn't have tried it with Bull Goldfield. I'm too sharp for you, and I don't like to be duped. Now get your coat and haul that pretty ass out of here."

"You can't do this!" She pounded his chest.

He laughed and flung her back.

A wild swing landed a fist on an iron jaw. She fell back, gripping her hand.

He took another drag. "That the best you can do?"

"No." She backed away. "I can do better." She reached into her purse and leveled a nickel plated automatic at his chest.

"Hey, don't play games." The cheroot fell to the floor as he edged toward the door.

"*You* don't dump *me*, you..." He had tricked her and tricked her bad. She had actually fallen for him, believed all his lies. Now they were so abominably clear. But nobody dupes Isadora Hawthorn. Particularly not this womanizing bastard with his honey tongue. It thrilled her to see he knew she would kill him.

Thunder shook the house. The lights flickered and went out. She let the gun drift to her side as if it were a serpent coiling to strike. Another flash froze him stereoscopically as he reached for the door. Darkness returned. The door slammed open and his footsteps retreated down the hall towards the atrium. Rain roared across the roof.

She found the door and waited. Her breath was steady and deep, her pulse a low drumbeat in her ears. A series of flashes flooded the glassed atrium, the paneled upper hall, the wide staircase, draperies, framed portraits, and Bull, about to flee downstairs. She raised the gun and fired.

* * *

Fast Nickie Macchetto pressed his slender frame into the shadows of the servant's quarters and watched the storm sweep across marsh and river towards the estate. Thunder boomed in the distance.

Perfect, he thought. Just perfect. The storm will cover me while I'm inside and the rain will wash out any tracks. I won't even have to watch where I step.

He checked his watch. Eight-fifteen. A trickle of sweat ran down his back although the night was cool and each blast of air from the storm cooled it further. Isadora would be pissed if she knew he had decided on his own to come ahead of schedule. She was too careful sometimes. Told him to come after midnight when the moon was down. Moon, no moon, he was just as good. A cat burglar like the movies called it, quiet and quick. Like Cary Grant in "To Catch a Thief." A real pro. But earlier, as he passed time in a cheap motel over in Bluffton — close enough to be convenient; far enough to be inconspicuous — he had seen the weather report and knew the storm would be perfect cover. Why lose sleep working late at night? He could get in, hit the safe, and be out in thirty minutes, maybe less. Then back for a good night's sleep after a few drinks at a dive he fancied. There was a waitress there who had come on to him. Maybe he could get more than sleep. Isadora would never know, upstairs with Goldfield, just as planned. "I'll screw him to sleep and stay with him to be sure he doesn't interrupt you, in case you make any noise. The butler sleeps in the quarters, so he's no worry."

In case he makes any noise. That irked Nickie. How long had they worked together, four, five years? Well, before he went up this last time. And that wasn't his fault. Some asshole squealed on him. But it wasn't because he, Fast Nickie Macchetto, had made any noise.

They had a great scheme. Isadora as an art dealer could get into a rich guy's home and case the joint to find the location of the safe — those guys really did hang a painting over the safe, just like in the movies. Then she set up the hit with him as the yegg. Yegg. He liked that word, got it from some movie he had seen, an old black and white with George Raft. Isadora knew art and he knew safes. Hadn't found one he couldn't crack. And he never made any noise. There was the bonus, too. A cut from Isadora's scam. She doctors the paintings of that numbnuts in New York who lets her handle his work but never checks on her. Some hoity-toity artiste named Gaetano too full of himself to worry about money, so she sends him the profit from the first sale, then sells and resells the original to rich guys who know how to make money but don't know shit about art. But she's careful. "Never more than three times, maybe less depending on how it feels, always a small town far away from the last, always someone stupid and rich," she warned. "Then get another painting and do it again."

A blast of storm-cold air pressed him against the building and brought with it the smell of marsh and rain. Nickie checked the time again. Over thirty minutes since the butler left the mansion for the servant's quarters. He's settled, time to get busy. He eased into the shadows under the covered walk to the mansion. He was a shadow among shadows, black from sneakers to ski mask and gloves. Lightning flashed, coming closer. The door was easy. He had it picked and was inside in seconds and neutralized the security system with the code Isadora gave him.

The kitchen was dark. He eased toward the den just off the wide staircase that led upstairs. The den held the safe Isadora had found behind the portrait of Goldfield's great-great-grandfather. He moved with the flashes, as the eerie blue light showed him the route ahead, and in the intervening darkness used a tiny pen light. The gloves came off, pocketed, so he could work the safe. There was an almost sexual pleasure of entering uninvited and undetected into someone's home. Like doing it to a sleeping woman.

When he reached the lower hall the house shook with a peal of thunder and he stopped, astounded at what he saw. Goldfield's famous gun collection adorned the walls of the foyer. Nickie wasn't much for guns, preferring the knife to intimidate. But he had never cut anyone. Only a threat. You threaten some guy with a gun, he might shoot first. But a knife would stop 'em, make 'em think, give you a chance to get away. But this display was impressive.

Handguns, rifles, shotguns, flintlocks, old and new, in every conceivable shape and size, festooned cabinets, walls, and shelves of polished oak in the foyer and continued into other rooms. The place looked like a gun store, like a museum. A set of ornate dueling pistols, filigreed metal and polished wood, caught his eye. Mounted upright in their antique case, each asked to be held, balanced, and sighted. Fascinated by their beauty he hefted one of the pair, surprised at its weight. He wondered if anyone had been killed with those. They came from a long time ago, when guys went out and had duels. Stood apart and shot at each other, just like in the movies. He shivered. He could never face someone only yards away with a gun, calmly taking aim to fire while the other was doing the same.

He heard something!

Muffled voices came from upstairs. His neck hairs prickled. Across the hall, almost hidden in the thunder, an eerie squeak sounded. Should he get out and forget the safe? Upstairs a door banged open. What the hell was going on? Another flash. A man up there ran towards the stairs. Goldfield! Nickie's chest tightened. He needed time…how?

The pistol! Fire a shot. Not to hit him, just to scare him back. Give time to get out. Forget the safe and get out. He raised the gun. Nothing! The trigger was loose. He remembered it had to be cocked. In his panic he barely managed to get the hammer back. A long series of flashes silhouetted Goldfield against the atrium at the top of the stairs. Nickie threw the gun up and fired.

* * *

Annabelle Goldfield leaned against the wall of the tunnel. She shivered in her mackinaw, knit cap and woolen clothes, but from the task at hand as much as from the cold. The beam of her flashlight penetrated the narrow darkness only a few feet. She felt as though she moved through a starless universe. She thought of the people past who had fled down this tunnel. In the Revolutionary War, Goldfield ancestors as they slipped away from British patrols; in the Civil War, slaves who ran to the river to start the journey north up the Underground Railway. Legend had it that the ghost of a slave shot by Goldfield's great-grandfather haunted the tunnel and sometimes uttered plaintive moans that could be heard up in the house. She whirled at a sound as a rat scurried into a crevice. It was a tunnel built for rebels, used by rebels, and now she, a rebel against her husband's years of faithlessness, reversed the direction to come up from the river and into the mansion. She came up to kill her husband. A pistol trembled in her hand.

Even in her anguish she moved with a certain grace, with an air of sophistication. How reasonable it had seemed. Could her aristocratic mother and father believe it? Never! She hardly believed it herself. But she had good reason. Finally she would get revenge for her husband's years of philandering. He bedded women from Beaufort to Shanghai without the least regard for her feelings, and often flaunted his latest conquest in her face. In her staid old South Carolina family, divorce was not an option. She was patient, hoping he would grow out of it, and even countered with a few affairs of her own. But she was always discrete, unlike her husband. The resentment had been there for a long, long time.

At her Thanksgiving party a week ago Bull had openly flirted with Isadora Hawthorne, the art dealer recently arrived in Beaufort. Annabelle knew he had been seeing her almost since the day she arrived, and she was furious that he would so mockingly ruin her party.

Until then it had been clandestine. But Bull never kept his liaisons secret for long. To him it was a game to taunt her as he played his paramour like a fish only to eventually dump the beguiled woman.

He announced to the crowd of guests mingling on the lawn that Isadora wanted to learn scuba diving and escorted her to his yacht moored at the estate's dock. They were gone for hours. He returned smug as a cat, twirling his gold key chain, a habit he knew infuriated her. He announced that Ms. Hawthorne had a touch of *mal de mer* and he would drive her home. They left with the slut attached to Bull's arm. A longtime friend sidled up to Annabelle and whispered, "Why don't you kill him?" That was when it all fell into place. "I think I will," she said. Her friend had no idea she was serious.

Annabelle shivered again in the damp tunnel and checked her watch. Almost eight-thirty. He had told her he had work to do tonight and wanted to be left alone. So she went off in her own yacht and anchored three miles south in Port Royal Sound, something she often did when he was in one of his moods. But now she was back and by now Wilson would be in quarters and the mansion quiet. She pressed her ear to the secret door into the house. The key turned easily in the lock.

The ancient hinges complained briefly as she swung the door open to emerge below the main staircase. Behind her the door, disguised as a tall cabinet, swung slowly closed and the latch clicked into place. The house was dark. A long rumble of thunder was just fading away. She moved to the base of the stairs and found the familiar outline of the newel post. Across the hall there was no light in the den where she expected him to be. He must be upstairs — good God! What if *she's* here? Would even Bull have the gall to bring her into this house? Of course he would! That was why he wanted "to be alone." Voices came down from the bedroom. Did something move across the foyer? Wilson? She turned to flee back down the tunnel. Before she could, a door upstairs slammed open. Footsteps sounded from above. A long series of flashes brought to her startled eyes the figure of Bull at the top of the stairs. Her heart fluttered in her throat as she raised the pistol and fired.

Chapter 2

Earlier that same day, someone else had been interested in the Goldfield estate.

Reuben Conner sat perched in the skeleton of an immense storm-washed tree embedded in the beach of Repository Cove. Out in the Beaufort River channel a shrimper, trawls out, a cloud of gulls in its wake, growled homeward. He had climbed ape-like into the tree with powerful arms and shoulders, his prosthetic legs useful only for support. Beached beneath the tree was the boat he had rowed down the river from Pigeon Point. Working against the tide had raised a sweat and his shirt was open to the southerly breeze coming up from Port Royal Sound.

Across the River lay the Goldfield estate, Riverbriar. Poised on a bluff, white Georgian columns gleaming in the late afternoon sun, the mansion was the lone centerpiece on this stretch of the river, and the focus of Reuben's attention.

To the west lightning and thunder from a bank of dark clouds announced the first big front of the fall. The air had already cooled, although it had been a pleasant day for December: sunny, temperature just into the seventies, and a light breeze.

Reuben's hard eyes locked on the mansion and he cursed Bull Goldfield with every obscenity gleaned from five years as a Marine. He had not killed in a long time, not since Viet Nam where he left two legs and a career in the Corps. Bull Goldfield was a man who needed killing.

He pulled an unopened bottle of bourbon from his pocket and propped it in the fork of the tree. He appraised the bottle as one might an old friend. Down deep he knew it was anything but. He could smash it against the tree and watch the contents and shattered glass cascade down to the sand. Or he could open it and feel the burn of the liquid down his throat, feel the warmth spread and numb his mind to unwelcome thoughts. Thoughts that terrified and disoriented him. He hardly remembered buying the bottle, only a few hours earlier, blinded as he was by rage after Goldfield had thrown him off Riverbriar. Bad enough that with two artificial legs he was no match for Goldfield, but to be humiliated in front of his daughter was worse. And after Goldfield made a play for her — Cissy! And she only thirteen. The rage returned as the scene replayed in his mind: Goldfield as he came out of the mansion with his arm around her, she there to collect for her paper route, trying to pull away, while he talked in her ear and let his hand roam where it shouldn't. Reuben, hired by Goldfield as gardener, was below them trimming azaleas.

Reuben lapsed into another long string of obscenities. Bad enough that bastard played around with grown women, but children? His Cissy? He had exploded up out of the garden and mounted the stairs on metal and plastic legs only to be hurled back down by Goldfield and ordered to leave. And beyond today's humiliation there burned in his mind the memory of Cissy's older sister, Cassy, dead now three years, her body found in this very cove. Had Goldfield done it?

His hand dropped to where he used to keep his combat knife in his boot. But it was years gone, along with his legs. And Doc Reuchmaire had taken his gun. Maybe he could get another.

The strange electric sensation began. It came up from his heart and spread out in a wave, just as it had years ago when he had the gun and was going to shoot Hildy that day when he really felt the need to stop her. Stop her vulgar, violent attacks on Cissy that demeaned her so, just as he felt when he was the object of Hildy's scorn. Hildy deluged him with insults day after day, hour after hour, until he had to find a way to end it. That was when he realized the gun was in his hand and that he was going for her just to get the meanness off her face, to make things easier for Cissy and himself. And then Doc Reuchmaire appeared with that little, friendly, apologetic smile that said things were really okay and reached out a hand for the gun, not insisting, but in a way that made him feel that it was what he should do. Hand it over and let Doc deal with it. He did, and a flood of relief told him he had done the right thing.

He saw Doc was pleased with him and it was going to be all right.

Hildy was mean even before they were married, back when he needed to get over Nam and the loss of his legs, every day a struggle to escape the pit of post-trauma. Mean, but available. He was too depressed to notice. When pregnancy forced marriage on them, he began to see just how abusive she was. To him, to Cassy, and to Cissy when she came along. She got worse after Cassy's death, and he did too. Back to the bottle and the terrible rages Doc Reuchmaire helped him get over. It took a long time, but at last he was out of it. For good, he felt.

His mind slid from that memory to another. He was back in Nam, his platoon under ambush, surrounded by explosions. Men dove for cover; some died as they did. The lieutenant tried to organize a withdrawal but went down with an arm blown away. Reuben saw a marine drop. He got to him and got him on his back and headed for the rear while bullets and fragments whistled past. The weight of the man and gear was almost too much but he made it through the fire and confusion all the way back to their lines. Friendly arms pointed directions. Safety was within reach when he stepped on the mine. One of their own for God's sake! A terrific blow slammed upward through his legs and hurled him into the air. Everything was confused. He felt so weak. While they tourniqueted his bloody, mangled legs he saw the man he had rescued, his back laid open by shrapnel and his organs showing. He had been dead the whole time. That was the last he remembered before he passed out.

He emerged from the vision. A warm satisfaction washed away the electricity. He had done all he could even though the man was dead, just as Doc Reuchmaire had told him again and again until he believed it. He had done all he could.

The shrimper had gone and the channel was empty. Waves from the long wake slapped gently on the sand. In the distance thunder rumbled. The clouds over the marshes rose into big, brilliant cauliflower heads and seemed to jostle one another in a race for the town. Be rain tonight and cold tomorrow. The real start of winter. But with the perversity of this semi-tropical Lowcountry weather it would likely warm again in a day or so and make mockery of the Christmas decorations beginning to appear.

He had begun his career down here, at Parris Island, just down the river. Something about the wide stretches of water and marsh rippled by unhindered breezes, so different from the rolling Georgia Piedmont where he grew up, drew him back. Or maybe it was the memory of what he had and what he loved, the Corps, before he lost his legs. But all through the pain and discouragement and tedium of rehabilitation, he knew when he got finished, this was where he would settle.

He picked up the bottle of bourbon. The cap twisted off easily. He let the contents sprinkle down onto the sand. He drew back his arm to throw the empty bottle into the river. Then he remembered what Cissy would say about the environment. He smiled, and his dark eyes softened and the harsh lines around his mouth relaxed. She was the sensible one. She brought conviction and stability to his life. How could she be so different from her mother? What did it matter? Hildy was out of their life, divorced from him and gone back to her family in Alabama, and he didn't care as long as she was away from them. He pocketed the bottle and stared across the river at the mansion for a long time. Finally he swung down out of the tree and untied the boat. He needed to get across before the storm hit.

As he pulled across the river his heavy shoulder muscles rippled beneath the thin shirt. Aided by his long smooth strokes, the small boat scurried along before the breeze from the sound. The storm's arrival would reverse and build the wind after which the trip across would be difficult without a motor. The route to Pigeon Point Landing took him close in to the estate, where he slowed and eased along a short distance off the high bank. Rumor had it that there was a secret entrance along here. He came to a storm-wrecked framework of a Civil War dock used by privateers evading the Yankee blockade. It had last been active in the twenties when the Goldfields ran illegal whisky. A few pilings still showed above water, but at high tide only eddies marked their position.

Cissy said kids used to slip around the boundary fence and dive off the dock until the time Goldfield scared them off with a shotgun, wounding a kid in the process. They never returned and a year later a hurricane demolished the structure. He backed water at the dock, a likely place for an entrance, but found nothing. Resuming his way along the shore he spied through a stand of marsh grass a low stone ramp and above it a path descending the bank, both nearly obscured by undergrowth.

He grounded the boat onto the slope of the ramp and got out. The door was cypress and looked old, but the hinges had little corrosion and were cleaned and oiled. He tugged at the round iron handle. The door thumped against the lock, but would not open. Close inspection revealed faint scars around the keyhole indicating recent use.

The path up the bank was faint and partially overgrown, with a few footprints all but weathered away. He went up the path just high enough to peer over the edge. There was the mansion not two hundred yards away, an easy shot with a scope.

He went back down and stared at the door with fierce intensity as though his sight could throw it open. Behind him the storm clouds rose and obscured the sun.

Chapter 3

Dr. Reuchmaire was bundled against the cold in a huge fur-lined Russian coat and black woolen hat, refugees with him from his profitable, and until three years past, enjoyable, career as a psychiatrist in the nation's capital. But his blood was Southern, by birth and preference, and he shivered even beneath the warm clothes. It was so unusually cold that Captain Semmes had refused to accompany him into town, the cat preferring to remain at home curled on the sofa.

General Stuart had been persuaded to come along, reluctantly, even though protected by his very own doggie coat, a wee woolen Union Jack appropriate to his Yorkshire heritage and purchased by his master on one of his semi-annual trips to England and Europe. In spite of the protection, General Stuart was not pleased with the cold. He pranced in agitated circles around the doctor's feet, his mincing steps seemingly an attempt to minimize contact of each tiny paw with the frigid concrete. His tiny jaws, tilted upward as though a wolf baying at the moon, emitted an ear-splitting howl, astounding in such a small dog. The doctor called it the General's Rebel Yell. Marla, Dr. Reuchmaire's girlfriend, called it a primal scream. The rest of Beaufort said it was an Excedrin headache.

"Tsst, General Stuart, tsst." Reuchmaire absently gave the leash a gentle tug. The doctor's hearing was not what it used to be, and he was not as appreciative, so to speak, as the general populace of the piercing wail. Also, he loved the little dog and felt, as owners of offensive pets often do, that the General could do no wrong. The Yorkie raised his plaint to an even higher level.

Reuchmaire tuned out the wail (something only he could do) and cocked his head one way and another to try to find a favorable angle from which to view the oddly colored marshscape behind the window his breath was fogging. The late morning sun, unsullied by the clouds being carried out over the Atlantic by the departing storm, cast images onto the glass from the quaint storefronts across Bay Street. The pastel reflections nearly obscured the painting, but he could see the hues were bright, almost garish, and not at all like the real marshes in the Lowcountry. There were purples and reds and magentas, an unusually dull green, perhaps as a counterpoint to the brighter accents, and a pale yellow sky. He sighed, straightened, and brought out a handkerchief to clear his glasses. "Interpretism! Modern impressionism." Leaning close for another look, he could not believe what he saw.

"That is a fake. Cleverly done, but none the less, a forgery. *Sacre!*" He punctuated his comment with a pop on the sidewalk with his jade-handled umbrella, careful to miss General Stuart who was circling left at the moment, still in full voice. A frown, rare on the doctor's pleasant features, appeared above hazel-brown eyes from which compassion flowed for patients, friends, acquaintances and just about anyone other than Bull Goldfield. Reuchmaire, at last aware of General Stuart's irritation, turned to the Yorkie, oblivious to the Rebel Yell which continued unabated. The only change was that General Stuart ceased to prance and sat, his muzzle aimed directly at his master.

"Tsst, General Stuart, here." Reuchmaire searched the pockets of his voluminous coat and brought forth a small paper bag from which he extracted something he knew would quiet the General. Stooping to the small dog's level, he held out a chocolate covered bourbon ball.

The uluation abruptly ceased. General Stuart inspected the morsel. Taking it carefully between his teeth he sprawled terrier fashion, rear legs splayed backward, and began to gnaw contentedly.

"The problem with small town galleries," Reuchmaire said to the happily chewing General, "is the limited selection. Limited selection and the ease with which the unscrupulous can cheat the ignorant. Unless, of course, some particularly talented and prolific artist selects a town such as Beaufort." During his three years of semi-retired psychiatric practice here such had not happened.

It was that practice which had enabled him to become somewhat of an art critic, a vocation for which he had not been schooled. One of his recent patients, a pleasant young man with nothing worse than an obsessive-compulsive personality, spent hours on the couch (actually in a chair) describing in intimate detail the nuances of painting. It served to avoid the real issues milling about in his subconscious, which Reuchmaire knew were an overprotective mother and a possessive wife. Although Reuchmaire found the discourses on painting rather interesting, he dutifully steered the young man back to the issues at hand and an eventual confrontation and resolution of his anxieties. But in the process Reuchmaire became educated in the various techniques used in art, of which he otherwise would be ignorant. Some of these he discovered were for less than honorable purposes.

In daily life, Reuchmaire often seemed distracted, or absent-minded. In fact he had a keen mind, high intellect, and a rapier-like wit, which he was ordinarily too polite to unleash. He bit his tongue rather than skewer some deserving oaf. He was as competent as anyone who practiced his profession and more so than most, but often lost himself in thought, mulling things Oedipal or anal retentive, while busy with errands or other daily habits. He walked into automatic glass doors that opened too slowly, pushed a door clearly labeled pull, or wrestled with the wrong side of doors with those confusing horizontal bars for handles which gave no indication of direction.

He squinted through the window at the placard beneath the painting. "Why, some fool has bought it."

The fool, the card noted, was Bull Goldfield. Goldfield was entrepreneur, gun collector, self-appointed authority on any subject under discussion, and heir to the Goldfield financial empire built from indigo, rice and cotton by his forebears. Little of these former staples of the Lowcountry was grown these days, but Goldfield subsisted opulently on the fortune (wallowed in it, Reuchmaire declared). It was a privilege the billionaire would take to the grave with him, since, having avowed no use for children, he had none — at least not by his wife of twenty years.

Reuchmaire pursed his lips at his reflection in the window of the town's newest and most prestigious art gallery owned, the card noted, by Isadora Hawthorne of New York. *Merde!* Another dishonest carpetbagger come south. Perhaps he should inform Mr. Goldfield that he was being duped. But Reuchmaire still smarted from yesterday's attempt to purchase from the obstinate billionaire the set of superbly preserved dueling pistols believed by Reuchmaire to have once belonged to a Reuchmaire forefather. Reuchmaire was still smarting from Goldfield's coarse refusal.

"Well," Reuchmaire decided, "he can bloody well look out for himself." He reset his hat at a jaunty angle and checked his reflection. Thanksgiving had indeed added a few pounds. Ah, but it's exaggerated by the coat. Yes, definitely the coat. Obviously the coat. Nothing to worry about. After Christmas — certainly not before turkey with oyster stuffing and Marla's special brandy-cranberry sauce — he would rejoin the health club he rejoined every January. By the end of February he would again be down to a hundred and sixty. Give or take five pounds. Maybe ten. And probably give. Maybe fifteen. Above what his doctor wanted, but a figure — and eating style — at which he felt comfortable.

Overall he was quite content. If not the best psychiatrist in Beaufort, and perhaps all the Lowcountry, he considered himself among the best. He was friendly, polite, a good conversationalist (he knew how to listen) and had no vices other than the tendency to curse in French, a product of his twice yearly vacations in Europe. With a comfortable and enjoyable job, and a vivacious girlfriend, life was good and he was home. The last thing in the world he considered himself to be was a sleuth.

He had a tidily short beard, which he allowed only himself to trim. Or occasionally Marla when she begged — he loved it when she begged. It had just the right amount of gray to look Freudianly distinguished, and that, he insisted, appealed to patients. He hooked the polished jade handle of his umbrella — a constant companion, rain or shine — over a forearm and began to search his pockets. A pair of small scissors appeared in delicate fingers. He could have been a surgeon but for his distaste for blood (he had passed out cold at his first operation in medical school). He began to trim a few errant hairs.

At that moment a scream broke the morning calm. General Stuart's ears pricked up. Down the street Reuchmaire caught a flash of movement. A small, wiry man leapt onto an idling motorcycle, the strap of a woman's purse slung over his shoulder. A screech of tires left the woman waving frantically on the sidewalk. Thief and machine hurtled in Reuchmaire's direction.

"The blackguard," said Reuchmaire, and slipped the end of General Stuart's leash over the gallery's doorknob. He moved quickly between two parked cars and braced a foot on a bumper. The effort would take all of his five feet five inches. As the cyclist shot past, Reuchmaire hooked umbrella handle in purse strap and hung on. The rider gave an anguished yelp and landed with a thud at Reuchmaire's feet. The riderless bike clipped a lamp post, jarring loose one of the city's newly hung Christmas wreaths, then circled to return like an obedient horse where it fell to a sputtering halt.

Reuchmaire rubbed his arthritic right shoulder. Naturally it had to be the one to bear the worst shock. He peered into the mousy face of the culprit. "Well, well, Fast Nickie Macchetto. I see your kleptomania is acting up again. That will get you another three to five at Allendale."

The thief's eyes bulged and he gasped for breath. A hand snaked inside the motorcycle jacket and a knife flashed in the sunlight.

"Tch, tch, Fast Nickie. Armed, also. That's a bad boy — and ten to twenty." Reuchmaire spanked the umbrella's handle against the threatening hand to send the knife skidding. The doctor brought forth a pair of manacles and linked the thief to the wheel of his vehicle.

Satisfied that the culprit was secure, Reuchmaire went over to the fallen purse and began to gather the spilled contents. A solitary key with an unusually large barrel and stem caught his eye. He dropped it into the bag along with a diamond-studded gold key ring and chain containing several conventional keys (the owner was no pauper), a wallet, a checkbook, an address book, an envelope containing what seemed to be money, a nail file, a compact, various other odds and ends indigenous to a woman's purse, plus a guillotine.

A crowd began to gather. The first to arrive was Police Chief "Harry" Doyle. His large, doughnut-enhanced frame trotted — as fast as he was ever known to move — from the direction of Blackstone's

Deli. He puffed with the effort, while the jowls of his friendly-hound-dog face worked on what Reuchmaire knew was a helping of breakfast waffles. Harry reholstered a phone with one hand and rested the other on the handle of his service automatic. He leaned over the prostrate form. "Whatcha got here, Doc?"

"Attempted robbery, Harry."

"Yeah, I saw it all. Nice work. I see you still have the bracelets I loaned you — say, you never did tell me why you wanted them."

"Um, never know when they might come in handy." No need to explain that he and Marla used them to play their slightly steamy version of cops and robbers. He quickly shifted back to the culprit. "Our friend here is Fast Nickie Machetto, A.K.A. Nickie the Cat, late of the state prison at Allendale and apparently soon to be again."

"Dr. Reuchmaire! Dr. Reuchmaire! Oh, how can I ever, EVER thank you!?" A tall, trim woman in a cashmere coat came clipping up on high heels. An upturned nose and pinched mouth gave a coquettish appeal to a face framed by a head scarf restraining unruly brunette locks. She appeared to be having a bad hair day.

Reuchmaire winced at the mispronunciation of his name, made worse by her accent and word inflection.

"Rock-more, madam," he corrected. "ROCK-more, not Roosh-mare."

"Oh, yes, I should have remembered. The excitement, I guess. I do apologize. EVERYONE knows you. You are THE best known doctor in town, and SO distinguished."

"Well, a common mistake." Reuchmaire smiled, smoothing his beard. The woman was a good judge of character. As grandfather Reuchmaire said, 'Everyone can recognize flattery, but no one can resist it.' He admitted he was no exception. "Your purse, madam. Perhaps you should check the contents."

"Oh, I'm sure it's all here." She glanced inside and extended a gloved hand. "I'm SO glad to meet you, and such a DRAMATIC introduction."

"You seem to know me, ma'am." Reuchmaire bent and brushed lips against doeskin. "You have me at a disadvantage."

She tittered at his flourish. "Why, a TRUE Southern gentleman. How gallant. I am Isadora Hawthorne, of New York."

She seemed to think he should know her. His mind was blank, but she was vaguely familiar.

When he failed to respond, she said, "Yesterday you left your card at my gallery. I make it a point to check on prospective customers, and well, EVERYONE knows you, and their description was just PERFECT. You must come by."

"Yes, well..." His interest in Ms. Hawthorne's gallery had ceased with his discovery of the copy in the window. Furthermore, this was not a flower of Southern womanhood he had rescued but an entrepreneuring carpetbagger. A dishonest one, at that. He should have let the thief go. He quickly chastised himself for such a thought — it was too late now, anyway.

"Oh, I can't take time now," she said, with a wave of her hand. "There's the hairdresser, and, ah, several other things. But please, please come by again. I just adore people who have a real interest in art. And I have a WON-derful selection. I know we can find something to please you." She tripped off with an over the shoulder wave and a pleasant, "Ta, ta."

A police cruiser hurtled around a corner and screeched to a halt, lights flashing. Out leapt a lanky young deputy with drawn gun.

"Dammit, Buster," Harry drawled, "put away the hardware. I said it wasn't an emergency. The Doc had the man down before I called you."

The chagrined youngster holstered the gun. "Well, heck, nothin' ever happens in this town. Only time I ever get to use the lights is on speeders, and we ain't had one of them in three months."

Harry sighed. "Just take him down and book him for attempted robbery."

"Armed robbery, Harry." Reuchmaire used a handkerchief to retrieve the knife.

"Oh, yeah. Thanks, Doc. And send Sam over with his wrecker to get the cycle."

Buster drove off with Nickie slumped in the back seat, and the crowd filtered away, leaving Reuchmaire and Harry to await Sam.

Hands deep in pockets, Harry stomped his feet to keep warm and narrowed his eyes into the expression he used when deep in thought. "So, what do you think, Doc?"

Reuchmaire quit trying to remember what it was about Isadora Hawthorne that seemed so familiar and brought his attention to the game. "I think…rook to Q - B five, takes knight."

Harry fished in a jacket pocket and found the dead stub of a cigar. "Ahh, Doc, what've I told you? The black queen. Always the black queen. She's the key." He put the stub in his mouth and began to chew on it. "That's your move, huh?"

Reuchmaire nodded firmly, although he knew he was in trouble. Harry didn't make mistakes, not at chess. A former high-income lawyer in a prestigious Atlanta firm, he was practiced at complex strategies and thinking on his feet. Five years, one ulcer, and a mild heart attack earlier Harry decided it wasn't worth it. He chucked the job, the Mercedes, the six-figure income, packed up wife and kids and came back to his home, the Lowcountry, and became Beaufort's enormously popular Chief of Police. Leaving the courtroom behind had not eroded his skills at chess.

Harry sighed. "Okay. Queen to Bishop seven. Mate in three moves, unless you're clever. But all you can do now is delay the inevitable."

Reuchmaire had once again blundered into one of Harry's traps. He ground the tip of his umbrella into the pavement to ease his irritation. "Don't you even want to study my move?"

"Tell you the truth, Doc, I was expecting it." He rubbed the back of his neck in an embarrassed gesture.

"Oh."

"Well, here's Sam," said Harry, as he began to wave pedestrians away with one large arm while guiding Sam in with the other.

Reuchmaire tried to assemble the chessboard in his mind. It was so hard to remember the board without his Chessmaster. He sighed dejectedly. Some people's talents lay in one direction, others elsewhere and his, he admitted, were not for spatial visualization. Particularly when his thoughts were so busy with other things — psychiatry, patients, the remarkable intricacy of the human mind, and what project

Marla might be cooking up to involve him in.

"So, what do you think, Harry?" he asked, as they watched Sam secure the cycle on the flatbed.

Harry took the cigar out of his mouth, looked at it, and replaced it. "Guess I'm not sure. Seems straightforward enough, but that Hawthorne lady gives me an itchy feeling."

"And when you itch, something ain't right."

Harry squinted after the departing wrecker. "Um hum, sometimes. And sometimes it's just a chigger bite. Anything of interest in her purse?"

"Just a rather unusual key and a guillotine."

"Come again?"

"A small one, like so." Reuchmaire held up index finger and thumb to indicate the size. "A novelty, for trimming cigar tips. Almost bought you one the last time I was in Paris."

"Only top quality cigars need clipping."

"That's why I brought you cognac."

"Guillotine. Funny thing for a woman to carry around."

"Maybe she smokes cigars. After all, sometimes a cigar is just a cigar."

"What?"

Reuchmaire smiled. "Nothing." He rubbed the fingers of his right hand together beneath his nose. "She does wear a most interesting fragrance. Most interesting. Well, I'm lunching with Marla. I'll come over Saturday and you can try to improve my game."

Reuchmaire departed with a jaunty wave. He retrieved General Stuart, snoring off the effects of the bourbon ball at the gallery, and sauntered off towards the Smith-Barney office, casually twirling the umbrella on one arm with the Yorkie cradled in the other. Humming "Bonnie Blue Flag" he paused the twirling to again bring to his nose the fingers of his hand that had clasped Ms. Hawthorne's. Where before had he smelled that sweet, penetrating odor?

Chapter 4

"Greedy, greedy, greedy!" Isadora Hawthorne glared at her reflection. She left the mirror in the rear of her gallery to pace up and down among oils and watercolors, glad for once to be free of customers. Back at the mirror she shook the key at her image and said, "I've told you over and over, 'Don't try for too much,' and yet you did. Now you've got this damned key and can't get rid of it. Worse, that nosy Dr. Reuchmaire knows you have it. Didn't he look into the purse before he returned it? He must have seen it."

She paused at a seascape slightly askew, one she had done herself but signed with Gaetano's name (he was absurdly easy to copy), straightened it, and resumed pacing. She had tried several times to dispose of the key. She thought of flushing it down the commode but feared that it would somehow clog the pipe. A plumber would wonder why such a key was there. She could have put it in the trash, but someone might stumble across it, perhaps a scavenger at the landfill, and trace it back to her. There was the river. But if someone saw her throw it in it might get back to Reuchmaire and his friend the police chief. There were dozens of ways to relieve herself of the key, but in each she found a flaw. Now she began to rationalize ways to keep it.

Her plan had been to get the key to Nickie so he could go back and hit the safe, getting in through the tunnel in case the police were still watching. It had taken a cash bribe, also in her purse, to keep him from taking off after the previous night's turmoil. Bull bragged about the "cash on hand" he kept in the safe. At least a hundred grand, he said, pocket money. And her check was there, the one she insisted he hold until she found the "original" of a Gaetano he bought, one she had copied herself. The one on display in the window was the doctored original she sold to Bull, "discovered" to be a forgery, and brought here to the gallery to be restored to its original condition and sold again to a dupe in another town. Her copy was in the back room ready to go to the mansion, where now it would never go. The cash and the check were worth another attempt. But Nickie was in jail and she was stuck with the key. Damn Reuchmaire!

She put the "out to lunch" sign on the door and made a cup of very hot tea. After last night, she felt she would never be warm again. And her hair was a mess. She sipped eagerly, scalding her lips but not caring, and let each hot swallow burn down into her stomach. It helped, but tea was not her drink. She needed a bigger jolt.

A cup of espresso with two sugar lumps and a lemon twist was the answer. She set the tea aside and brewed a strong, hot cup. Just like in the Village, back in New York, where she had taken many a cup with artists and musicians. How she longed to return. It was there she met Gaetano, lover of seascapes and marshscapes, a good (although not great) artist, taken a few years back with the South Carolina Lowcountry on a happenstance trip. Lazy and egotistical — typical Italian! typical man! — he fell easily into her scam. After she slept with him he was even more malleable. She convinced him to stay in New York and paint from photographs of the Lowcountry she sent. She would sell his paintings down here where they would be popular.

How she wished she were back in Manhattan surrounded by skyscrapers and an ocean of people in which to lose herself. She would be there again as soon as she could skip this unbearable burg where mosquitoes, flies and no-see-ums vied for her blood. And the smell! A nauseating fishy odor of swamps and tidal flats she got sick of, growing up here. And the people! With an impossibly slow drawl, they took forever to complete a sentence and cherished the Civil War as though one of those generals, Lee, or whoever, might any day march right down Boundary Street. To think she might have returned to stay in this backwater as Bull's wife.

She wondered if anyone would have recognized her if she had. But she had been here unrecognized for months. It had been chancy, she admitted, to come back here for a scam, but she wanted to get even with these people, with the upper crust for whom she was never good enough. As a teen she was ostracized by Beaufort's elite whose ranks she once dreamed of joining. But her parents weren't rich enough. Weren't rich at all, she bitterly recalled. She got some satisfaction out of conning the sons of wealthy Beaufortians with her underwater trick. She and — what was her name? Marla something-or-other, Baxter or Bailey or something like that. Marla was good for small bets but wouldn't go along with anything bigger. And Marla wouldn't do drugs, so they parted company, she to New York and Marla to Las Vegas married to a sweet-talking gambler. No one in this jerkwater town appreciated her real talent, painting. That was a long time ago, but she had not forgotten.

She cleared out after high school to head for New York and the big time. The first thing she did was get rid of her Southern drawl and force herself to sound like a New Yorkino. She had not said 'ain't,' 'honey,' or 'y'all' for thirty years. During that time she cajoled, manipulated, begged and screwed — besides actually painting and being good at it — her way into prominence. But that wasn't enough. Something inside always reached for more than was in her grasp, and she wasn't particular how she got it. When she chanced across Nickie and devised the plan for their scams, he came along.

Then six months ago, after she and Nickie had cooled it long enough after their last action, she decided it was time to go again. She smiled grimly at the way she kept Nickie out of circulation. As she suspected, he couldn't stay away from burglary, it was just in his blood, like conning people was in hers. They were up in Columbia two years ago, on their way back from Texas and Nickie, who trusted her far too much, flat out told her he wanted to hit a place on his own, a big mansion out in Heathwood just to keep his hand in. So she made an anonymous call that got him sent up. The old Columbia Correctional Institution closed shortly after he arrived, so they sent him down to the Allendale facility for two years. A nice, convenient way to keep him on ice. She even went to pick him up when he got out, just to show she still trusted him. His luck was rotten, she agreed, and suggested it was one of his so-called friends, Greasy Malone, that turned him in. She had heard, she told Nickie, that Greasy was worried Nickie was taking over his territory and wanted him out of the way.

About that time she heard of Bull in Beaufort. Allendale was just up the road, so the idea hit her that it would be a great trick to come back after all this time and see if she could pull it off. And she would have if she hadn't gone crazy and fallen for Bull. Goddam him anyway!

She reviewed for the umpteenth time the previous evening. Had she overlooked anything? The gun was safely hidden with Bull. And she even remembered to find the empty shell. Details! Success always depends on little things, the details. But now her scheme to have Nickie hit the safe and return the key to the mansion was foiled by Dr. Reuchmaire, self-appointed paladin.

Did he suspect anything? She didn't like the way he looked at her. Psychiatrists could do that, see inside to what someone wanted to hide. And the chief. He had given her a strange look. She calmed herself with a sip of espresso.

Closing the office door to keep smoke from the gallery, she pulled from her purse a fresh pack of Marlboros and the small guillotine. How she missed the robust flavor of Chesterfields. Camels were all right, but they didn't quite measure up. She tried cheroots, but they were bad for the image. Billionaires were unfailingly chauvinistic. Image is everything in a scam. Marlboros would have to do. She opened the pack and withdrew a cigarette, inserted it in the guillotine, and neatly lopped off the filter tip. She tamped the cigarette firm, lit it and inhaled deeply. Dangling the cigarette in one corner of her mouth, she cocked her head to keep the smoke from her eyes. She methodically beheaded each cigarette and imagined each severed tip as the head of Dr. Reuchmaire.

Feeling better, she slipped into her coat and freshened her makeup for her appointment with the hair-dresser. How irritating to have to return so soon, money down the drain. But it was a necessity. Salt water ruins one's hair.

An inspiration hit her. She could return the key. At the right moment she would slip in through the tunnel and leave the key behind. Not immediately, but later, after the police questioned her and found out nothing. Wait! Even better, she would get Nickie in with her to do the safe. They can't hold him for murder without a body. She would tell the chief she would not press charges for the attempted robbery, that she just wanted to forget the matter. They would have to let him go. And what if they did find the body? Nickie takes the rap and she insists she must return to New York, that the whole episode has been just *too* upsetting. Then she would leave this burg behind for the second and last time.

How clever I am, she purred to her reflection as she tied her scarf. I just needed to get the wheels turning so everything will work out. But first to the hairdresser's.

* * *

Annabelle had taken a sleeping pill and awoke after noon, feeling not at all refreshed. In spite of the drug she had slept fitfully, the image of Bull at the top of the stairs appearing in surrealistic dreams. The yacht, bow into a brisk wind coming down the Intracoastal Waterway from Beaufort, bobbed nervously on the tide. The firm slap of wavelets would have made the cold clear day exhilarating were it not for the grogginess and the memory. A shudder ran through her slender body and she pulled the Mackinaw closer. Huddled in the aft chair in the lee of the superstructure, she held a cup of hot, black coffee in both hands, savoring the warmth as she stared blankly at the distant outline of Parris Island. The popping of small arms fire from some Marine exercise seemed to rouse her. Beneath an expensive silk kerchief, tied tight against the breeze to keep her disarrayed hair from further abuse, her brows knotted in a frown.

"Perhaps it was all a dream," she said aloud to no one, for she was alone and had been since she anchored here the day before. But it was no dream and the weight of the pistol in her lap was all too real. She had been thinking about the gun. What should she do with it? She could throw it over the side, but the du Ponts might notice. She glanced at their boat a hundred yards away. They had been up since before she awoke, fishing and paying her no real attention as was their habit. Down here in the Sound, a favorite fishing and socializing spot among the yachting crowd, protocol was an occasional wave or a pleasantry unless an invitation was extended. A book lay open over the gun to hide it, although she knew no one could see. She felt better with it hidden.

She had brought it above decks to drop it over the side when it occurred to her that it must be returned. The police would notice it missing, but if it were back in its place, who would be the wiser? But how? And then she had an inspiration. She rushed below to the stowage locker and found just the things she needed. How ironic that Bull would assist in her plan.

She started the engines, feeling her spirits surge with the rumble of the twin Diesels, and weighed anchor. It was a plan and it would provide action and that would be a tremendous relief. She went below to get another cup of coffee and stretch a bit to relieve the stiffness of sitting so long. She reflected bitterly that she was too old for this sort of thing.

Back at the helm she began to realize how much this was going to change things. And how! Bull wouldn't run around on her anymore. That brought a short, sardonic laugh. But could she pull it off? Sure, she told herself. No one had seen her. No one could connect her to it. Just be your calm, collected, indifferent self, just as you handled all his affairs, never letting on how it burned inside.

How naive she had been to marry Bull, confident her charm and beauty would change his ways. But that was twenty years earlier when she was in her thirties, still believing she was the college belle she was when she graduated summa cum laude from Furman and had a trail of beaus a mile long. 'Beaus.' She smiled wistfully at the archaic term favored by her mother. How proud her parents had been over her 'snagging' Bull, as they put it. A great match, a great blending of fortunes. She sighed, and her spirits sagged. Fortune was one thing, happiness another. Wasn't she due some happiness after all those years of abuse and humiliation? Yes, she insisted, trying to feel justified.

She surveyed what lay ahead and began to think how to handle the inevitable questions. I can carry it off, she told herself with more conviction than she felt. Steering to the right of the channel to pass a barge coming down the Intracostal Waterway, she held her face out into the wind, letting the cold cut like a knife until tears flowed down her cheeks. She hoped it would clear her mind and drive away the haunting image of Bull at the top of the stairs and the terrible, oppressive realization that she had shot another person, that she had killed her husband.

Chapter 5

Reuchmaire entered the Smith-Barney office and stopped before the receptionist's desk where Perky Pattie (Pubescent Pattie, he secretly thought of her) was busily typing.

"Hi, Dr. ROCK-mooore!"

"Good day, Patricia." Reuchmaire swept off his hat and bowed. He was always flattered at the way she accentuated his name, just for him.

"And, helloo, General Stuart," she crooned, added a terribly unmilitary salute, and jumped up to take the Yorkie her arms.

General Stuart grinned happily and tried to lick her face.

"So, Patricia, how's my favorite Olympic swimmer?"

"Dr. Reuchmaire, I'm not an Olympian. I haven't even gotten through regionals yet. They're next month."

"But you're the best swimmer in Beaufort, and probably South Carolina." He felt great pride for Patricia and for Beaufort, his adopted home, for producing such a fine athlete. At the same time he was envious of her ability, and in awe of the regimen and effort — and often pain — any athlete must endure to be successful. In college — all those years ago! — his only activity was bridge (at which, he recalled, he was fairly decent), and he did that mostly to avoid studying. He could throw a long and sharp spiral and ran well, but shivered at the thought of what it took to play football, hour upon hour of tedious drill, often requiring that he hurl his slender body (in college he was quite trim) into much larger, more muscular and savagely determined teammates. He projected that opponents would be considerably worse. Ergo, bridge.

Patricia blushed and lowered her eyes. "Well, I hope so. I guess we'll see."

"I'm sure we will. Was I of some help on your term paper?"

"Oh, YESSS! I got an 'A.'" She swatted the air with a fist. "The only one in Psych 101. You saved me hours of research and Professor Hardiman — we call him Old Hardass — said it was OK to use you as a reference. I've got it right here." She set General Stuart down and stretched across the desk to reach a green folder. "You sure do know your Jung, Dr. ROCK-more."

"Hopefully." He resisted an urge to give her petite bottom a pat, and chastised himself for such a lascivious (but appropriately Freudian) impulse.

She proudly thrust the paper at him, and he leafed through it, giving it the attention he thought would please her, inwardly gratified that she had chosen him as a resource.

"Jimsy, let Pattie get her work done. Come on in here." The smooth Southern brogue, not sticky sweet but pure Lowcountry, came from the first office down the hall. Bowing again, Reuchmaire excused himself and found Marla busy at a computer.

She waved him to a chair.

General Stuart tottered in trailing his leash. Bourbon balls had the most curious effect on his walk. While his head and front legs proceeded in his chosen direction, his hindquarters slued slowly from one side to the other, as though on a caster. It was surprising that overall he moved in a straight line, but he did, occasionally emitting a small but distinct, "hic."

"Bourbon ball," Marla said, with a reproachful glance at Reuchmaire. She paused in her typing long enough to scoop up the Yorkie and give him a few gentle chin chucks.

The General responded with grunts of satisfaction, then retired to a doggie bed Marla kept prepared for him in the corner where he curled up and shortly was emitting a soft snore.

"Jimsy, chocolate is toxic to dogs. Not to mention the alcohol."

Reuchmaire gave his best remorseful pout. "It's such a small amount surely it can't matter. And it quiets him." He added pointedly, "As does food me."

"I'll be ready in a jiff, Jimsy, soon's I make Goldfield another wad of cash. As though he needs any more."

Reuchmaire grimaced. "Beaufort's favorite billionaire."

"Now, Jimsy. Goldfield may be a jerk, but he's a rich jerk, and right now he's making me a bunch of *dinero. Comprende*?"

"He has a set of pistols I want," he said, somewhat wistfully, leaning his chin on the handle of the umbrella. "A remarkably well preserved and beautifully filigreed dueling set, real flintlocks — Frenchlocks as they were originally known — circa Revolutionary War. He won't sell. I even offered more than they're worth. Quite a bit more."

"Now there's a headliner." She blew him a kiss while her scarlet nails clicked over the keyboard and the printer disgorged a sheet of stock purchases. A fashionably short business suit revealed long shapely legs which she used to swing her chair around. Removing her horn-rimmed glasses she picked up the phone. "Just let me tell him the sale's complete."

He had never understood the market with all its ups and downs, buys and sells, margins, shorts, and what not, and was content to let her increase his already sizeable estate without guidance (rather, misguidance) from him. She was good at it and, unfortunately, knew it, which meant it was unlikely she would quit anytime soon. Which was good news, bad news. Good news that it made him wealthier, bad news that she spent less time with him. "I'm hungry." The umbrella began a paradiddle on the floor.

"Jimsy, you want me to make lots of money don't you?"

"No!" Not true, but there was this thing of image.

"Jim-see. I'll just be a moment." She rolled smoky-blue eyes at him. Getting no answer she hung up the phone and tapped the pen thoughtfully against curls silvered to hide the gray. "That's strange, he told me he'd be home this morning."

Reuchmaire stood emphatically. "No doubt he was called out."

Smoothing her suit to six feet one inch of slender curves, she pocketed her glasses and reached for her coat. "You ol' bear. You can't be that hungry 'cause I just fed you breakfast three hours ago."

"That doesn't mean I can't be hungry."

They both looked to General Stuart still snoring away, nodded in mutual assent, and eased out the door.

Patricia, fingers on automatic, piped them out the door. "'Bye, Dr.

ROCK-more. 'Bye Ms. O'Shae."

Marla waved a finger. "I'm not available, hon, 'til I'm back — unless Harrington calls. He's a must. And if General Stuart wakes up give him a walk."

"Yes, ma'am. Have a good lunch."

Out in the crisp air, Reuchmaire asked hopefully, "Want to take your car?"

"Jimsy, to Plum's? It's only two blocks. And you can use the exercise." She gave his tummy a pat.

"I've got a coat on."

"You didn't have no coat on last night, lover boy." He grimaced and took her arm. "Let's go."

"So, what was the commotion earlier? Buster went by like a bat out of hell. He scared ol' Mrs. Henry so bad I thought she'd fall off her porch."

"Well, well, a real crime in Beaufort," She said after he told her. She snuggled into the depths of her coat and scrunched closer to him. "Jesus! Where'd this weather come from?"

"Marla, dear, it's unladylike to use profanity."

"Well, excuuuse me. Doesn't seem to bother you with Perky — make that Pubescent — Pattie." She giggled at his expression. "You talk in your sleep, Jimsy. Bet you have some great fantasies about her."

"Marla!"

"Don't be such a fuddy-duddy. You spend too much time with your mind on the couch."

"If we spend much more time on the couch they'll have to put me in a home."

She hugged closer. "You silly."

"Why, look at this." He stopped before the front of a shop window with a display of Confederate flags, gray uniforms, old volumes, and guns. "A shop of memorabilia…from the War of Secession. And look! A .36 caliber Navy Colt, vintage 1861. Octagonal barrel. Walnut handgrip. It's hardly scarred. Why, I believe it's authentic, not a copy. Let's go in."

She tugged his arm. "Jimsy, darling, I don't have much time. You come by later and reserve it and I'll give it to you for Christmas."

"Would you?"

"Let's see how much it costs. By the way, I believe it is more commonly known as the Civil War."

"That's what *Yankees* call it."

"You lived up there for thirty years. I would have thought —"

"Never!"

"I bet you've got a stash of Confederate money somewhere. But you haven't touched that leather-bound volume by Freeman I bought you last Christmas."

"Oh, no! I could never read it."

"What?"

"It's General Lee's biography."

"Aaand?"

"I might find something that would tarnish his image. Robert E. Lee was the exemplar of Southern genteelness, flawless and beyond criticism."

A smirk crept across her face. "You're serious."

He nodded and raised his nose a notch higher.

She laughed and tugged at his arm. "I do declare — make that d'clayah — you are a case. Com'n, I thought you were hungry."

He stuffed his hands into the coat's deep pockets and allowed himself to be led away. His mind filled with the vision of a smoky battlefield, staccato rifle fire, harsh flat crack of cannon, yells, screams, flashing bayonets among charging men and horses. That pistol might once have been held by Great-grandfather Reuchmaire, Colonel in the Beaufort Irregulars (attached), aimed at a blue-clad foe. Then he remembered. Grandfather Reuchmaire was a field surgeon and never in battle. Well, he sniffed, perhaps some other relative, a great-grandcousin or such, wielded that sidearm in defense of the Old South. He felt certain of it. And if it wasn't true, it should be.

Plum's Restaurant, oak-paneled, cozy, with Sea Island decor and a waterfront view, was a lovely place to spend a cold afternoon, sipping toddies and watching any boats audacious enough to brave the chill — there were always a hearty few — idle by on the Beaufort River. They were barely seated when her beeper went off. “Sorry, darling, but that’ll be Harrington. A big money customer that won’t wait.”

“Aren’t you going to eat?”

“Can’t. You go ahead. This’ll take a while.”

“I wish you’d quit that job,” he grumbled, but dutifully rose to hold her coat.

“Get the she-crab bisque,” she said, cheerfully ignoring him. “It’s fantastic, and I’ll buy.”

He sat back down, stiffly to show he was not to be mollified. Her job was a constant irritant, and she seemed to think she could just buy him off. However, he was quite hungry and he had heard that the bisque was wonderful. The shrimp salad too. And there was nothing wrong with accepting a free lunch.

Marla tugged on gloves and kissed his forehead, leaving a crimson smear. She reached inside his coat, handed him his handkerchief, and added, “I’ll fix dinner tonight, and then we can…well, you know.”

He watched as her heels clicked a rapid departure on the polished hardwood floor. *What a woman,* he said to himself with just the tone he remembered Gable using in *Gone With the Wind.* The rich aroma of she-crab bisque floated from the kitchen and brought him back to the menu.

A cappuccino topped off lunch and left him pleasantly drowsy. What to do with the rest of the day? Marla likely would be all afternoon at the office. If she worked late, as usual, she’d renege on dinner, too. *Mon Dieu!* But then they could go out to eat somewhere with real butter and rolls and he might manage to sneak one past her ever-watchful eye. He patted his waist again and realized he had begun to do it subconsciously and more frequently. But it really, really was mostly the coat he insisted to Freud’s glaring image rising in his mind.

He banished Freud to the nether regions and ordered another cappuccino, to which he added a brandy, and leaned back to enjoy the view. Out on the river an occasional off-season pleasure craft eased past, trailing a cloud of steamy exhaust. After the storm the previous night the day had calmed and a brisk breeze, beginning to lighten toward early afternoon, blew downriver toward the sound.

Fast Nickie drifted into his reverie. Tomorrow was lecture day at the prison. He'd have to get up at dawn to be up to Allendale by eight. But it was an opportunity to pull Nickie's sheet and see if something was missed during rehab. Why would a recently released criminal so quickly regress? And threatening him, his former doctor, with the knife? That just wasn't Nickie. He hadn't been out long enough to get that discouraged. Something else, or perhaps something Reuchmaire had missed in treatment (unthinkable!) drove him back to crime.

Ah, the intricacies of the human mind, he thought, shoving Nickie aside with a long sip of coffee and brandy. Just when you're sure you have someone figured out, off they go in another direction. He would be happy enough just to figure Marla out. He propped his hands on umbrella handle, and his chin on his hands and dreamily remembered the day two years ago when they met.

The circumstances were indeed dramatic, something he did not do just every day and would not have done had it not been Reuben Conner. He had just taken a pistol from Reuben, one he had pressed to his wife's head. Reuchmaire had shrugged off praise from amazed citizens who quickly surrounded him. It did give him a glow to be the hero, even if momentarily — his fifteen minutes. But he had felt no danger. Reuben was his patient, and he knew Reuben better than Reuben knew himself. Mrs. Conner was the object of Reuben's anger. Reuchmaire knew, as did everyone in Beaufort, how infuriating and impossible to deal with she was, a regular female Bull Goldfield. She was the one who should be in therapy. As he talked Reuben into handing over the gun, Reuchmaire's real fear was that it might accidentally go off before he could get it away. As soon as he got it, Reuben deflated like a balloon, the tension and anger gone. Mrs. Conner, stone white and mute for the only time he had ever known, let her amazingly docile self be led away by the EMS.

Reuchmaire put an arm around Reuben before surrendering him to the police and told him to come by for a chat, not suggesting it as appointment so much as a friendly visit. Reuchmaire's subsequent testimony got Reuben a probated sentence. The thanks in Reuben's eyes was a greater reward than the admiration from the bystanders.

And at that moment this silver-haired amazon walked up and asked him out to dinner. What does one say, he asked himself, when riveted by the most intriguing eyes he had ever seen, smoky blue and seductive, in the face of a stunningly beautiful woman a foot taller than oneself? For an instant he thought she was one of the movie stars frequently on location in Beaufort. One accepts, that's what. That is, if one ain't crazy. The rest, as they say, is history.

Pattie plopped into the chair across the table and his daydream vanished. She handed over the leash attached to General Stuart. The General sat, tongue lolling, and fixed Reuchmaire with adoring eyes.

"I gave him a walk." Pattie was all teeth and big brown eyes. "The old slave driver sent me over to tell you she's going to be late. She'll see you at the house at seven o'cl — ooh, are you having brandy? With coffee? Buy me one Dr. ROCK-mooore, pleeese."

"Pube — er, Patricia! You're underage."

"Am not. I've been legal since October."

He fixed her with his no-nonsense therapist stare. "Sex is eighteen, Patricia. Drinking, twenty-one."

She screwed a finger into a dimpled cheek. "Oh, yeah, well..." Leaning close she whispered, "But you could buy another and slip it to me."

"Slip it..." He fought to keep a straight face, tossed off the coffee, and smothered laughter with a napkin. "Patricia, my dear, as much as I regret it, I am not to be the instrument of your downfall into ruin and degradation."

"Hanh?"

"Never mind. Please tell Marla I'll see her at seven. Come along, General Stuart." He bowed and left, leaving Pattie gaping after him.

* * *

The day had warmed. Birds flitted among the magnolias and live oaks. A brisk walk by the river, down by the salt grass expanses and out to Pigeon Point would be just the thing to pass time and remind him why he had decided to run to this uncomplicated, charming town away from the grind and rush and politics of Washington, and an irritating ex-wife.

In the beginning, when he was young, eager and naive, he enjoyed it. Later it became simply a job. Finally, when he found himself possessed of the psychiatrist's bane — nodding off during a patient's anguished revelation — he knew it was time to leave.

In the nation's capital even psychiatry was submerged in politics. In thirty years on the Potomac he had treated senators and congressmen, their wives, husbands, lovers, children, children's lovers, and lover's children, their politics as well as their problems ranging from the international to the domestic, from the mundane to the scandalous. He wondered if there was a normal person in all of that tangled, convoluted metropolis. But then, what was normal? Was he normal?

He remembered Pattie's innocent — or Freudian? — request. Laughing aloud he almost collided with prim Mrs. Taliaferro, market basket clutched to her bosom, who rounded the corner of a building. General Stuart backed to the end of his leash and gave a disapproving yip.

Mrs. Taliaferro, startled, adjusted her pince-nez and recovered with a gracious smile but cast a wary glance at the General with whom she had been at odds since the Sunday he gave his rebel yell in church right in the middle of Mr. Taliaferro's sermon. Reuchmaire, nodding off, had chanced to place the tip of his umbrella on the General's tail.

"Why, Doctah Rockmowah," came the liquidy drawl, "whatevah is so amusin'? Shuahly not somthin' Ah did?"

Mrs. Taliaferro tended toward paranoia, and though she covered it well with her manners there remained on her face that slight disdain Lowcountry natives held for anyone other than Lowcountry natives. This was especially true of "upstaters," even though they were fellow South Carolinians, and very especially towards Yankees or anyone who might have voluntarily chosen to live among those former invaders of her homeland. Reuchmaire was aware that he fell into all but one of these categories. He appreciated Mrs. Taliaferro's indulgence, sharing as he did, their mutual dislike of the opposition in the "recent unpleasantness."

He bowed and tipped his hat. "Why, ah, the weather, Mrs. Taliaferro. The weather. Isn't it grand? I just burst out spontaneously."

"Well, yes, Ah suppose so." She agreed, looking not all that certain. "Howevah, Ah always feel a change in the weathah signals a change in fowtune. Somethin' unexpected may come our way." She eyed General Stuart again with a forced smile, hitched up her shopping basket with both hands and turned to go. "Hope to see you in church, Doctah." She eyed him over her glasses. "It has been a while, hasn't it?"

Reuchmaire bowed and tipped his hat. "I shall endeavor, Mrs. Taliaferro, I shall endeavor."

"It would be best," she said over her shoulder, "not to bring the dog."

Old Mrs. T was the ship of state for the local chapters of the Daughters of the American Revolution and the Daughters of the Confederacy, vice-president of the former and president of the latter. She exemplified the feeling among many older Beaufortians that the conflict which formed the nation could easily be wedded with that which tried to tear it asunder. It all had to do with forebears. As Grandfather Reuchmaire used to say, South Carolinians are like Orientals; they grow rice and worship their ancestors.

"Why don't you slip it to me?" he snickered when Mrs. T had sailed beyond hearing. Ah, innocence. He found his handkerchief and wiped away a tear of amusement. Marla was right, he did fantasize about Pubescent Pattie, er, Perky Pattie.

"Tch, tch, Reuchmaire," he admonished, "you're letting your id slip rein." Now then, what would Freud have said about it, or Jung?

When he first came to Beaufort he declared himself retired. He put aside the previous thirty years, and looked forward to doing nothing. He would read, work on his golf game, and find a bridge club to join. That lasted about three months. He could not divorce himself from psychiatry. He loved it too much. There was great comfort in helping others, of feeling that he made a difference in their lives. Mostly, though, he remained intrigued by the workings of the mind. What a powerful force it was! It had changed history more than once. Failure to reach a compromise often had cataclysmic results on either the personal or national level. And what is psychiatry but a pursuit of compromise, and life but a continuum of priorities? It was so simple to see; so difficult to unravel.

So, he had opened a practice in Beaufort. But in deference to the easier schedule he had promised himself, he limited his patients and took time for things that thirty years in Washington had kept him from, namely enjoyable close relationships with people he loved. His relationship with Marla was his most important. Chess with Harry second. As it turned out, his patients mostly came from the less-well-off of Beaufort society. The socialites and "old money," for the most part, went off secretly to pricey shrinks on Hilton Head or up to Charleston or Atlanta.

He charged his patients what they could afford and never pressed for a bill, even accepting barter in seafood from local fishermen, or in fresh vegetables from their wives who gardened. If the AMA found out he would probably lose his license, but he found that he didn't care, or maybe he thought that not even that massive bureaucracy could be so obtuse as to deny help to the needy.

But this day was too beautiful even for psychiatry. The crisp air quickened his pace, and he began his next strategy against Harry. A crisp day for crisp planning. He popped his umbrella emphatically on the pavement and caught it on the rebound. General Stuart, sensing the mood, gave a bark of agreement and pranced merrily ahead to the end of his leash. One of these days he would beat Harry fair and square. It was difficult when not entrenched in his den, Chessmaster glimmering on the computer, coffee at hand, and Grandfather Reuchmaire's *The American Chessplayer's Hand Book* in hand.

He opened the board in his mind and set the pieces. What to open with? Queen's gambit? No, something less familiar. There was a match he recalled. Gibaud vs Lazard in 1924. The shortest recorded match between two masters. Harry knew it. He had shown it to him early in their competition. What if he could catch Harry preoccupied with another matter and guide him through the moves of the loser Gibaud by repeating the moves of Lazard, the winner? What a delightful experiment. It just might work. The trick would be to catch Harry off guard. That was the rub. Harry was never off guard at chess.

His walk carried him down Pigeon Point Road in front of the Goldfield estate. Old, gnarly trees gathered in brooding groups behind an iron fence, as though to prevent a clear view of the mansion whose columned presence could only be clearly seen through the gate and down a long avenue of ancient live oaks. Reuchmaire continued down the road to where it ended at a bend of the river that formed Pigeon Point. The tide was making its slow return over wide mud flats rich with the smell of the Lowcountry. Later that night the mud and scattered oyster beds would be covered.

"Well," he said, panting a bit as he fanned himself with his hat, "that little jaunt should draw some points from Marla."

The Goldfield estate stretched from the point half way to town. It was isolated and beautiful. The mansion was unchanged since Revolutionary days until Bull Goldfield took over. Its columned splendor recalled the grandeur of antebellum days, nights of jasmine and magnolia, and lovers strolling beneath a pale moon. Reuchmaire loved the myth. Loved the oh-so-American spirit of The Lost Cause, the underdog struggling against superior odds. His vision of the South was of gallant warriors who defended home and hearth against Yankee intrusion. There was a kinship. He was a South Carolinian. After all, was he not named for grandfather Reuchmaire whom great-grandmother Reuchmaire had named for General Pierre Gustave Toutant Beauregard himself, the first leader of the Army of the Confederacy? Some in the family whispered she had done so with *raison*. Was it possible? A Reuchmaire forebear involved in a scandal? No! Although, Grandfather Reuchmaire did mention that Great-granny was a high-spirited lass and sometimes impetuous.

He shivered in the breeze across the point, glad today for the coat and hat. Placing hands on umbrella he stared out over the wide river, dreamily becoming Rhett Butler incarnate on a sleek and speedy sloop as it eased downstream to slip past the Yankee blockade.

And she would come on deck, large beautiful eyes beneath auburn ringlets. Hoop-skirted and wasp-waisted, she glanced fearfully into the drifting fog and trembled with dread or cold. "Miss Patricia, ma'am, my coat," he said, draping his captain's coat over her shoulders. "You'll catch your death."

"Oh, Captain Reuchmaire, how gallant. But what of you?"

"It's nothing, ma'am, I'm quite used to it." He grasped a line of rigging with one hand and stared into the fog as though possessed of some inner sense that could penetrate the mist. After a long drag on his cheroot (forgetting he did not smoke), he said, "Thickest fog I've seen, but we'll get you to Charleston before light of day, and you'll be reunited with your father."

"But the Yankees have blockaded the port."

He laughed carelessly, amused at her concern. "The Yankees don't know these waters like I do. Amongst the islands are secret passages. Rest assured, ma'am, we'll get through. Now you'd best get below and out of the cold...

The thrum of a power boat brought him back to reality. Just docking at the estate's pier was Mr. Goldfield's yacht. Reuchmaire squinted. Yes, it was *Mr.* Goldfield's. The ensign bore the circle and upward angled arrow above the family crest. Annabelle Goldfield's, in just one of many eccentricities of that marriage — if it could be called a marriage — would have flown the circle and cross. Finding his bifocals he brought out a handkerchief and gave them a good cleaning, then put them on. "His" and "Hers" lettering respectively he knew graced the fantails of the otherwise identical yachts, but even with the glasses he could not be certain of the lettering. Just the thing, matching monogrammed yachts. Well, he sniffed, it was possible for the occasional Clemson grad to be hugely successful.

The figure of Goldfield appeared and ascended the wooden walkway from the dock up the bluff. It was Goldfield's outfit: navy blue blazer, white pants and the only orange and white striped captain's hat in all of Beaufort. He was never seen in anything else when aboard. What a silly display of collegiate loyalty. An orange hat for the Clemson Tigers, arch rival of Reuchmaire's alma mata, the University of South Carolina. Although ever faithful to the garnet and black, *he* would never go to the extreme of a captain's hat in those colors. Even if he had a yacht. A simple football pennant on his study wall, Gamecock emblems on his tumblers, matching bed linens and bath towels, a few other touches and, of course, season tickets to all home games in Columbia. His car did not count. Even though trimmed in black, his Porsche was really more of a maroon than a garnet. Some might argue otherwise, but it was definitely maroon. Porsche didn't have garnet — he had asked.

So, the billionaire had been out for a cruise. That explains why Marla couldn't reach him. Having enough of the breeze and the chill, Reuchmaire started back along the path towards town. But a quick snort from General Stuart and a sharp tug on the leash turned him back. The General's little tail vibrated with energy. He strained at the leash, staring intently at the distant figure. A little butterfly of thought fluttered through Reuchmaire's mind. Something about what he saw wasn't exactly right. The person was just now mounting the mansion's wide front staircase. Reuchmaire fingered his beard and considered: how interesting are the basic instincts within the spiral helix, for even at this distance he could discern the subtle difference in carriage that delineates woman from man, the stride, the swing of the arms. Of course, it is possible he was mistaken, but he thought not. He gave a tug at the General's leash and turned to retrace his steps, wondering who would perform such a charade? Or for what purpose?

Chapter 6

General Stuart, sitting beside his master's chair waved a paw and fixed Reuchmaire with his most wistful gaze.

"General Stuart's ready for his," Reuchmaire called to Marla in the kitchen. To the Yorkie he whispered, "Better go. You'll like it better than what I'm getting."

"Com'ere General," Marla called, "grits and ham and redeye gravy."

"Lucky dog," Reuchmaire muttered as the Yorkie scurried for the kitchen.

He tucked a napkin under his chin and placed chin in hand beneath a furrowed brow. "You know, there's something very familiar about that Ms. Hawthorne, but I just can't place it."

Marla arrived at the table with a tossed salad and bread. "About who?"

"Isadora Hawthorne."

"Who's she?" Marla surveyed the table, nodded approval and returned to the kitchen.

He speared a tomato and popped it into his mouth. "The owner of that new art gallery. I feel I've seen her before." She returned with plates of steaming pasta mixed with broccoli, zucchini, and sun-dried tomatoes, lightly oiled. "Be careful, it's hot."

He stared at his plate. "What is this stuff?"

"Pasta primavera."

He wanted to look displeased but could not ignore the pleasant aroma. "Do I like it?"

"Cleaned your plate every time." She poured them each a glass of Chardonnay.

"No meat?"

"No."

"No cream sauce?"

"No."

"No cheese?"

"A little Parmesan — a little."

"I don't like it."

"Oh, Jimsy, you do too. We have it every time Edwin visits — it's his recipe — and you love it. Pasta and veggies lightly mixed with olive oil. Just the thing for you."

"If it's Edwin's I probably just say that to please him. He's an insufferable health nut."

"He is not. He's just careful about what he eats, just as you should be. Then you wouldn't have to rejoin that health club every year."

He rotated a piece of broccoli on his fork as though examining a lab specimen. Inwardly, he knew it was good for him, but he was fighting a lifetime of deep-fried eating habits. "It's your fault for fixing such grand meals for Thanksgiving. And Christmas."

"That's rationalization, darling," she smiled sweetly, offering a basket of sectioned French bread with a dish of minced garlic and basil in olive oil. "You don't have to eat them. But it's only twice a year, and mostly low-fat anyway. Except for the oyster dressing, but that little bit won't kill you."

He grimaced, irritated at being out-psyched, and broke a piece of bread in two. He looked hopefully for butter. She slid over the plate of minced garlic and basil in olive oil. "No butter. This is much tastier and much healthier for you."

"It isn't making me feel healthy."

"You gotta eat it first, butter brain."

He tried his exasperated exhale, but she just kissed at him and began on her food, taking dainty bites of vegetables and wrapping the pasta with fork and spoon as expertly as any Italian. One thing that had attracted him to Marla, other than her physical charms, was the way she fielded the hot little verbal grounders he shot at her and tossed them right back at him.

He dabbed the bread in olive oil, like a swimmer toe-testing a pool, captured a small amount of basil and garlic, and gave it a critical appraisal before taking a bite. "Oh, my, that's rather spicy. And good. Have we had it before?" He popped the remainder into his mouth and reached for more.

Marla looked at him with adoring resignation. "Every time Edwin comes, and sometimes in between."

"Oh." He dipped another piece of bread.

She took a sip of wine and thought for a moment. "Aha! Now I recognize Ms. Hawthorne's name. Gail says she's been in Beaufort since October. Gail keeps me up with all new arrivals, and the rest of the gossip."

"Gail?"

"My hairdresser. More news than the *Gazette* and knows more than the CIA about what you don't want her to know. She said you were in Ms. Hawthorne's gallery last week. You didn't like the marshscapes. Pass the Parmesan, please."

He looked up from another raid on the olive oil. "She is good. But I don't mean familiar like that. I mean like I saw her some time ago. Last summer, maybe." He rolled some wine around on his tongue and nodded approval. "Excellent Chardonnay, my dear. Ms. Hawthorne is a dealer in altered paintings. Gail tell you that?"

"Well, no," she said, adding a dusting of the pungent cheese to her primavera. "Going to turn her in?"

"Art is not my business. Besides, she's duping Bull Goldfield. Someone who does that can't be all bad."

"Tch, tch, Jimsy."

A forkload of pasta stopped en route to his mouth. He had just noticed she was wearing her body stocking.

She caught his glance. "Got to work tonight."

"Whaaat? This isn't Saturday."

"Special event. Some Arabian emir is here to pick up his airplane from Gulfstream. Bernie asked for me, said he'd pay double."

"You're only supposed to work Saturday."

"Now, Jimsy, when and where I work is my business. We agreed. I don't tell you how to treat your patients, do I?"

"Well, no." He crunched a piece of cauliflower, thinking this was really not such a bad dish. Perhaps there might be enough for seconds after she left. And maybe some frozen yogurt — no fat, of course — for dessert. Ice cream, he knew, was out of the question.

"Exactly so," she said, and gave his head an affectionate pat on her way to the bedroom. She returned in jeans and flannel shirt to give him a big hug and kiss. "You just finish eating and curl up with a book. I'll be back by eleven, and then…" She trailed off into a sensuous purr, tickling his ear with her fingernails.

He felt compelled to make one last jab, even though it contradicted what he told his patients. Having the last word was not the way to peaceful relationships. But somehow what was sauce for the goose did not always suit the gander. Particularly when he was the gander. "You make more than enough as a broker. I can't understand why a woman of your…uh, your…" Too late he realized his blunder.

"Of my age?" she cooed, slipping on a pullover.

"Well, yes. Of your age."

"Dear, Sally Rand worked until she was sixty, and I'm only fifty-three. Don't you think I have the body for it?" She performed a quick bump and grind.

"Of course you do," he admitted. There must be a better gambit. 'Dear' was her warning that she was tired of the conversation. "But you're lucky. If I had your genes —"

"Hah! Genes?" She popped each part of her anatomy for emphasis. "A butt lift, a boob job — lift, not silicone, it's all me — and a face lift. Plus two hours each and every day of aerobics, weights and stretches. Honeychile, it don't come easy." Her eyes even more than her tone indicated it was time to fold his tents. He wound pasta onto his fork and produced his remorseful look. It didn't work.

"Aaand, the two-a-day facials and body toning ever since the ten years I was in Tinsel Town don't hurt a thing." She moved to the closet and extracted a large flat case.

"You forgot your time on the Strip," he muttered. She wheeled around with tightly pursed lips and hands on hips.

He changed the subject, a figurative white flag. "Hey, this stuff is really good. Really, really good." He began to chew with relish.

"Jimsy, you're a case." The flares subsided. A slight tilt of her head meant she accepted the peace proposal.

He breathed easier. She rarely exploded, but when she did he battened hatches and ran for cover. Her angers were brief, and happily non-violent, but she could skewer him with a fury of sarcastic ripostes. He hoped for a better end to the evening, even if she did have to work. There was always later.

"Las Vegas?" She continued as though nothing had happened. She found her purse and extracted compact and lipstick. "Nah. I was young then. Didn't know my bod'd ever be old. Couldn't believe I'd live past forty. I was nineteen when I started dancing. Lasted 'til I was thirty on what Mom Nature gave me and that was old for that town. So, I guess you're right, the genes help, but they can't do it all."

He finished his pasta and swept the plate with a piece of bread, then took another for one more dip into the olive oil and garlic. "And," he continued on a positive note, but not quite yet ready to give up, "you have certainly done a superlative job of staying fit. But, being trim is one thing, and I have to admit I have not understood your desire, perhaps I should say, your need, if I were to speak psychologically, to be a fan dancer."

That she did not show irritation told him that it was over. She would allow him a few more parting shots but the subject was essentially closed, and the field, once again, was hers. She slid her arms around his neck. He knew what was next, and he loved it.

"Jimsy, darling, it's just my thing. I've told you that a thousand times. And I'll keep my word. Promise and cross my heart. Just 'til I'm fifty-five. Then I'll quit and you can stop asking me to marry you, 'cause I will."

"You could do that now."

"Aww, Jimsy," she fawned — a ploy he knew she knew he could not resist — "it just wouldn't be the same for the customers. Besides, I crave my freedom. Just two more years, really just a year and eight months. You can wait that long, can't you? For me? Hmm?"

He refused to give in to her nuzzling, but he couldn't hold out much longer. "Fan dancing is a thing of the past," he insisted. But his composure began to slip.

She gave him a big smooch and giggle. "Won't quit, will ya'?" She went to get her coat from the closet and tucked the box of hand-made pink fans under an arm. "Well, you'd think so. I thought so. But maybe that's why I'm so popular at the Lion. It's so old it's new. Those topless and totally nude places leave nothing to the imagination. With my fans I don't show 'em a thing 'cept some skin, same as what they'd see at the beach and probably less. But it's what they can't see that's so alluring. And, honeychile, I got one thing that works anywhere, anytime — class. That's what keeps packing 'em in. And as long as they come, I'll dance." She gave him one more kiss and said, with her face in his, "End of subject."

He nodded complacently. In his mind he saw her gliding across the stage behind the floating fans. It was a remarkably sensuous vision and a tingly warmth crept over him. He had not told her he had a secret desire to watch her perform. But incognito. He feared if she knew she would take it as approval. He had tried to think of a disguise, but could not resolve the problem of his distinct, peppery beard. He would not part with it even temporarily.

At first he wondered if he was in fact perverted. But if they got to watch, he got her in the flesh, so to speak. A common sexual fantasy among men is to visualize one's lover with another man. Ah, the mind. Such a tangle of intrigue. Could he wait? Of course. He wasn't about to let this lady get away. Two years or ten, he would wait. But he didn't want her to get complacent. Did they really need to be married? Not as far as he was concerned, but being a dedicated Son of the South, he felt that for appearances they should be. So he often asked. And it would add a certain comfort of permanence. But that hadn't helped his first marriage. Of course, his first wife was not Marla — not by a country mile.

She checked the fans and closed the container. Blowing him a kiss she opened the front door and almost collided with an angelic young girl with a newspaper sack draped from her shoulder.

"Cissy Conner," Marla said, "you gave me quite a start." A small shy smile appeared. "Sorry, Mrs. O'Shae. Hello Dr. Reuchmaire."

Reuchmaire got up and came to the door. He always enjoyed seeing Cissy.

General Stuart appeared from the kitchen licking his chops. He pranced up to the girl, his eyes aglitter and his tiny tail a blur.

"Ohh, General Stuart," she cooed, "hi there." A good ear scratching was heartily approved of by the General.

Marla took Cissy's arm. "You come right in out of that cold, darlin'."

"Here's your paper, Mrs. O'Shae. Sorry it's late. There was a special edition —"

Marla tossed the paper aside. "Oh, don't you worry about that. I've got to run, but you come in and have some hot chocolate with Dr. Jim."

"I can't, Mrs. O'Shae. I've got to finish my deliveries."

"How's your father, Cissy?" Reuchmaire asked, trying to sound matter-of-fact.

"Well, okay."

"That doesn't sound, 'okay'. Is something wrong?"

Cissy twisted a strand of blonde hair and looked away. "Well, he had a fight with Mr. Goldfield yesterday. It really has him down, worse than I've seen him in a long time."

Small world, Reuchmaire thought, catching himself before he said it aloud. He was astonished to hear Marla blurt out, "Is he —?"

"Oh, no ma'am. He's not drinking at all, not for over a year."

Reuchmaire knelt down and took a small cold hand in his. "Cissy, you tell him I said 'hi,' won't you? Tell him to drop by, if he'd like."

She nodded with her shy, appreciative smile. "Yes, sir, I will."

"Cissy," Marla said, "you go get in my car. I'll drive you to the rest of your deliveries."

"Oh, Mrs. O'Shae, you don't —"

"Cissy, that's an order."

"Yes, ma'am." The soulful eyes beamed thanks.

"I thought you were late," Reuchmaire whispered, when Cissy was out of hearing.

"Not that late." Marla buttoned her coat, her face screwed into an expression that said she was plotting something.

"I'll be glad to drive her."

"You're a dear, Jimsy, but I want to talk to her. Won't take long. Besides, you haven't had your seconds." She grabbed a fur hat and fitted it in a mirror beside the door. "I've got to get that girl a bike. It takes her forever to deliver those papers. She shouldn't be out this late and in this cold."

"Perhaps you should buy her a car."

"She's not old enough — oh, stop being sarcastic."

"You can't take care of them all, my dear."

"You sound like a republican."

"I am a republican."

"Um, hum. That's why you've been treating her dad for nothing. You finally brought stability to their life."

"So, buy her a bike."

"You think Reuben wouldn't sell it to get booze?"

Reuchmaire pondered. "I doubt it. But, knowing him, he probably wouldn't let her take it. Pride, you know. Won't accept charity."

She squeezed his hand. "I've got to go. You finish dinner and think of some way for us to get her a bike. Hey! You can give him a post-hypnotic suggestion."

He gave her an irritated look.

"Well, *think*," she said, and closed the door. After another plate of pasta, pleased with himself for not having a third, he searched the freezer for ice cream but had to settle for frozen yogurt. Satiated, he even took his dishes to the sink, a strict rule at Marla's, never done at his place except when there were no clean ones left. He even rinsed them and put them in the dishwasher. Then, supervised by General Stuart, he lit a fire, a rare event for Beaufort. He fiddled for a while with Schubert on the baby grand but was badly out of practice and soon gave up. At the window he surveyed the cold moonlit night where moss hung like frosty gray ornaments in the trees. All of his John Wayne videos were at home. Was a quick trip worth it? The cold seeped, nay, seemed to flow, under the window sill. He shivered and turned back to the fire. There was a Roosevelt biography here he had not finished. He put Mozart on the stereo, unplugged the phone, and nestled into an overstuffed chair by the fire.

The General reminded him with a sharp yip that dessert had not been served. Shortly the Yorkie was munching a bourbon ball by the fire while his master sipped brandy and read.

Reuchmaire set the book aside. Flitting in and out of his mind was his little butterfly, an elusive thing that teased the edge of his consciousness and said there was something important just under the surface. Suddenly it emerged. Reuben. What will be the effect of his fight with Goldfield? Even though Reuchmaire had been positive in his reply to Marla, it was the sort of question psychiatrists dreaded and never really knew the answer to.

He ruminated over it for the better part of an hour. But there was nothing to do. He knew he worried too much about his patients, but he couldn't help it. Well, he had sent the offer through Cissy for Reuben to come see him if he needed.

Finally, relaxed by the brandy, the fire and the book, he began to nod. In a foggy half-dream he almost realized what had been so familiar about Isadora Hawthorne. But before he could grasp it, he and the General were sound asleep.

Chapter 7

Marla turned her Suburban off the highway onto the dirt driveway to Cissy's home. It was a modest frame house with a neatness about it common to homes where ends did not quite meet but personal pride did its best.

"I'll just wait, hon, until you see that your dad's home."

Cissy was out of the car in an instant and up worn wooden steps. Before she vanished inside she tossed her newspaper sack onto a porch swing, old and wooden but comfortable looking. Shortly the screen door banged in her wake and she piled back into the car.

"He's not there."

"Hon, what's the matter?"

The girl crossed her arms and stared at the floor. "I'm scared. About Dad's fight yesterday with Mr. Goldfield."

Marla reached over and took a small cold hand in hers. "Do you want to tell me about it?"

Cissy chewed her lip for a moment in silence. "Since it's you, I guess it's OK. Dad blew up because…because of something Mr. Goldfield did…to me."

"Hon! What happened?"

"I went to collect, and Mr. Goldfield asked if I wanted to see the mansion. Usually Wilson — he's the butler — pays me, but he was gone. I'd never been inside, so I said sure. It's so elegant and big, like something a king would live in. He showed me through the whole thing and told me about his great grandfather who had married his great grandmother when she wasn't much older than me. I thought he was just being friendly. Then all of a sudden he grabbed me and kissed me, right on the lips. He told me what a great paper carrier I was and that in a year or so he would let me come to work for him in the house…"

As she talked tears began to run down her cheeks. Marla fished a box of tissues from the console.

"I was so scared, Mrs. O'Shae. I mean, what kind of a man is he? Doesn't he remember Cassy?" Marla drew the girl close, patting her head, and tried to think of what to do. Get a gun and shoot Goldfield. No, be sensible.

"He's a bad man, darlin'. Now don't you worry. We'll protect you. We'll deal with Mr. Goldfield later. Right now we need to find your dad. Did you tell him what happened?"

Cissy blew her nose. "No way! But he saw when I came out of the house. When Mr. Goldfield let me go I ran for the door, but it was locked. I didn't know what he would do. If he grabbed me again I was gonna kick him hard as I could right in the...well..."

Marla stifled a smile. "Good for you."

"But he just opened the door and led me onto the porch. That's when Dad saw us. Mr. Goldfield was putting his hand on me...well, here. Like he was taunting Dad. Dad was right by the steps trimming the bushes. I've never seen his face like that. I've never seen him move so fast. He came up the stairs and grabbed Mr. Goldfield by the throat..."

Cissy wiped away tears. "He really meant it, Mrs. O'Shae. He might really kill him. I've been afraid to tell anyone."

"Oh, hon, I don't think —"

"You didn't see him, Mrs. O'Shae. And then Mr. Goldfield threw him down the stairs. Dad can't fight as good as Mr. Goldfield 'cause of his legs. Mr. Goldfield just threw him down and laughed. If know if Dad had had a gun right then he would have shot him."

"Shh, hon, never mind. Now you listen to me. That man will never harm you. Never! You understand?"

Cissy nodded and managed a smile.

"Good. You believe me, 'cause it's true. But now we have to find your dad. Maybe he went out for a...maybe he went out." Marla feared they would find Reuben drunk in a bar. Was Cissy right? Was her dad angry enough to do something really desperate? She tapped her fingers on the steering wheel in time to her thoughts. Maybe she should tell Jimsy. Maybe she should tell Harry.

Cissy read her thoughts. "He really doesn't drink, Mrs. O'Shae. Honest. I'd know if he did."

Not at all encouraged, Marla remembered the first time she saw Reuben, when he had a gun to his wife's head on the courthouse steps. Marla just happened by in time to see Jimsy take the gun away. Of course, she didn't know it was Jimsy at the time, but it was the most heroic thing she had ever seen. But if Reuben did it once...she forced the thought away. With what she hoped was an encouraging smile, she said, "OK, hon, let's go find him. Any ideas?"

"Sometimes he goes to the library. Sometimes he just walks, to help him think, or he goes to the health club. He says it works off steam. But maybe he went somewhere to be alone. He does that when he's feeling down. He rows over to Repository Cove and sits up high on that big dead tree. That's where they found Cassy."

"I know," Marla said gently.

"He's taken me there. It's beautiful. Herds of fiddlers scoot across the sand, like a miniature cattle stampede. The smell of the marshes is so strong and good, and birds come by so close you can almost touch them."

Marla backed the SUV out of the drive and headed toward Beaufort. "We'll find him. If we can't, I'll stay with you 'til he comes home."

Cissy dabbed her eyes with a tissue. "But, don't you have to go to work?"

"Oh. Thanks for reminding me." Marla steered with her thighs while one-handing a number on a cell phone. "I've got to get this thing hard-mounted with a speaker, like Jimsy has," she said while the phone rang.

"Yeah," said a hoarse drawl at the other end.

"Bernie, Marla. Look, hon, I'm running a bit late."

"Late? The emir —"

"Bernie, I know the emir is coming."

"Coming? He's here!"

"Bernie, this is important. I'll be there as soon as I can. Stall the son-of-a..." She threw a quick smile at Cissy. "...the son of a sheikh, or whatever he is."

"What the hell am I gonna —?"

"Bernie, dear, that's the way it is. Get Pipsie, she's a good filler."

"You said you'd be here."

"Sweetie, if you don't like it, you dance for his majesty. I'll be there as soon as I can. And don't forget I get a bonus for tonight. 'Bye." She handed the phone to Cissy. "Put this back in the console, hon. Now, let's start looking down at the boat dock."

Thirty minutes later they were headed back out of Beaufort. All the likely places had been searched, except the bars. Marla didn't push it when Cissy insisted he wouldn't be there. Hope? Denial? She didn't know, although she felt surely that was where he was. But she went with Cissy's judgment. It at least spared the girl embarrassment if she was wrong. Her heart sank when she saw a patrol car in the drive.

Two figures were talking on the porch. The tail of an old pickup protruded from behind the house. It was Reuben's all right, stenciled with 'Conner Lawn Service, Beaufort's Finest,' and the bed filled with mowers and other lawn equipment.

"Dad!" Cissy yelled, and bolted from the car.

Reuben hurried down the stairs to swing her in his arms. "Lord, girl, where have you been? You sure gave me a scare."

Marla breathed a sigh of relief. Reuben was sober as a judge.

Buster came down and listened with casual interest while Cissy spilled out the tale of looking for her father. He looked as though he had expected the conclusion.

Reuben shook Buster's hand. "Thanks for coming out. Sorry to trouble you."

"No problem. Glad the girl's safe." He touched a finger to his hat and drove off.

The affection that flowed from Reuben's eyes told Marla that Cissy was in safe hands and that she was fortunate to have this man for a father. She gave herself a mental wrist slap for doubting Cissy. She gave Cissy and especially Reuben a real hug.

She sped toward Savannah, trusting to luck to avoid a ticket. She would atone for being tardy with a special performance and maybe his majesty would favor her with a big tip.

Up SC 170 out of Beaufort, across the Broad and Chechessee Rivers and on towards Savannah she kept the needle on eighty. The troopers mostly stayed over on the interstate. Salt marshes, pine forests, occasional shacks, mobile homes and paint-peeling, wooden churches flashed by. Traffic was light. Long straightaways made passing easy and her radar detector remained mute except for occasional spurious pulses which she ignored. She slowed only when she hit the heavier traffic on the four-lane just outside the city.

Delayed by stoplights and traffic she had time to think. The earlier conversation with Jimsy, one they often had about her dancing, came back. Why did she get such a charge out of dancing? For one thing it reassured her that she still "had it." Fifty-three, but with body of a thirty-year-old. Well, maybe thirty-five — OK, forty. But it was also what she got from the audience. They fed her, she fed them. She loved the way they watched, mesmerized or leering or respectfully lascivious, but every one of them entertained, even the few women who showed up. But mostly it was the satisfaction of something done really well. She sought that of anything she did. It was part of her and had been as far back as she could remember. Jimsy would just to have to understand. She knew she was good and she was going to enjoy it as long as she could.

But a contrary thought usually crept in about this time. If she did "have it," why had she been unable to hold three husbands? Jimsy had insisted that it did not mean she was a bad wife, perhaps she was just not a good selector of husbands. He was sweet to say that, but she decided after a few months with him that she had placed too much emphasis on the physical aspects of relationships and not enough on the mental. Jimsy stimulated her mind in a way others hadn't, and that in turn stimulated the physical, and so on. It was just a terrific relationship.

She was sure when they married it would work. Even though he kept asking, she knew it didn't matter to him whether or not they were. He was a man of principle and felt he should insist. She adored that. But first, she had to finish dancing. Age fifty-five. That would be her final year. Then she would dance only for Jimsy, when he begged. She loved it when he begged.

Who would have thought she would marry a psychiatrist? She had thought for most of her busy — make that turbulent and erratic (not erotic, but there was that, too) — life that she needed a shrink. But not to marry. After her third unhappy marriage she had gravitated back to Beaufort, seeking comfort in the marshes and beaches she loved and had so regretted leaving after high school. She had thought she wanted the big time, the glitzy life, her name in lights and all that. Like her old high school cohort, Grundel…Grundel something or other, Smith or Smuts, or something like that who had headed off to New York. She hadn't seen Grundel in years, and just as well. Grundel was bad news, drugs and stuff.

It had taken Marla thirty-five years and three husbands to realize that the big time wasn't really where it was at. Right here in Beaufort was where she was happiest, particularly with Jimsy. She would never forget the way he just walked up to Reuben and took the pistol. She *had* to meet him and the quickest way was just to walk right over and ask him out to dinner and hope he couldn't hear her heart hammering. Things had been wonderful since.

A frown creased her forehead and she tossed back silver locks in an irritated headshake. Her dancing career would end next week if that jerk Goldfield closed the Lion. Was there anything in the Lowcountry — anything profitable — that he didn't have control of? That horny, obnoxious, self-aggrandizing, philandering, perverted, child-molester! He was angry because she had refused his advances. When she turned him down, he drew himself up like a rooster, and crowed in his raspy accent, 'Well, awl raht then. S'pose I jus' clowse th' Liion.'

"Somebody ought to shoot that jerk."

* * *

Cissy tied an apron around her slender waist and began to set the table. "Dad, it was my turn to fix dinner."

In the small kitchen Reuben spooned collards from a kettle into a large bowl. He looked up, smiling. "You needed to do your homework."

"I know. I should've stayed in and gotten it done. But I didn't know where you were."

He brought the collards and a plate of corn on the cob to the dinette to join a steaming bowl of black-eyed peas. "No problem, kiddo. I should have left you a note. We'll swap dinner. You can do tomorrow night. Get the cornbread out of the oven, please, before it burns."

With potholders she extracted the hot pan. Mingled with the aromas was the sweet tang of Reuben's aftershave, and with it relief eased over her. She could gage his mood by the growth of beard. When he was really down he might go two or three days without shaving and his shoulders would slump. She could never shake the fear that he might return to drink. But it had been a year now that he was sober, and each day was another victory. This morning when she saw he hadn't shaved, her heart fell. The fight with Mr. Goldfield had done it. Now she had to see how he would handle it.

But tonight he was sitting erect, like his Marine Corps picture she kept in her diary. Seeing that, she knew things were all right. He said grace and she thought of the food spread as grand as any banquet, the sweet hot smells, the warmth of the house, and their togetherness. The terror of yesterday, his fight with Goldfield, were forgotten. She added her "amen" at the end.

"I just fixed vegetables," he said.

She cut the cornbread into squares, moving the knife with a slow and steady draw, just as he taught her. "That's fine. We had fish last night; I'll do chicken tomorrow."

"Saves some money," he explained.

"And is healthy," she added. "Like this. I got it instead of butter." She offered a container of non-fat yogurt.

"Healthy, huh?" A smile touched the corners of his mouth. "If Nam didn't kill me, I don't think food will."

"Dad, it can too." He was being stubborn again. Parents! They thought they knew everything. "I've been on the Internet with this guy in California, and he steered me to a bundle of Web pages about food and how to eat — why are you shaking your head?"

"Internet. Web. I had pen pals. All this electronic mumbo-jumbo is too far-out for me."

He was baiting her and she knew it. It was a game they played, poking fun at their differences. "'Far-out?' Oh, wow, are you out-of-date. That phrase is *archaic*."

"Don't you mean *awesomely, totally* archaic?"

And so it went, one riposte answered by another, until they had finished the meal, sometimes lapsing into uncontrollable laughter when the insults became absurd.

After dinner she brought the empty plates to the sink where he was washing. "Dad, all kidding aside, I do need to upgrade my computer."

"I thought you just did that."

"That was nine months ago, and it really wasn't enough then. The speeds now are, well, awesome."

"Got the money?"

"Yes, sir."

"Need a subsidy?"

"No, sir. I saved enough from my route."

He rubbed his forehead against hers. "Young lady, you are a jewel. Well, if you've got the money, what are you asking me for?"

"Well…" she shrugged and plopped her hands against her sides. "Well, because you're my dad. Because maybe we need the money for something else."

His eyes moistened. He chucked her chin and said in a husky voice, "Nothing we need more than to keep you up with the rest of the world."

She gave him a big hug. Encouraged by his mood she asked, "Dad, are you okay about yesterday, with Mr. Goldfield?"

Her heart chilled when the smile left his face, and she wished she hadn't asked but at the same time knew she had to. After a pause he said, "Yeah. That's over with. I shouldn't have blown off like that, shouldn't have let you see me lose my temper. Shouldn't have lost my temper in the first place. Goldfield's a snake not worth soiling my hands with." He took her by the shoulders and looked into her eyes. "This I promise you, kiddo. That man will never touch you again. You believe me?"

She felt the strength of his hands and saw the meaning in his eyes. "Yes, sir."

"Good. Now, how about a game of backgammon before bed?"

"Sure." She went to get the board. Setting it up she asked the other question bothering her. "Dad, you didn't tell me where you were tonight. You know, when I couldn't find you."

"I went back to Goldfield's place. We left so fast yesterday I forgot my tools."

Chapter 8

"Jimsy, wake up."

"Hmmph — what?"

"It's just me."

He blinked and yawned. Marla stood over him, her fan case under an arm.

"Ah, yes. What time is it?"

"Almost midnight. The emir insisted I have a drink with him. Now don't worry, it was a big group and he was a gentleman."

He yawned again and tried to get his mind in gear. He was not a night person. "You, um, sound a bit tense."

"Does it show? Sorry. It's Bull Goldfield. He's a real pain in the…neck. Not enough that he tells me how to manage his stocks, now Bernie says he's going to close the Lion. I won't have anywhere to dance. The jerk."

Reuchmaire tried to look disappointed. "Really?"

She put her fans in the closet and closed the door with a bang. "Somebody ought to do this town a favor and shoot him."

"Marla!"

"Just kidding. I'm for hot chocolate. C'mon." The sound of the phone came faintly from the bedroom. "Unplugged the phone again, didn't you? Now who could be calling at this hour?" A moment later she yelled, "Plug in the phone, Jimsy. It's Harry."

"Hi, Doc," Harry said, with a cheerfulness that grated on Reuchmaire's groggy mind. "You awake?"

"Kind of. What's up?"

"Goldfield's missing, and it looks like foul play. Can you meet me at his mansion right away?"

* * *

The Porsche's headlights cast eerie shadows down the twin lines of oaks bordering the long estate drive. It was hard-packed dirt with thin grass along the center strip, much the same as it had been in antebellum days, and one of the few things on Riverbriar that the eccentric billionaire had not fiddled with. Reuchmaire would not have been surprised to find neon arrows flashing directions from entrance to mansion. He yawned for the umpteenth time and checked his watch. After midnight! He was glad for Marla's coffee, and wondered again why Harry had called him. He was flattered, of course, but his previous assistance had been on misdemeanors. A missing person was something else — and a bit exciting. Although it seemed hardly something a psychiatrist could help with.

What strange circumstances. Only two days before he had been here to make Goldfield an offer for his dueling pistols. The billionaire's refusal, a donkey-like bray, was uncalled for and it had stung. Marla was right, Goldfield could be a real jerk.

Reuchmaire stopped the Porsche in the circled drive at the rear of the tabby-walled mansion, got out, and sleepily held the door open for General Stuart to hop out. After several inert moments the frigid air revived him and he remembered he had left the General snoring beside the fire at Marla's. He closed the door and headed toward the house. No doubt it was the finest old structure in Beaufort. Goldfield never failed to point that out, always with a lengthy explanation of the process of making tabby, a mixture of ground oyster shells, whole oyster shells and sand, which formed the sturdy walls of this and many other old Lowcountry buildings. As Goldfield told it, his forebears invented the process. In his obdurate style, he modified interior and exterior over the pleas of Mrs. Goldfield, Mrs. Taliaferro and the rest of the D.A.R. and the Daughters of the Confederacy.

Most prominent of the changes was an atrium. It had required the sacrifice of an upstairs bedroom and downstairs sitting room. The area, open to the outside and the sky, contained plants, shrubs and flowers around a fountain. Reuchmaire shuddered at the obvious expense of the project. The bedroom was originally the master and the Daughters were certain both George Washington and Jefferson Davis had slept in it — not at the same time, of course, Mrs. Taliaferro always quickly pointed out. Goldfield said it added character.

Reuchmaire lifted the yellow police tape with his umbrella and slid under. He thought the atrium presented a snaggle-toothed appearance in the face of the otherwise beautiful old home.

The wide rear stairs led up to a porch and doors which opened into a small foyer from which separate oak-paneled halls ran around the center of the interior to the front of the mansion. Reuchmaire followed one to the large front foyer where, he knew from his previous visit, the two hand-carved mahogany doors led to an elevated porch above a lawn spreading to the river. This was the true front of Riverbriar which had greeted sail, paddle-wheel, and steam boats since Revolutionary days. When the sun set, it was said, there was no lovelier view across the Beaufort River than from the columned porch. Reuchmaire, not of the Beaufort aristocrats, did not know, and felt it was something he could live without since the opportunity would require association with Goldfield.

Goldfield's gun collection filled the foyer and adjoining rooms. A wide central staircase, carpeted in rich red, with a solid, cream-colored bannister and mahogany railing, rose to the upstairs hall where the glass wall of the atrium glared in reflected light. Reuchmaire decided that under certain conditions, say with a full moon and clouds showing through and the lights low, it might be picturesque, even romantic. But it was not what one expected to see in such a setting.

Harry, cigar stub in mouth, was standing at the base of the stairs squinting up at the atrium. One heavy arm was draped on a newel post, the other hand thumb-tucked into his utility belt which defied gravity by clinging, beneath his ample stomach, to his hipless waist.

Nearby on a Louis XIV chair sat Wilson, the butler, a slight, balding black man. Wearing a sour, defensive expression, he mopped his forehead with a handkerchief and stared at the floor. He rose to take the doctor's coat and hat, surprised when Reuchmaire kept a firm grip on his umbrella. Goldfield ancestors glared from wall portraits as though in disapproval of this late-night intrusion. Uniformed officers moved about in adjoining rooms.

Reuchmaire stared horrified at the empty space on a shelf where the dueling pistols had been. "Someone stole —"

Harry gave an amused shake of his head. "We impounded them. Exhibit A."

Reuchmaire sighed with relief. There was still a possibility he might obtain them. "I see — impounded them? Why?"

Harry took the cigar out of his mouth and scratched his head. "Well, this may be more than just a missing person case. Seems our friend Fast Nickie left his fingerprints all over one of those pistols. And it's been fired recently."

"Fast Nickie? I don't believe it. He would never use a gun."

Harry shrugged. "Maybe. Problem is, I can't say if you're right or not 'cause as of right now we've got a gun with fingerprints, but we're missing a very important item."

"What's that?"

"*Corpus delicti.*"

"A body?"

"Yep. But we have another suspect. You know Reuben Conner?"

Reuchmaire nodded and suppressed another yawn. "I treated him for Post Traumatic Stress Disorder. He had a rough time in Viet Nam, and there was the death of his daughter and a lousy marriage."

"He happened by here earlier to pick up some tools, according to Wilson."

Reuchmaire started to say, "So?" but a yawn overwhelmed him.

"Would he kill anyone?"

"Good grief, Harry, I don't know. It's possible — under enough stress anyone might commit murder — but, Reuben? Well, I don't think so. He's been out of therapy for quite a while, and I thought he was doing all right. Ask me again tomorrow when I'm awake."

Harry patted Reuchmaire's arm. "Sorry, Doc. Not trying to pin you down. It's just that if it is murder, Reuben could have a motive."

"Didn't mean to snap. I'm not at my best in the middle of the night. How was Reuben involved?"

"Seems he and Goldfield had an altercation yesterday afternoon."

Reuchmaire nodded. "Cissy said something about it."

"Well, Goldfield called me and said he wanted a restraining order on Reuben. Well, you know how explosive Goldfield is. He's made similar threats before, so I didn't think anything of it when he didn't follow through. But now, well…"

"You think Reuben was returning to the scene?"

"Just considering all the possibilities."

"Is there any coffee?"

Wilson returned from the coat closet. His Lowcountry brogue was as slow as his movement. "Yes, suh. In the kitchen. Ah'll get it."

Harry took Wilson gently by the arm and smiled. "This is tough, Wilson, I know. We'll go with you, and you tell Doc what you found."

The kitchen was a dichotomy of marble counters, old wooden cabinets and shelves with modern electrical appliances housed in polished wood. Reuchmaire felt torn between past and present. While Wilson made coffee Reuchmaire pulled Harry aside. "Harry, I don't belong here. If this is what you think, it's murder, a felony. I'm a psychiatrist, not a law officer. I wouldn't know the first thing —"

"You know people, Doc," Harry soothed. "And that's important. I think it'll be real important before this thing's cleared up. The mayor's already on edge about what effect this may have on tourism, so I'd like to get it wrapped up real quick."

There was irony in Reuchmaire's smile. "Murder's more likely to attract tourists."

"Could be, could be. People seem attracted to the morbid. However, his honor thinks otherwise."

Reuchmaire nodded thanks for the coffee to Wilson, whose stress was obvious, and offered the butler a chair. Reuchmaire's empathy kicked in, enhanced by those traits necessary to any good psychiatrist, the ability to ignore folly and forgive frailty while maintaining a countenance so beatific as to make the Pope jealous. He simply could not refuse someone in need. It would be horrible to have something like this crash into one's life. He felt the strain himself, and he was an outsider, merely an observer. He tested the coffee, hot and delicious, and it infused him with renewed vitality. The cobwebs cleared, and he banished doubts about his usefulness, now genuinely interested and capable of investigative thoughts. "Where is Annabelle?" he asked, pleased with himself for so quickly coming up with a legitimate question.

"Off on her yacht. Seems Goldfield ordered her out of the house so he could, ah, get some work done, if you get my drift. She hasn't returned."

"Wilson," Reuchmaire said, "this is superb coffee. I don't know when I've tasted better." Another of Grandfather Reuchmaire's adages: oil the gears with a compliment and they turn smoothly. In this case it was easy duty. The coffee *was* superb. "I know this is a trying experience for you. What a terrible thing to have to contemplate, Mr. Goldfield missing, possibly come to harm. But perhaps it is not as bad as it seems." To Reuchmaire, Wilson was a patient with a problem to extract. He pulled a chair close, to show he cared about what was said. A touch that worked well in the office. He felt it gave one the sense of confiding in a close friend. "Now, Wilson," he said gently, "it will be most helpful if you can tell me what happened."

With an occasional shake of his head, as though he didn't himself believe the events, Wilson recounted the time since he last saw Goldfield. Harry sat nearby and drank coffee generously endowed with sugar and cream. He helped himself to a second cup, waving Wilson down when the butler started to rise, and sipped with a large pinky projecting beside the delicate china.

Wilson concluded, "So you see, suh, yesterday evening, early, along about six, I believe...yes, it was just about dark. Mr. Goldfield told me he would be working late and did not want to be disturbed. I fixed his dinner, corned beef sandwiches, on rye with mustard, horseradish, onion and pickles, and went to quarters."

Reuchmaire's saliva glands made a Pavlovian response and his stomach gurgled a reminder that it had been several hours since he had eaten. Such a sandwich would be delightful. He tried to ignore his stomach, which seemed to be competing with him for the floor. "And you were in your quarters all night?"

"I returned twice, once at about seven-thirty, to fix coffee. I left it in the kitchen, like he wants when he is, ah, working late. The second time was a little before ten, as the storm was ending, to check the house." Wilson jerked at another loud intestinal complaint from Reuchmaire. "Would you like something to eat, suh. I can fix —"

"No, no, thank you, Wilson." The gentleman in Reuchmaire automatically declined. One always refuses the first offer. Reuchmaire, the gourmand, immediately regretted it. Gourmand and gentleman often had such disagreements. A sandwich would be delightful, but he was bound to *the code.*

"I'll take one of those sandwiches," Harry said.

"Certainly, suh. And you, doctor?"

Reuchmaire was astounded. How could Harry allow his stomach to overrule his manners at a time like this? How could Harry be so coarse about food and so good at chess? On the other hand, why did anyone think the way they did? Why did he dream of pubescent Patty when he had marvelous Marla at his beck and call? Sometimes he wondered if he understood the human mind at all. Well, as Grandfather Reuchmaire said, 'I often think that everybody in the world is crazy except you and me, and sometimes I'm worried about you.' However, since Harry had broken the barrier… "Yes, I believe I will." He quickly added, "If it's no trouble."

While Wilson made the sandwiches, Reuchmaire toured the kitchen. It was as expensively furnished as the rest of the house, and gleamed like a showcase. He took the lid off the coffee urn and inhaled. Delightful. Perhaps he should consider ground instead of instant. But the *cost*…. He inspected spice racks, appliances, shelves, and cupboards while Wilson glanced up from time to time to comment on the contents. He opened the side door and looked out. A covered walkway led to an adjoining brick building.

"That leads to my quarters." Wilson sliced the sandwiches into neat halves and served them on china plates.

"Door was unlocked," Harry said.

Reuchmaire looked at Wilson. "Perhaps Mr. Goldfield went out and left it unlocked."

"Oh, no, suh. Mr. Goldfield was very careful about security."

"I see. Then is it your impression that Mr. Goldfield was alone? Perhaps someone else might have failed to lock it."

"Maybe someone in a big hurry," Harry said through a mouthful.

"I, ah, I couldn't say, suh. He was alone when I first went to quarters. I didn't see him when I was preparing coffee, and I remained in quarters until this morning."

"And you heard nothing?"

"Well, the storm was coming. That was about eight. Quite a bit of thunder." He paused and found a cloth to wipe a drop of spilled coffee from a countertop. "I might have heard voices, but I'm not sure. The bedroom is so far from the kitchen."

"The bedroom? Does Mr. Goldfield usually work in the bedroom?"

Wilson's lips closed in a thin, distressed line.

Reuchmaire reworded the question. "Did you have reason to think that someone else might be here?"

"Not…then. Although, it would not have been unusual." The butler's face showed an inner struggle, and he blurted, "Dr. Reuchmaire, I have been a very loyal servant to Mr. Goldfield. I have never approved of his private life, nor of the way he treats Mrs. Goldfield. But I do as I am told, and I don't ask questions."

Reuchmaire considered how far to push. He finished the sandwich and picked up his coffee. He was quite envious of the quality. He fancied himself a connoisseur of instant coffees. Even though he had to admit it was somewhat bitter and lacking the flavor of the grinds Marla bought, instants were much cheaper, especially if one looked for bargains. Hers were easily as good as Goldfield's. He turned back to the butler. "So sometime later Mr. Goldfield may not have been alone."

"Yes, suh. This morning in the hall beside the stairs I found this." He handed over a lace hanky. "It's not Mrs. Goldfield's. Too fancy for her taste. Then I knew. About last night, I mean. He wasn't alone."

"And do you know who it was?"

"No."

Reuchmaire turned the hanky in his fingers. Likely Wilson did know the owner, but refused to say. Who was he protecting? The embroidery was so elaborately filigreed that he almost missed the initials GS as part of the design in one corner. He was about to hand it to Harry when an odor caught his attention. He abruptly put the hanky to his nose and inhaled. A very familiar scent. "Then, Wilson, Mr. Goldfield was not around this morning. You thought that not unusual?"

Wilson stiffened. "I assumed he had gone off with the owner of the kerchief. That would not have been unusual."

"When did you decide to call the police?"

"Late this afternoon the maid called me upstairs to see the floor in upper hall. In the cracks between the boards there was something she thought was dried blood."

"And where was the maid yesterday evening?"

"She leaves every day at five. There's not a maid in Beaufort will live in quarters here. Not since the unfortunate incident with the Conner girl."

Reuchmaire remembered. Two years previously it had come close to getting the billionaire run out of Beaufort, if anything could. It concerned Cassy, Cissy's older sister and then only sixteen. Goldfield hired her as a maid. Shortly afterward she got pregnant and insisted it was Goldfield's child. He denied it, claiming she was just after his money. She was brave enough, with Reuben's support, to go to court. Just before the trial, Cassy's drowned body turned up in Repository Cove. The coroner said publicly it was an accident, privately that he couldn't prove foul play but there might have been. Had Goldfield paid to have Cassy murdered? Had he done it himself? The only things for sure were that it closed the issue and drove Reuben back into depression.

Indirectly it was the first time Reuchmaire had crossed paths with the billionaire and it ignited an abiding mistrust for anything Goldfield did. Nothing since had occurred to change his view.

Reuchmaire suddenly remembered something from that afternoon. "Wilson, what about Mr. Goldfield's yacht? Is it here at the estate?"

"No, suh. Mr. and Mrs. Goldfield keep their runabouts at the yacht club. Just use the dock here for convenience stops. Their big boat is on loan to the Jeffersons. They're down in the Bahamas."

"They call those big twin diesels runabouts?"

"Yes, suh."

"*Sacre.*"

Wilson collected the empty plates, rinsed them and put them into the dishwasher. "Will that be all, suh?"

"Yes, thank you, Wilson. Good night."

Reuchmaire was thinking of the figure he had seen that afternoon entering the mansion. The clothes were Goldfield's, but the appearance...he wasn't sure.

"Com'n, Doc. I'll show you around." Harry led the way from the kitchen. "There's a patio being added on the east side. Nothing there that might hide a body. Biggest thing seems to be the stain."

The constable's investigative team, requested by Harry because the much more densely populated Beaufort county (thanks to Hilton Head) had more resources than the town, and because Goldfield was a VIP, was waiting in the foyer to ask if there was anything else he needed. They had dusted for fingerprints, collected a sample of the questionable substance (yes, they thought it was blood), searched for unusual objects, found none, and since there was no body to examine, wanted to go home. Buster and another officer were still here if he needed any help. Harry agreed and dismissed them.

In the paneled upper hall were portraits, antique furniture, drapes and the windowed wall of the atrium overlooking a courtyard containing a fountain surrounded by plants and shrubs. The far side was open to the night. Reuchmaire shuddered at the thought of the expense of the project. Posh drapes were drawn back from the glass. Reuchmaire's sympathy went out to the Daughters. This was indeed an abomination of an historical treasure. What if the rumor was true? Jefferson Davis himself might have trod this very floor. Goose bumps prickled his spine.

He studied the drapes and the atrium glass. There were ratchets to allow upper panes to be opened. Along the base of the drapes was a discoloration. A touch of his fingers disclosed dampness. One of the windows must have been left open during the storm and the drapes closed over the wet floor. How careless! To allow such expensive material (it felt like velvet) to be ruined was unforgivably wasteful. If he had such a house he would see that things were better taken care of. At least there were no Clemson pennants on the wall.

"Over here, Doc," Harry called from where the bannister curved away from the stairs.

"Blood?" asked Reuchmaire.

"For my money it is. The lab boys will tell us for sure, and if it's Goldfield's type. See how it's collected in the cracks. Looks like someone made a hasty attempt to clean it up."

"Not a very big stain," Reuchmaire observed. "Maybe four or five inches across."

Harry nodded.

"But no body."

"No body. And no shells."

"Shells?" Reuchmaire could not imagine what sea shells might have to do with this. The walls of one of the downstairs rooms, a lounge of sorts, were decorated with a variety of sea life, large and perfect horseshoe crab shells, star fish, at least one sailfish, and a display case of sand dollars, conches, periwinkles. But none had seemed to be missing and there was no reason why one of them might have found its way up here.

"Cartridge shells, Doc. No cartridge shells. If this blood came from a wound it likely was done with a knife, or some other sharp object, a bludgeon, or something similar, or a gun."

"Oh." Reuchmaire felt foolish, then he brightened. "Or the culprit may have been smart enough to collect the casing. Or use a revolver."

Harry nodded. "Right you are. See, you're beginning to think like a cop. I told you you'd be helpful."

Encouraged, Reuchmaire used his umbrella to point downstairs. "From down there, someone looking up this way would see a person silhouetted against the glass. But it happened at night according to Wilson. Ah, but the moon was up. But there was the storm. Most interesting." He looked again at the drapes. "Damp from the storm. And with the storm — lightning!"

Leaning over the railing to the side of the staircase he asked, "What is that thing mounted just below? It looks like a camera."

"It is. Night vision camera covering the foyer."

"Really? I didn't even notice it the other day."

"Yeah, Goldfield was a bit paranoid, particularly about his guns."

"Ah, Harry, but just because you're paranoid doesn't mean they aren't out to get you."

"What?"

"Never mind. So what does the camera do? Set off an alarm?"

"Don't know. I think it just views. If there's a display somewhere we haven't found it. Maybe it feeds to the regular TVs."

In the master bedroom, the bed was made and the furniture undisturbed. Reuchmaire ran his hand over the rich upholstery and finely polished furniture, giddy over the money represented in this room alone. He jerked his hand away as though he had been burned. "Fingerprints!" He may have disturbed fingerprints, a critical mistake.

Harry chuckled and replaced an exquisite ceramic vase on a table. "We already dusted. Found some prints from the maid, and from Wilson, but none from Goldfield."

"None?"

"Nary a one. Kind of unusual not to find a guy's prints in his own bedroom. I'm thinking someone wiped the room."

Near one window Reuchmaire found a long burned spot in the carpet. Tapping it with his umbrella tip he clucked, "Such a waste. This expensive carpet ruined by someone's carelessness — Mr. Goldfield's, no doubt. The man has no sense of value."

Harry's casual, "If you can afford it, I guess you can do what you want," caused Reuchmaire to grimace.

Reuchmaire toured the room, examining everything with great care. Uncertain of what to look for, he hoped he would know if he saw it. He was beginning to enjoy himself. A nightstand by the bed appeared antique, but there was new lacquer on it and the front had a false drawer. He ran an exploratory hand under it and encountered a button. *Voila!* Out slid a control panel and CRT.

Harry grinned. "There's our recorder for the cameras. Well done, Doc. There'll be a tape that might show us something."

Three other bedrooms and a library yielded nothing of interest other than the fact that Mrs. Goldfield's bedroom was on the opposite side of the house from her husband's. "I just don't understand," Harry said, "why people get married if they aren't in love."

"Ah, Harry, people marry for many reasons. They marry for convenience, for necessity, out of boredom, to please others. Sometimes they marry for love, or what they think is love. Rarely do they marry for the right reason. It's what we psychiatrists thrive on."

Harry gave Reuchmaire an odd look and moved on. A former bedroom, now a gun room, contained supplies and equipment for servicing guns and loading cartridges.

"Had to pick the lock," Harry said. "No key in the door."

"The paranoia," said Reuchmaire.

"Right."

"Rather an antiquated lock. Must take a large key."

"This whole place is antiquated, except for the parts Goldfield insisted on changing."

Inside was an impressive collection of high-quality equipment. Dies, presses, vises, a forge for melting lead, small barrels of shot and a stack of lead ingots.

"Quite an operation," Reuchmaire said amid the sweet smell of solvent and gun oil. "But again, such carelessness." His finger along a counter surface came up with a film of solvent. "Someone didn't clean up very well."

"Jeeze, these things are heavy," Harry said, lifting a keg of shot. "Well, nothing in here that tells us anything, except that he loaded his own ammunition."

Back at the top of the stairs Reuchmaire tapped his umbrella thoughtfully on the stained boards. "We know that in addition to Goldfield there may have been two other people in the mansion last night, Fast Nickie and whoever dropped the hanky. Assuming Nickie doesn't go in for lace hankies. Assuming we discount Wilson."

Harry took the cigar out of his mouth. "Doc, the butler never does it. You watched Wilson. You think he's guilty?"

There are few things, Reuchmaire reminded himself, that humans do better than lie, but he shook his head. “No, but I think he hasn’t told all he knows. He seems to be protecting someone.”

“Maybe the hanky’s Nickie’s. He’s got peculiar tastes.”

A wry smile came to Reuchmaire. “Probably not that peculiar.” Two separate events came together in his mind. He felt he might know to whom the hanky belonged, but he felt too amateurish to speak. Harry was the professional and he just an advisor, and a novice at that. Maybe he would mention it later, if it seemed important. A call from below drew them both to the top of the stairs.

Buster was down in the hall beside the stairs. “Just found this.” He pointed into the shadows. “It’s a muddy footprint, faint but discernable. Small, like a woman’s.”

“Perhaps three people,” said Reuchmaire.

Harry nodded. “Curiouser and curiouser. Any ideas?”

“I think we should to talk to Nickie. Find out what his shoe size is.”

Chapter 9

Isadora tossed in the grip of a strange dream. She was in her art shop, alone, although there were people at the door waiting to get in. She had the key to the door in her hand and went to admit them, but when she saw their faces she stopped. They were all Dr. Reuchmaire! She looked around and all the paintings in her shop were of Bull. Her breath came in panicky gasps. Suddenly Bull was beside her, touching her with his skillful caresses. The Reuchmaires at the door had gone, and she began to relax into Bull's embrace, feeling the fire mount. Abruptly the floor became water. Bull slid down into it and floated away through some undefinable passage. His face, with that supercilious smirk he so often wore as though he knew something she didn't, remained. The phone rang, and the terror returned. It was Dr. Reuchmaire, she knew, calling to ask questions. She shrank away, afraid to answer. The phone rang again.

She sat up in bed, trembling, and reached for the light. She blinked at the instrument on the bedside table. It rang again. She was sure when she answered she would hear Reuchmaire's voice.

"Isadora, it's Nickie."

She squinted at the clock.

"Isadora?"

"Nickie, for Christ's sake it's 3:00 a.m. Where are you?"

"In jail. Where'd you think?"

"Have you lost your mind? I told you not to call me." She spoke in a whisper as though she could be overheard.

"The chief's out at Goldfield's place. No one's here but a deputy and he's out front. The phone's just outside my cell. I can reach it through the bars. You oughta see this place. It must be a hundred years old. I could break out in a New York minute."

She thought it over and decided jail was the best place for him for now. "No, you don't want to do that. I've refused to press charges. They can't hold you —"

"Listen, you don't understand. *You don't understand.* They're trying to hang a *murder* rap on me. For Goldfield."

"What? That's ridiculous! They have no grounds."

"I don't know. What if they do?"

She had to get him to shut up. Bad enough that he called her. That was a dead giveaway. She gambled that no one else was listening. "Look, Nickie," she soothed, trying to keep the urgency out of her voice, "it's going to be OK, trust me. Listen, if you're not out by tomorrow, next day at the latest, I'll pay your bail and we'll head out. How's that?"

"Well, yeah, I guess..."

"Good. Now hang up the phone and don't call me again. Understand?"

After a lengthy silence she heard him sigh. "Yeah, okay," and he hung up.

"Jesus!" She lit a cigarette and sat in bed smoking. "That stupid little jerk. She had half a mind to head out and leave him here in this jerkwater town. Then she thought of the safe and the money and knew she wouldn't leave. Nickie still had some use, and she needed to hang around for appearances. She crushed the cigarette into an ashtray and turned out the light. No reason to worry. These hick cops haven't even connected her to Bull yet, and they probably wouldn't. Hell, he screwed around so much it could have been anybody with him that night. A tremor ran through her. But it hadn't been "anybody." That bastard. She drifted off dreaming of Bull poised at the top of the stairs, and a glow of satisfaction lulled her to sleep.

* * *

Fast Nickie sat on the edge of the bunk, head in hands, and wondered how it all got so screwed up. This whole thing was like some movie. He should have been up in Norfolk by now, two states away and holed up, waiting for Isadora to call. Holed up and counting his share of the Goldfield take, playing some pool, chasing snatch, maybe even putting a couple of big ones on a horse. After a heist he always felt rich. Instead, here he was in jail, held not just for attempted robbery but maybe murder. *Murder!* He could not believe how fast it fell apart. "I didn't kill Goldfield," he muttered. "I couldn't have! Could I?"

He wasn't sure anymore. All he clearly remembered was Goldfield at the top of the stairs, silhouetted against the glass. He deliberately aimed wide and almost collapsed himself when Goldfield dropped like a rock. Then he was running out of the mansion and off the estate to high-tail it on his motorcycle back to Bluffton.

When Isadora called the next morning she sounded like nothing was wrong. Cool and collected, like always. She just called, she said, to confirm the plans for the purse snatch. This time, she said, there was something extra. There would be a key in her purse for him to use and get back into the mansion. Before he could protest she told him the plan and said there was an advance in her purse for him, just a fraction of what they'd get from the safe.

He was to make the hit at eleven-thirty on Bay Street, same routine they always used. Away from the gallery so it would seem random, she said, just as an added precaution to avoid any connection between them. She was real careful that way, a real nut for details. He pictured the way she talked with her head tilted up in a slightly snooty way, the phone held with an arched wrist and her pinkie out, just like those aristocratic babes in the movies. Probably the way she was just now, when he called her. She could have been in movies, he thought. Her face was OK, not so much pretty as sexy, but OK. And she had a fine body, kind of broad-shouldered and athletic, but a slender waist and great legs. He had the hots for her all right, but never had the courage to make a pass. The superior way she acted, the businesslike way she handled their operation, made him think that if he ever did, she would just laugh. Besides, he was not one to mix business with pleasure.

Unable to sit still he began to pace. He took quick drags on a cigarette while his free hand ran repeatedly through his long dark hair. There was another problem. He had gone to the mansion early that night against her plan. He thought he would be in and out while she was upstairs with Goldfield, and she wouldn't even know. But now the whole thing was screwed up, and she might blame him. She could be dangerous. It was in her eyes sometimes. A hard stare that went right through him as though he wasn't there, as though she was looking at something only she could see. It was a look common to career criminals, which he knew he was but in a minor way. The others who had that look were killers, and it scared him to see it in her.

That morning he had grabbed her purse and roared off, just as planned. Everything was just like their last operation out in Texas until Dr. Reuchmaire stepped in. Nickie laughed. Who would of thought the doc would do what he did. Just like a movie hero. Pretty neat trick with that umbrella of his. He never would of thought of it, he told himself, as though proud of a friend. Nickie rubbed the knot on the back of his head, admiring the doc's courage. After all, it was kind of like he was *his* shrink, the way they worked together in stir up at Allendale. Well, they didn't really work together, Doc just counseled him like, but it was almost the same.

Hope stirred in his narrow chest. Maybe Doc Reuchmaire could get him out of this mess. At least get him off the murder rap. The doc knew he wasn't a killer.

He lay down on the bunk. Yeah, the doc would know. He began to relax. How had Cagney done it in the movie he saw the other night? He put his hands behind his head and closed his eyes like it wasn't such a big deal, like he could handle it.

* * *

The sound of the cellblock door awakened him. He leapt off the cot and grabbed the bars, looking quickly from Dr. Reuchmaire to Chief Doyle.

"Well, Nickie," Reuchmaire said reproachfully, "here you are again in the slammer."

"Doc, what is this? I didn't kill no one."

"Who says you did?"

"He did. Chief Doyle."

"Well, Nickie. You did pull a knife on me yesterday."

"I was seein' stars, Doc. I didn't know it was you. I never would have, not you."

"Nickie, we have a gun with your fingerprints on it."

"What're you talking about?"

"Goldfield's dueling pistols, Nickie. One of them has been fired and has your prints on it." Reuchmaire watched the delicate fingers, so suited to working safes, tighten on the bars. He wondered whether under different circumstances Nickie might have become a highly successful concert pianist.

"That can't be. She said..."

"Yes, Nickie? Who said?"

Nickie closed his eyes and leaned against the bars. "I don't know, seems like somebody said something, but I can't remember. I just didn't do it, I'm tellin' ya."

Reuchmaire pursed his lips. Either Nickie was a superlative actor or he really did not believe he had shot anyone. Knowing Nickie better than Nickie did, he opted for the latter. "Maybe you should tell us what happened," he said, and leaned close with the same sincerity he had used with Wilson. "Truth is always best isn't it, Nickie. Just like we used to talk about."

Nickie nodded. "Yeah, yeah, 'to thyne own self be true.' Just what you used to tell me back at Allendale. Or was that the chaplain?"

"Well, do you want to tell me? I'll be more sympathetic than a judge."

Nickie found a cigarette pack, crumpled it, and threw it in a corner.

Reuchmaire extended a fresh pack. "I took the liberty. I believe this is your brand."

"Thanks. Thanks, Doc. You always was a good guy." He lit a cigarette and sat on the bunk, smoking nervously. "Okay," he said finally, "Okay, I shot the gun. But I didn't mean to hit 'im. Honest to God, Doc, I was just trying to scare him back to give me a chance to get out. I was there for the check, not to kill anyone." He came back to the bars, his eyes pleading. "That's the honest-to-God truth, Doc."

"You were there for what?"

Nickie looked confused. "The safe, Doc. To hit the safe."

Reuchmaire tapped the umbrella briskly on the floor while he thought about Nickie's slip. Finally he said, "Ah, Nickie, so quickly back to a life of crime."

"Yeah, well, I guess I just wasn't meant to be on the outside…but, you do believe me, don't ya, Doc?"

"Yes, Nickie, I do."

Nickie sagged against the bars and emitted a long sigh. "Thanks, Doc."

"By the way, Nickie, what's your shoe size?"

"My size?" He raised a foot and looked at it as though he might find a number printed on it. "Ten D. Everybody kids me about my big feet. I mean, compared to how small the rest of me is."

"Okay, thanks Nickie."

Back in the outer office Harry lit a cigar and said, "Well?"

The umbrella tapped a rapid pace on the floor while Reuchmaire stared out the dark window. He could see the lights of the marina down on the river. "I don't know. We have the gun. We have his prints. What about powder traces?"

"None, but he could have taken two dozen baths by the time we got him."

Reuchmaire rubbed his eyes. "Harry, I am too exhausted to think. I'm going home to bed. Call me tomorrow if you want, but not too early."

"Sure. Thanks, Doc. Appreciate your coming out."

On the way to his car Reuchmaire pulled his coat tighter in the predawn cold and grumbled at the unseasonable weather. What an astonishing night! Even as tired as he was he felt exhilarated. He was actually part of a felony investigation. He even thought he had been of some service. There were so many things to consider. However, there were two things of which he was certain: first, if Nickie did shoot Goldfield he did not mean to, secondly, Nickie, like Wilson, was withholding something.

Chapter 10

A weary Reuchmaire returned home at 5:00 a.m. Barely able to keep his eyes open, he longed for Marla's coffee but longed more for sleep. He was almost home before it occurred to him that her place in Old Beaufort, on the exclusive historical area known as "the Point," was only a short distance from the Goldfield estate and closer than his house out on Dataw Island. He had also left General Stuart asleep by the fire. But he was too weary to backtrack, and the General would be fine with Marla.

The land east of Beaufort, to which U.S. Highway 21 led after crossing the Woods Memorial Bridge from downtown, was a series of smaller islands comprising the larger expanse of Lady's (originally Ladies) Island. All were islands, some literally, some not, due to meandering tidal creeks and marshes that cut the land into irregular segments, like pieces of a giant jigsaw puzzle. Living there, Reuchmaire felt no sense of being enisled. After the large Woods bridge over the Beaufort River he had only to cross a small one across a thin finger of the Morgan River, and another two over tidal marshes within the confines of Dataw. The land, although low lying, for the most part was firm ground above sea level.

He waved to the guard as he drove into the entrance of Dataw Estates. He knew that back at her place Marla would be just getting up, cheerful and alert, to do her exercises before leaving for work. He was in no mood for that. A great mystery of his beloved was how she could day in and day out force herself to perform the rituals she claimed kept her feeling young and vital. They were painful even to contemplate. But her devotion was exemplary, and he could hardly complain about the results. She would be at work precisely at eight-thirty, daisy-fresh and ringing like a bell, exuding a *joie de vivre* that would last the rest of the day whether it be eight hours or eighteen. And today she would do it like any other day but on only four hours of sleep.

He, on the other hand, needed eight hours straight without interruption plus a firm cup of coffee to hope for the smallest degree of civility. Any less and the psyche devils would poke their hot little pitchforks into his eyelids, resulting in behavior irritating even to himself. When he departed the police station he had not even registered on the chess move Harry included in their parting remarks. His mind was awash with a sea of clues, non-clues, assumptions, truths, and pure guesses Harry had presented as they covered every inch of mansion and estate. He felt as if he had been through a wringer. This was far beyond the simple cases he had assisted with before, and he was not certain he was up to it. He knew he was not if it included many more nights like this one.

At this early hour, the pivoting bridge was closed. He sped over it with a sigh of relief and reached home within a few minutes. But Harry's move had vanished into the mists. All he remembered was Harry's sympathetic smile, which probably meant the game was over. He would have to call later and ask if it was and Harry would laugh, knowing the reason. Harry, who worked long hours and was often called out suddenly in the dark of night, had not appreciated Reuchmaire's plight. But he was quickly apologetic when it was tersely pointed out. They got along well, due largely to Harry's virtue of not letting his ego overrule his judgment. And, of course, there was his own even temperament, no small thing, Reuchmaire modestly admitted.

At his front door he reminded himself that one person's calling lay one way, another's another (he sounded confused even to himself). His was given to shrewd daytime analysis preceded by sufficient sleep. He yawned, and fumbled for his keys.

He was startled to discover that his front door was unlocked. He was certain that he had locked it. He *always* locked it. His heart beat a warning. With the umbrella held defensively like a sword, he entered. The house was dark, just as he left it — no need to light empty rooms; his bill was high enough as it was. Even a single lamp added up over time. A street light, filtered through a magnolia and partly opened blinds, afforded a dim view. Nothing moved. There was no sound. Or was there?

He heard something in the kitchen. Should he turn on a light? No. He would be blinded by the glare. But so would the intruder. He stopped in the center of the living room. It took all his will to force himself onward. He slipped out of his shoes at the parqueted dining area, crossed silently, and paused at the kitchen doorway. Why was he doing this? He should race outside and call for help, pound on a neighbor's door, or — of course! Call Harry on the cell phone in his car. But he was stopped by another thought. What if it isn't an intruder? What if it's a mouse, or — of course! Captain Semmes! That was it. Wouldn't Harry have gotten a laugh if he called him to arrest a cat.

He relaxed and reached for the light switch under the calendar. But his hand stuck in mid air. *Something had moved.* Something big, like a man. A shadow within the darker shadows by the refrigerator. *There is someone here!* In his house. On his property. To steal his possessions. *Sacre!* What nerve!

Anger overcame fear. He released the catch on the umbrella's handle and slid the enclosed *epee* free of its case. He never thought he would use it. He never thought he *could*. He detested the sight of blood. The shadow turned his way. Fear overcame fury. But it was too late. He snapped into *en garde* and bellowed, "Stand and deliver!" embarrassed as hell at the tremor in his voice.

The figure was too close. Instantly it was inside his reach and had him clasped in a crushing bear hug. The arms tightened, lifting him clear of the floor.

A voice roared in his ear. "Jimbo!"

Reuchmaire, returned to the planet of the floor, peered at the shadowed face. "Edwin?"

"Where the hell is the light switch? I've busted my knees twice."

Sagging on weakened knees, Reuchmaire leaned on the counter. His hand found the light switch. He and his cousin squinted at each other.

"Edwin, it *is* you. What are you doing here? How did you get in?"

His cousin opened the refrigerator and fumbled around. "Jimbo, you gave me a key. Don't you remember? Getting senile? And you only five years older than me. Is that what I have to look forward to?" He closed the refrigerator and set a can of cat food on the counter. "Your cat's hungry. Don't you feed him?"

Beside the refrigerator sat a gray and black tabby. He had one full ear and the other reduced by half, a kinked tail, and a left eyelid drooped by a scar. His back had a curious bend to it that gave him a slightly hump-backed appearance. The good right eye watched Edwin with great interest.

Reuchmaire retreated into the dining area and slumped into a chair, letting the blade sag to the floor. He glared at the tabby. "Some watchcat. He's always hungry."

Edwin spooned cat food. "So, where'd you get the pig sticker? By the way, 'stand and deliver' is a highwayman's challenge. You know, 'stop the stage and hand over your valuables.'" He placed the dish before the loudly purring Captain Semmes.

"It was all I could think of." Reuchmaire resheathed the blade and laid the umbrella on the table. "What are you doing here? And at this hour?"

"Doing an article on how to eat healthfully in the midst of cholesterol-saturated Lowcountry food. Tough assignment. I was out logging some time in my plane yesterday and got held up in Atlanta by weather. By the time it cleared Houston was socked in, so I thought I'd just hop down here for a visit and get this article done. The editor's threatening to take back my advance."

Reuchmaire yawned violently. "In the middle of the night?"

"No. Although I believe that editors do hang by their feet in caves, I think they only work during the day — oh, you mean why am I here in the middle of...well, hardly the middle of the night. It's after five. It'll be daylight soon. I got in last night about eight. You weren't around, I had already eaten, so I hit the sack and got up to get an early start." He rummaged in the pantry. "Got any grounds?"

Reuchmaire shook his head.

Edwin found a jar of instant, made a face, shrugged and searched for a cup. "I always forget where you keep things."

"Left cabinet." Reuchmaire leaned down to stroke Captain Semmes who had come over to rub against his leg.

"Where'd you get the cat? Didn't have him when I was here last."

"Captain Semmes went through a boat propellor —"

Edwin laughed. "Captain Semmes. Captain of the CSA high-seas raider Alabama. Why does that not surprise me?"

Reuchmaire ignored the remark. "A patient of mine was fishing out there in the creek and saw him fall off a shrimper. He pulled him out more dead than alive, broken back, deep lacerations. He brought him here and I got him to the vet. Touch and go for a while. The vet was surprised he lived."

Edwin placed a cup of water in the microwave. "Lucky kitty, in a manner of speaking. By the way, what are you doing up now? Want a cup?"

Reuchmaire shook his head and fought down another yawn. "It's a long story. I'll tell you later. I need to get to bed or I'll fall over." He came over and embraced his cousin. "Good to see you again. Make yourself at home."

Five minutes later Edwin looked up from newspaper and coffee at a distressed Reuchmaire in garnet pajamas sprinkled with black figures. "Hey, nice P.J.'s. Little gamecocks, aren't they?"

"I have made a terrible blunder." Reuchmaire fumbled among papers by the phone, found a pen and scribbled briefly.

"I am supposed to be at Allendale State Prison at nine to conduct a class, but I would be incapable of functioning. Please call Warden White at this number — he won't be there until eight — and give him my profane, uh, profuse apologies. Tell him…" He wondered what he *should* tell him.

"I could tell him you're unconscious, which seems to be the case."

Reuchmaire scowled. "Funny. Tell him the truth. I've become involved in a case, perhaps a felony, with Chief Doyle.

"Wow! A felony? Tell me about it."

"Later. Just call the warden, please, and my office and have my secretary reschedule tomorrow's — er, today's appointments. Unless there is an emergency, and I'll see that after noon. Make that after three. No, just wake me up. Fortunately it is a light day. Then unplug the phone." He trundled off to bed.

* * *

A ravenous Reuchmaire awoke at two in the afternoon. His stomach felt like a big empty pit. Not too surprising. He had missed both breakfast and lunch. Unthinkable! He would never make a good law enforcement officer. So far, being a detective was not all that much fun. In the shower he let the hot water soothe tight muscles not used to all night investigations until he thought of the cost of all that hot water going down the drain. Quickly, he shut it off.

Toweled, dressed, and refreshed he pondered the first item of business: where to have lunch? He went to the kitchen for a glass of milk and found that Edwin had been shopping. How thoughtful. But was there anything edible in the cornucopia of food with which his normally empty 'fridge fairly burst?

"Jimbo, up at last," Edwin heralded, as he entered the back door and set another bag of groceries on the counter. "Have a seat and I'll fix you a turkey sandwich."

"Turkey? Isn't there any ham?"

"Too much fat and salt. You'll like this. Trust me." Shortly Reuchmaire accepted a neatly sliced turkey on rye (made with cottonseed oil, Edwin explained) with mustard (no mayonnaise), tomatoes, avocado, and lettuce.

Edwin started on one for himself. "In Houston I can get turkey breast pastrami, which I like better, but this is hickory smoked and quite tasty."

"Well, it is rather good," said Reuchmaire through a large bite. "Do you suppose I might have another?"

"Well…oh, all right, and for dessert, an apple."

Reuchmaire sighed. "How long are you staying?"

"Unfortunately, not long enough to get you trimmed down, cuz," said Edwin, taking a bite of his own sandwich as he brought it to the table. "Now tell me about this case you're on. The paper says you're a hero. Captured the murderer single handed."

"Alleged murderer," Reuchmaire answered. He had to admit he was in fact somewhat of a celebrity and wondered why the paper had not asked for a picture. He'd best dig out a good one in case there was a follow up. "And I'm really only on the case as an advisor."

The doorbell rang and Harry came in twirling his Stetson. "Something wrong with your phone? Hey, that sandwich looks good."

Edwin found the end of the cord and reconnected the phone. "I'll make you one. Have a seat. Sleeping beauty didn't want to be disturbed."

"Doc," Harry said, "the lab checked out the blood."

Edwin's eyebrows shot up. "Blood?"

"Type O, same as Goldfield's, and it had been dry at least twelve hours when the maid found it. Which means the murder must have been committed during the night — the night of the storm. Sometime between six in the afternoon, when Wilson last saw Goldfield, and five the next morning."

"Murder?" said Edwin, handing Harry the sandwich.

Harry said through a mouthful, "Of course, we don't know for sure that it was murder. Not without a body."

Edwin's head swivelled from one to the other. "Will you two tell me what's going on!"

Harry told him and Edwin let out a long whistle. "So, what's next?"

"This," said Harry, and produced a video cassette. "Remember the night vision camera, Doc? That control panel you found was for a recorder that comes on with the camera, which is motion activated. Where's your VCR?"

The three gathered around the screen as the replay began.

"That's Nickie!" exclaimed Reuchmaire. "He's firing upstairs toward the atrium. Um, why is the picture green?"

"I.R." said Edwin. "Infrared. Sees in the dark."

"If it's infrared why is the picture green?"

"That's how it transmits."

"I see," said Reuchmaire, not seeing at all. Harry rewound the tape. "Watch. Nickie looks at the guns, picks one up, then something upstairs startles him. He fumbles with the gun and fires. That's why the picture washes out, from the muzzle flash. The fuzziness from time to time is from the lightning flashes, not strong enough to completely blank it but enough to make it fade. That sure looks like Nickie, no question. Now, after he fires, he stares up past the camera. He slowly mounts the stairs and disappears off camera. Less than a minute later he runs back down the stairs and out of the picture."

"Rerun it, Harry," Reuchmaire said, his eyes narrowed in thought. Again the three watched Nickie fire, pause, go slowly upstairs, then run downstairs.

"Something is there," Reuchmaire said. "Something I can't quite place. Again, Harry. This time watch the right side of the picture just as Nickie fires. There seems to be another flash almost at the same time."

"Probably lightning."

"No, it's much smaller — there! See it."

"Humph. Not sure. Let's do it again."

This time the three of them agreed that there was indeed another faint flash from off-screen right but overridden by Nickie's shot and the lightning.

Harry was dubious. "I don't know. I think it's lightning. What else could it be?"

"Is there another camera? One for the other side of the foyer?"

"It's mounted but not working yet. You know how Goldfield monkeys with the house, adding one thing and another. He just got it in a week ago."

"What does it matter?" asked Edwin. "You've got the shot of this Nickie. What more do you need?"

Reuchmaire leaned back and clasped his fingers behind his neck. "We have a picture of Nickie firing the gun. But what did he hit?"

"He hit Goldfield," said Harry. "That's why we found the blood. Nickie shot Goldfield and hid the body somewhere. All we got to do is find the body and I'll bet you'll find a fifty-four caliber ball in it."

Reuchmaire shook his head. "I still cannot accept that Nickie shot Goldfield. A gun is not Nickie's weapon. He couldn't hit Goldfield if he tried, unless he stuck the gun in his gut when he pulled the trigger."

"Lucky shot?" Edwin offered.

Reuchmaire scowled. But it was possible.

Harry thought for a while. "But, if he missed, why wasn't there a hole somewhere in the atrium glass? There was a whole wall of it behind Goldfield."

Reuchmaire jumped up. "I know why. Let's go to the mansion. And Harry, leave that film here. I want to run it some more."

* * *

Reuchmaire, Edwin, Harry and Wilson looked up at the glass wall of the atrium. "Remember, Harry, night before last the bottom of these drapes were wet."

Harry nodded, searching his jacket for a cigar stub.

"See, the material is discolored, even though it is dry. Now, Wilson, cannot those upper panels be opened from down here?"

"Yes, suh. And the night of the storm one was open, this panel here. And the drapes were drawn back." He turned the crank and an upper panel ratcheted open.

Reuchmaire popped his umbrella on the floor emphatically. "So that it rained in and got these drapes wet."

"Yes, suh, that's so. It was wet when I came up and closed it."

"And when was that?"

"About ten, suh. The storm was almost over and I remembered I had left the window open. So I came up and closed it."

"But you told us last night that after fixing coffee you went to quarters for the night."

Wilson fidgeted. "Yes, suh. I forgot that I did come up later to close the window."

Reuchmaire throbbed with excitement, barely able to allow Wilson to finish before plunging onward to the next question. "And when you were up here, did you see anything. Anything unusual?"

The butler shook his head. "Couldn't see much, suh. The power was still off and I only had a hand light."

"But you saw to close the window and saw that there was nothing on the floor over there where the blood is. Not a body, for instance."

"Oh, no, suh! I surely would have noticed that."

"And you saw nothing else? Not Mr. Goldfield?"

The butler turned his eyes from Reuchmaire's, and said, "No, suh. The bedroom door was closed, so I went back down."

"Um, hum. Thank you. That's all we'll need you for now."

Wilson nodded and shuffled off.

"Well, that narrows things down even more," Reuchmaire beamed. "The murder must have been done before ten o'clock, when Wilson came up."

"Or after," Harry said.

"I thought you knew when it was done," said Edwin.

"What?" Harry and Reuchmaire said together.

"It was right there on the tape we watched. Date and time, down in the lower corner. Didn't you see it? It said 5DEC2028, military time for eight-twenty-eight at night, December fifth."

Harry smiled and scratched his head. "Got by me."

Reuchmaire tapped his umbrella rapidly on the floor. "How unobservant of me. Edwin, you're a genius." He turned back to look at the open window. "So Nickie's shot could have gone out that window."

"Pretty unlikely," said Harry.

"But there is no broken glass."

"Easy enough to find out," said Edwin.

The umbrella stopped tapping. "How?"

"Plot a line. From down there where Nickie fired and out through the open window. Just a simple physics problem. We've got the line of flight and the angle of launch. Assumed, of course, but reasonably accurate. All we need is the weight of the ball, the muzzle velocity, and Nickie's height. Those old cannons fired a big ball, didn't they? Not much range. I'd guess that it didn't get off the grounds." He stood beneath the suspect window panel and aligned himself with his arms, pointing one down to where Nickie had stood and the other in the opposite direction toward the distant front of the estate visible through the atrium glass.

Reuchmaire clapped his cousin on the shoulders. "Edwin, you're a genius."

"Why, thank you, Jimbo, that's twice in one day. Maybe I should call Mensa."

Reuchmaire hooked his umbrella on a forearm and fumbled in his clothes for his notepad. He scribbled briefly and tore off the page. "Here's the data you need. You see, I was trying to buy those pistols from Goldfield. He was quite eccentric about them. About all his guns, actually. He kept them all loaded and primed. I tried to explain to him that it was bad for the barrel to have powder in it all the time. Corrodes it, you know. He just laughed. But he knew to the exact grain how much and what kind of powder he used." Reuchmaire sighed. "They are lovely, just lovely, and almost faultless, considering their age."

Edwin looked at the note. "What do I do with this?"

"You're a Georgia Tech grad. Use that electronic slide rule you carry around and plot the line."

Chapter 11

"Well, kiss my blue britches with me in 'em!" Marla plopped down her coffee cup and slapped at a picture on the front page of the newspaper. "Look at this."

General Stuart, sitting hopeful of handouts at Reuchmaire's feet beside the breakfast table, looked up curiously, as did Reuchmaire who stopped applying a thick layer of marmalade to toast and crooked his neck to see. "That's Isadora Hawthorne, the art dealer," he said. "She's been oddly quiet over the incident with Fast Nickie. And, she refused to press charges. Rather puzzling."

"Ha! Isadora Hawthorne indeed. That's my old swim team mate, Grundel Smith. No, Schmidt. Hair's a different color, but that's her mouth and nose. Haven't seen her in twenty-five years, not since our ten-year reunion. She still has that snooty look from back then, like she's above you. But the guys seemed to like it."

"Grundel Schmidt," Reuchmaire said, munching thoughtfully and breaking off a piece to slip to the General. A faint bell rang in his memory.

"So, she's an art dealer — Jimsy, please don't feed the General at the table — well, that suits. The dealer part, I mean. She always had some deal going, usually a scam. One thing she did was impressive. She could walk the pool underwater."

"Do what?"

"Walk the pool. Back in high school we'd get pocket money betting the guys she could walk from one end of the pool to the other and back. Underwater. A hundred meters. She had to hold her breath almost two minutes. I'd set it up and she'd do it."

"Walking? Not swimming?"

"Right. Pretty slick for a couple of li'l ol' Beaufort girls, don'cha think?" Marla screwed a finger into her cheek. "She'd get a couple of bar bells from the gym to hold her down and just walk along the bottom. She could go almost as fast as swimming. She was like a fish, a real jock."

"How interesting," said Reuchmaire. "So she's from Beaufort."

"Just like me. After high school we went separate ways, me swept off my ignorant, impressionable feet by my first husband and whisked off to Las Vegas. He was a gambler, or thought he was. Grundel…I don't know where she went, New York, or somewhere like that. She wanted to paint, be an artist. Hah! She was an artist, all right. A con artist."

Reuchmaire tingled with a feeling of expectancy. Unconsciously he gave the General the last of his toast.

"Jimsy —!"

"Sorry."

The little butterfly began to flit around in his brain but refused to alight. His senses told him it had to do with Goldfield's disappearance.

Marla scooped up her dishes to take to the kitchen. "Maybe I should go by and say 'hi' while she's in town. Come to think of it she still owes me fifty dollars she borrowed at the reunion — goodness, look at the time!"

"I thought you were going to take today off."

"Sorry, Jimsy. Got some work I just gotta do. I'll work real hard — promise!" She held up three fingers and crossed her heart. "And tomorrow I'll fix a picnic and we'll go out to Hunting Island. Nobody's around this time of year. We'll have the whole park to ourselves. Now give me a kiss and don't forget to put your dishes in the sink. And remember General Stuart gets groomed today. His nails are way overdue for trimming."

Reuchmaire saw her to the door and returned to toast and coffee, marmalading another piece to share with the General. What could he do? She was too headstrong to argue with and too desirable not to have around. He was the psychiatrist. He was supposed to understand her needs. Yes, a little Freudian voice said, but it's entirely different when they butt heads with your own. *C'est la vie.*

Followed by the tapping toenails of the ever hopeful General Stuart, he went to the kitchen and searched the 'fridge for butter but found only no-fat sour cream. *Mon Dieu!* A bit of butter now and then was hardly a crime.

"Sorry, no butter," he reported to the General as he checked his watch. "Anyway, it's time for your appointment."

Grundel Schmidt, he thought, what is it about that name? Maybe Harry will know.

He got a houndstooth hat from the closet, an old favorite and appropriately sleuthish, and stepped outside for a weather check. High clouds, and the temperature was cool but almost balmy. A definite improvement after the freeze. He selected a light coat to go with the hat, and called Harry.

* * *

At eleven, Edwin arrived at the Goldfield estate in Marla's Suburban loaded with materials to construct a dig. Although boards and nails were easily available, a trip into Savannah had been necessary to find a transit with a laser marker. He also wanted to get a metal detector, which would have made things much easier, but his parsimonious cousin had balked at the expense of two "technological gadgets." 'What's a little digging,' he had said. Nothing, Edwin grumbled to himself as he parked near the area where his rough sighting indicated the ball might lie, if you're not the one doing it. Well, Jimbo was funding this scheme, which Edwin, in spite of his original enthusiasm, had become less sure of, so he had to comply.

He walked down to the house to explain why he was here and on the way rehearsed his story. He hated telling lies, even small ones, even for a just cause (which he fervently hoped this was). No one answered the bell. He rang again, shouted, and looked through several windows. No one home. Feeling very uncomfortable he used the key Harry had given him to unlock the door, and cautiously entered. When no one responded to further calls, he relaxed as much as he could. It felt creepy to be in someone's house without permission.

He positioned the transit at the foot of the stairs exactly where Nickie stood, then sighted a line at the atrium window he marked yesterday with masking tape, and recorded the bearing. He had to go find a ladder to reach the laser dot on the glass, from which he dropped a plumb. From there he sighted to the boundary fence on the same bearing, noted the precise spot, went down the ladder, and back out to mark the fence at the point where the transit was aimed. Now he had the line. If the ball had fallen inside the fence, as he hoped, they just might find it. Beyond was the road and beyond that tangled undergrowth where there was no hope.

It was slow labor, requiring him to move from one spot to another, adjust the ladder, and reposition the fortunately lightweight transit and make the long walk to the fence. A growl from his stomach reminded him it was past lunchtime. For that, Jimbo owed him dinner, and a good one. If he could find a restaurant with something not deep-fried or afloat in butter. He had brought an apple along, and he took time to stroll among the furnishings of the upper hall while he ate.

He was an engineer by education and a NASA pilot by trade. However, mild coronary artery disease and an unsympathetic bureaucracy grounded him from test piloting, and in disgust he took an early out to live on his government pension and be a writer. He enjoyed a comfortable but not extravagant lifestyle. Just to walk among this show of wealth was breathtaking, a journey through the palace of a king. He let not even a drop of juice from the apple reach the floor, and wiped his hand carefully on his jeans before venturing a shy touch of a richly upholstered chair or gleaming urn. It was careless to let these posh drapes get wet, but from the looks of the place Goldfield could buy another set — or ten — and not notice it.

There were plants in urns, antique chairs, an old chest, and swords hung among portraits along the paneled walls perpendicular to the atrium. At the glass wall of the atrium he peered into a small courtyard where shrubs and plants surrounded a small fountain. How odd and out of place it looked in this fine old mansion. His scientific eye missed nothing, not even a lone strand of cobweb hiding high in a corner. He came finally to a large portrait of Bull Goldfield. The billionaire stared arrogantly down from the wall opposite his bedroom. He was clad incongruously in a hunting outfit with a bright orange vest, adorned prominently with a gold key chain. Even if Jimbo had not called the billionaire a runaway egotist, the portrait made it obvious. Portraits, he maintained, reflected the inner person.

As he looked at the painting he noticed something not quite right about it. There was a small hole in Goldfield's vest, just about waist high. He brought the ladder over to get high enough to put his face to it. Small and round, only one thing would make a hole like that. With great care, still mindful of how expensive it must be, he eased the portrait to the floor and went to work with his pocketknife on the underlying hole in the wall. Shortly he held a small round piece of lead in his hand. "Very interesting," he muttered. Pocketing his find, he replaced the painting, finished the apple and went back to the survey.

Calculations complete, the point at which the errant ball fell (he hoped) appeared on his computer. To his relief it was just inside the fence. The fence of black iron bars, seven feet high and tipped with points, stretched a quarter mile in either direction, turned ninety degrees and hemmed the estate to the river. Down at the northern corner something brown and four-legged moved. A dog? It had not occurred to him that the estate might be guarded by four-legged sentries. Had he been clambering about the house, sighting lines and making calculations, with dogs loose on the grounds? All he needed was a Rottweiler or two to keep him company.

He cursed himself for opening his mouth about the damned trajectory. Why had he agreed to come out here? He edged toward the fence, thinking he should be home in Houston now, finishing the article, working on his book, writing op-ed pieces. Not nosing around here where he didn't belong waiting for a dog to rip his buns off.

It was a deer. He breathed again. The doe took a short run and cleared the fence in a long graceful bound.

"No dogs," he muttered, "no dogs. Just relax and do the work and get out of here." He went to work and outlined the plot with boards like an archaeological dig, which in effect it was. After a bit he yielded to the afternoon warmth and removed his shirt. The framework complete, he knelt beside it to check his calculations.

Absorbed in his work, he failed to notice Annabelle Goldfield's Mercedes purr through the gate and come to a stop just inside. After a moment's curiosity she got out of the car and sauntered over past the trees with her unhurried, aristocratic swing.

Edwin, absorbed in his calculations, was oblivious to her approach. He was unaware of the moment she took to remove her sun glasses and assay his broad shoulders and sweat-sheened back tapering into his tight, low-slung jeans.

"Dear boy, whatever are you doing?"

He leapt a foot in the air, scrambled to his feet and stammered, "Oh…yes, ma'am. Garden. Yes, garden. I'm installing a garden. Right here. In that outline." He thrust the calculator behind him.

She surveyed the boards, then him, with an amused air. "Isn't it small for a garden? There's quite a bit of open ground here."

"Small? Well, yes, I suppose you might say that." He looked around for his shirt. "But, um, well, that's what Mr. Goldfield wanted."

"I see. Well, the work must go on. So he contracted you before his disappearance."

"Yes, ma'am. That would follow, wouldn't it?"

She laughed and touched a hand to her forehead. "Of course. Couldn't very well afterwards, could he? Sorry. I've been under a bit of a strain these past few days."

"Yes, ma'am. I understand."

"Do you?" She looked dubious. "Why, yes, I believe you do. I can see it in your eyes. Thank you."

He nodded and picked up his shirt, startled when she slid her arm around him to take the calculator. She was tall and slender with ice-blue, inquisitive eyes. He had not expected Bull Goldfield's wife to be so attractive.

"My," she said, studying the instrument. "You use this for a garden?"

"I like to be accurate, ma'am."

"Apparently so. Good. I like men who are careful." She handed it back. "By the way, stop calling me 'ma'am.' Makes me feel ancient. I expect we're about the same age, anyway. How old are you?"

"Fifty, um, four. Fifty-four," he admitted. Women rarely unnerved him but she was keeping him off balance and seemed to enjoy it.

"Really? You look younger, but there, you see, I'm only a year older. Not enough to matter is it?"

"Um, no, ma — that is, no. I don't think so."

She laughed heartily. "You are a jewel. A rather sweaty jewel, at that." She shocked him again by running a finger across his forehead and flicking away drops of perspiration. "So you're the gardener my husband hired. What's your name, gardener?"

His mind swirled. Did it matter if she knew his real name? Did it matter if she knew he was here to prove that Nickie Machetto had not shot her husband? Which would throw suspicion elsewhere, perhaps on her. How did he get himself into these fixes? "Um, Erwin. Erwin Rottweiler," he blurted.

"A rather unusual name. But I like it." She cocked her head at him. "Is that really your name?"

He hated lying; he was lousy at it. "Well, of curse — of course. Why wouldn't it be?"

"One never knows. Well, Erwin, I need a drink. Would you care for something? Oh, don't look so shocked, I'm not above fraternizing with the hired help. It's the butler's day off and I want someone to talk to. Com'n." She hooked her arm in his and led him toward her car while he wriggled into his shirt.

She parked at the side of the house where there were bags of concrete mix, lengths of bundled steel rods, and a roll of plastic sheeting, some of which had been used to cover a double doorway gaping above a shallow square pit.

"A new patio," she said, skirting the pit. "Another of my husband's attempts to destroy the charm of this lovely old house. The work has been on hold since the, ah, other day."

In a glassed cupola overlooking the river she poured herself a glass of champagne. "What would you like, Erwin? I have scotch, bourbon, gin, vodka, beer…you name it. Mmm. Or this champagne, which is lovely and which Wilson keeps perfectly chilled."

"Well, ma — um, Mrs. Goldfield —"

"Oh, that will definitely not do."

"Well, what is your name? I need to call you something."

"Yes, I guess you do," she laughed. "Annabelle. But I prefer Andy. That's what my friends call me. Don't know why. It just showed up and stayed, like a stray cat. Do you like cats?"

"I have three, and a dog."

A wistful smile touched her lips. "I love pets, but I can't — couldn't — keep one around Bull. He hated animals." She abruptly hardened. "I guess you wonder why I don't act bereaved. Well, it is no secret that my husband and I merely tolerated one another. Actually, I hated my husband for the philandering womanizer he was. I am not exactly disappointed that he's dead."

There was a long silence in which she looked away from him and stared out at the river, her face an iron mask.

"No, that's not true. I didn't really want him dead. Just away from me. I let him have his affairs and he didn't pry into mine. Well, enough of that. I've ignored your drink. What'll it be?"

"Water will be fine," he said, feeling very awkward. His usually nimble mind felt like a flat tire. Through open doors came a marshy, damp, pungent smell. Tourists called it an ocean smell, but it was really a seacoast smell, the blending of tides and fens, brackish water, open mud flats and rotting marsh grass. It blended with her Chanel in a strange but pleasing way. *Eau de* Annabelle, he thought, wondering what she was up to or whether she was up to anything. This, perhaps, was basic Annabelle — Andy. How would he behave if his wife — if he had one — had just been murdered and he was the murderer? Hadn't he had thoughts, albeit fanciful, of strangling his obstinate ex during the conclusion of their bitter and tumultuous marriage? Perhaps Andy had done it; perhaps she hadn't. Whatever her internal workings, she had an *élan* that was contagious. He was beginning to like her.

She turned from the liquor cabinet. "Water? Surely you jest."

"Well, no. I don't usually drink this early in the day. A glass of ice water will be fine."

"Hmm. As you wish." She watched him as she made it as a cat might watch a canary. "You some kind of a health nut?"

"No, just habit. I like to be careful."

"Good," she smiled, handing him the glass. "So do I. Perhaps you can teach me how to be healthy. Come dance with me." She turned on the stereo and held out her arms. "Oh, come on. I won't bite."

Edwin gulped and set his glass down. This, he thought, is definitely above and beyond the call. If he were getting paid he'd demand a raise. Jimbo's going to hear about this, and from now on he can bloody well…

"But I might nibble a little," she said as she eased into his arms and destroyed his train of thought.

He stepped off into the music.

"Why, my goodness, Erwin, you know how to waltz. And quite well, I might add. How unusual in a man."

"I like to dance," he admitted. Light and dark patterns flowed through her eyes, like clouds passing on a summer day. There seemed to be a threatening storm behind her long lashes. The cupola opened into a more spacious room, a rec room in appearance, with Goldfield's guns adorning walls and cabinets and an occasional painting of a sailing ship or a seascape. Gliding over the parqueted floor with her close in his arms he began to relax. They spun out to the cupola door and the marsh smell and a cool breeze, then around the rec room past potted palms, a long leather sofa, an elaborate modern mahogany entertainment center from which Strauss flowed, and back to where they started.

"How wonderful!" she applauded and scooped up her glass. "I haven't felt so relaxed since…in days. You are a tonic for me, Erwin. Sure you won't have a sip?"

"Just a small one." His fingers overlapped hers on the glass. "Mmm, this is excellent."

"So, Erwin, gardener *extraordinaire*, you know champagne too?"

He took another sip, rolling it on his tongue and letting it slide down slowly. "No. But when it tastes this good, I know it's quality."

She went to the bar for a refill and sauntered back with one for him swinging casually in her hand. "I come from an old, respectable and veddy rich South Carolina family. I grew up with quality and I won't have things that aren't quality." The dark returned to her eyes and her bravado faded. "Except Bull. I guess I'm allowed one mistake, eh? But it was a doozy. Well, never mind...Erwin, you're not from Beaufort, are you?"

"Well, no, not exactly."

"Of course you aren't. There aren't any gardeners in Beaufort as good looking. And what do you do when you're not gardening? It rains here a bit."

"I write. I'm a writer."

"Really? What do you write?"

He shrugged. "Anything I want to. Novels, poetry, editorials."

"A writer. How convenient." To her wide mouth came a mischievous grin. "I have a little proposition for you, Erwin. Are you ready for it?"

"I, um, guess so."

"I want you to be my personal secretary."

"You *what*?" he gagged, choking on his champagne.

She came over and pounded his back. "Be my personal secretary. It would fit right in with your writing. Live here, enjoy this splendor, the good life."

"I, uh, I can't do that," he croaked.

"Oh, Erwin, of course you can. Ah! I know what it is. You're married. That's it, isn't it?" She gave his back one last slap and looked at him with deep seriousness. "Erwin, I'm not just your run-of-the-mill wealthy person. I'm disgustingly rich, I mean filthy, filthy rich — we're talking billions, here — and I'll be even richer now that — now that Bull's — out of the way." She took a quick sip and went on. "We can buy off your dear wife — she must be a dear to have picked you, you're such a charmer. It's really not a problem. Is it?" Her eyes flooded with desperation and the clouds gathered again. "Or are you in love with her? I guess I've been out of love so long I forgot that there are those who are."

"I'm not married," he said. "Divorced, a long time ago."

"What a relief! Then —"

"No. Annabelle — Andy. I can't." She couldn't be serious — no, she probably was serious. But he couldn't take her seriously — could he?

"Well, it seems perfectly reasonable to me." She smiled, but the clouds were building rapidly.

"It really is a nice — a generous offer, Andy, but I just can't."

"I see."

"I really am sorry."

"No, no, it's all right. It was a silly thing to say. You hardly know me. I hardly know you. It just seemed…well, I just…never mind.

He looked down at his glass, trying to think of something to say.

"Oh, JESUS!" She buried her face in her hands. "I've just been under such a strain I don't know what I'm saying. I'm sorry."

"Andy, I'm sorry. I really am. It's not you — it's, well, something else." He took her in his arms, patting her back softly. She nodded her head, not looking at him. Her perfume was nice. He tried to remember that she might be a murderess, but the length of her against him made it difficult.

"Andy, I'm not a gardener. I'm here looking for a bullet. If I find it, it will prove someone innocent of your husband's murder, but — it could implicate — you. My name's Edwin. Edwin MacMaster. I'm Dr. Reuchmaire's cousin. He asked me to come here and look for the bullet. That's what I was doing out front, when you came up."

"Well," she said with a slight laugh. "Well…"

He didn't know what else to do. He turned to say something, he wasn't sure what, just some attempt at comforting prattle. She also turned, drawing a breath to speak, and they stopped, startled, their faces almost touching. She blinked once, seemed about to say something, then her resolve fell away and she melted into his arms, pressing her mouth to his and opening her lips. Goldfield's murder faded from his thoughts and he was only aware of her body against his, the press of her breasts, her fiercely clinging arms, and her searching tongue. Slowly she pulled away and lay her face on his shoulder. "The pressure," she whispered, "has been enormous."

"I understand."

Her head moved slowly back and forth. "No, you don't. Thank you for caring, but you don't know what I know — don't know what I've done — what I've done." Her eyes cloudy with tears, she looked into his and said, "Edwin, Erwin, whatever your name is, you could do me the most immense favor if you would take me to bed and —"

He put a finger against her lips, and said, "I get the idea."

Chapter 12

Harry gunned the cruiser across the bridge just before it opened, avoiding a long wait. He headed out of Beaufort on U.S. 21. "Finished your shopping yet?" he asked.

Reuchmaire, slumped deep in thought in the right seat, looked up. "Huh? What shopping?"

"Christmas in two weeks."

"Good heavens, Harry. I haven't had time to think about that. This case —" He threw his hands in the air to emphasize his frustration.

Harry nodded, chewing his cigar. "Talked to Reuben about the other night. Said he was at the health club. You know, the same one you —"

"I know, I know. What about it?"

"After his altercation with Goldfield he went there to work off steam, as he put it. Exercise calms him down, he says."

"Works for many people," Reuchmaire said, and ran a hand across his waist, glancing to see if Harry had noticed.

"So he was down there until eight o'clock, stopped to get groceries on his way home, and stayed in for the night. So he says. Cissy confirms it, but she likely would in any case."

"So you've eliminated him?"

"Maybe. Unless somehow the scene we saw of Nickie had nothing to do with the — well, I guess we ought to call it a murder now that we've seen that film. The puzzling thing is that the camera was turned off at 8:32, just after Nickie left. It wasn't on again until you found the control box the next night."

"So, Reuben sneaks out of his place, goes to the mansion and shoots Goldfield? What does he do with the body?"

"Jehosephat, Doc! I don't know. Just something we have to consider. Like I said, don't expect an easy solution. Most of my time on these cases is spent thinking. Just thinking. Sometimes I take a pole and drop a line in the water and massage one possibility after another until I reach a dead end or find an answer. Sometimes the possibilities trail off to nowhere. Sometimes I get an inspiration. Pretty slow work, really."

"Ever hear the name Grundel Schmidt?" Reuchmaire asked. He scrunched into a more comfortable position from which to watch expanses of marsh and water drift by. Here and there among the swamp grass, rippled by the breeze and turned straw-gray for winter, a heron or an egret, a feathered statue, stared intently into a shallow pool. High up an osprey circled.

The Lowcountry was the place for him. Vast prairies of tidal water and sedge, aromatic mud flats, oyster beds, trees festooned with moss, brilliant flowers each spring, exhilarating summer storms, sometimes hurricanes with their drama and danger, and a genteel but opinionated people who spoke a soft, history-flavored drawl, the mildness of which belied their fierce inner passions. They were people for whom the South had never died, and for whose camaraderie he had longed during his thirty years away. Here he spent the holidays of youth. This was his childhood Xanadu. He remembered summer days with Edwin in beach houses on Pawley's, firecrackers on the beach, swimming, crabbing, droving herds of fiddler crabs across tidal flats....

Harry drummed his fingers on the steering wheel and muttered the name several times. Finally he shook his head and said, "Nope. Grundel Schmidt doesn't register. But there's a lot about this case that doesn't make sense. Not the least of which is we can't find the body and we don't have a motive if we did have a body."

The same questions plagued Reuchmaire and haunted his dreams. What sleep he got was fitful. His conviviality, on which he prided himself, suffered. Even Marla's coffee didn't help. He was merely a wide awake grouch and recently brought Perky Patty to tears with a sharp remark. After that he was careful to be more civil, although inside he remained in a black mood. He thought the whole affair would be simple. He expected to end the case swiftly by uncovering vital evidence missed by the professionals. Harry had smiled at his *naiveté*.

Questions, questions, questions! Why was Nickie involved in this? He was a thief, to be sure, but not a murderer. But there was the video, that incriminating tape that pointed so clearly to Nickie. And if Nickie had done it accidentally, as he claimed, what had he done with the body? And why couldn't he remember all that happened? There was some relationship between Nickie and Ms. Hawthorne. But what? Was she involved in the disappearance?

It was rumored she was having an affair with Goldfield, but rumors in Beaufort were often spurred more by imagination than fact. The juicier a tidbit, the wider it was spread and the larger it became until it resembled the actual event, if there even was an event, as much as an elephant would a mouse. Was she the one with Goldfield that night? In the same house he shared with Annabelle? Was Goldfield really that audacious? Did Annabelle's casual, almost frigid, indifference mean anything? Was she involved in a way none of them imagined? And hardly the least factor, where was Goldfield? As much as Reuchmaire disliked the billionaire, he feared that he had been done in. But by whom? And where was the body?

"Goldfield's dead," Harry said. "He wouldn't go off unannounced. That just wasn't him. He liked for people to know where he was, what he was up to. If he was kidnapped, we would have we heard from his abductors. And there was the bloodstain. Pretty conclusive, I think. We've got no grave, we've got nowhere someone could hide a body — unless there's some secret compartment in the house. Doesn't seem like someone would kill him and drive off with the body. Or is he dead? See, Doc. I keep going 'round in circles."

Reuchmaire abruptly sat up. "Harry, I've got it! Drag the river."

Harry produced his fatherly smile. "Pretty wide river. Cost a lot to drag it. Besides, anything dropped in usually shows up in Repository Cove."

Reuchmaire, feeling once again the tyro, nodded and laid his chin on the umbrella's handle, the shaft propped between his legs.

"I'll tell you what I think," Harry said, pointing with his cigar stub, "I think Annabelle did him in and dumped his body in the river."

"Annabelle? Really? Then why hasn't it shown up in Repository

Cove?"

"Don't know. Maybe some trick of the current. I checked the tide. At 8:30 that night it had just turned and was flowing out. The body's got to be downstream, out to sea by now, unless dead people can swim."

The little butterfly flitted through Reuchmaire's mind again. Annabelle? Not likely. No more than Nickie would use a gun. But he was relying solely on his intuition. A passing highway sign reminded him they had been steadily heading out of Beaufort.

"Where are we going?" he asked.

"Looking for someone."

"Who?"

"Tell you when we find her."

"Harry —"

"Be patient, Doc. Don't know why I didn't think of this before."

Reuchmaire retreated into silence. Harry would reveal what he wanted to when he wanted to. When he called Harry earlier he had hoped there would be a new angle on the case. Instead he was doing nothing more exciting than going on a drive in the country. Maybe he could get lunch out of it. Harry never missed lunch.

And there was chess. "As long as we have nothing else to occupy our otherwise fertile minds, shall we start another game? I believe you get the first move."

"Yeah, okay." Harry waved a hand absently. "Pawn to queen four."

"Knight to king's bishop three." It did not occur to Reuchmaire to be surprised at his quick response nor did he pause to wonder why he selected that move.

Harry watched a flight of pelicans skimming over a bend of Lucy Point Creek where it curved towards the highway. "Knight to Queen two."

Again the next move appeared in Reuchmaire's mind, as though from a teleprompter. "Pawn to king four." Where was this inspiration coming from? Usually he had to plot each move carefully on the computer. But this morning he was quick as a fencer, one thrust parried he quickly anticipated the next.

Harry's response, pawn takes pawn, came as expected. He added, "I think you're right about Nickie. I know everything points to him, but I don't think he did it. Maybe he fired that gun, but he didn't kill Goldfield. It has to be Annabelle. She had more than enough motives and they were all women. I think it just wore her down, all his playing around — right in front of her often as not. She's human. She just got fed up with it and decided to put a stop to it, once and for all. What do you think, Doc?"

Reuchmaire was convinced he knew who did it, and it wasn't Annabelle. And it wasn't Fast Nickie. If Edwin finds the missing ball, that will exonerate Fast Nickie. Then what of Annabelle? She said she was on her yacht in Port Royal sound all night. The Pinkneys, anchored nearby, confirmed her story. They would have heard her big twin diesels had she moved at all.

"Doc?"

"Uh — knight to Knight five." He was like an athlete 'in the zone.' Each move appeared with remarkable clarity. Realization struck. *It was Gibaud vs Lazako.* That was the match they were playing. Did Harry realize it? No. He was headed for defeat in two more moves. They both were unconsciously recalling Gibaud and Lazako.

"I meant about the case," Harry said.

Reuchmaire steadied his breathing. His palms were moist. This was it! In twenty-seven matches he had not won once. This would be Slippery Rock upsetting Notre Dame. If only Harry didn't catch on. He tried to sound calm. "I'm thinking. Your move."

Harry gave him a funny look. "Ohh, pawn to king's rook three."

Sacre Bleu! He had done it! "Night to king's six." He leaned back in triumph.

Harry took the cigar out of his mouth. "What are you grinning at? Wait a minute —"

Reuchmaire watched with glee as Harry's lips silently mouthed the moves.

"Well, I'll be danged, Doc. You'll mate in one more move, no matter what I do. Well done!" He stuck out his hand.

"Well, you were distracted."

"Still counts. Hah! That's rich. We just replayed Gibaud vs. Lazako, the shortest match ever between two masters. Did you know that? Guess our minds just followed procedure while we worried the case."

"The subconscious is very powerful." Glowing with pride, trying his best to appear modest, Reuchmaire beat a smart staccato on the floor with the umbrella tip.

He took a moment to adjust the black bow tie above the ruffles of his spotlessly white shirt, straightened the cuffs, pleasantly aware of the attractive fit of his tuxedo, and gave Marla a wink before turning to his next and last opponent, the Russian Master. Chinkinlogski (he couldn't remember a real master's name) was worried, as well he should be. He had played his best but the beads of sweat on his forehead signaled that he knew what Reuchmaire also knew: checkmate in two moves. There was nothing the Russian could do. Marla sat among the dignitaries in the front row of the gallery in the magnificent old hall in Moscow. Long legs crossed elegantly, svelte in a low-cut red velvet sheath, diamond earrings glittering like her eyes, she let an expectant smile edge her lips. In his wake, around the U-shaped table sat a dozen defeated opponents, each representing a different nation, all Masters. They, too, waited, eyes intent, for each knew Reuchmaire was about to complete a clean sweep of them all. Their faces reflected grudging admiration...

"Well, here we are," Harry said.

Reuchmaire came back from Moscow.

The creek cut lazily through a sea of sedge and came to meet the road. Patches of sunlight swept across the marsh beneath bright low morning clouds. Harry slowed to a stop on a bridge where an old black couple, man and woman, sat on the concrete rail. Each held a pole over the water, their hunched backs, jacketed against the chill and in the patient pose of fishermen everywhere, were to a light wind coming down off the Coosa River.

When Harry opened the window the breeze brought in the pungent smell of mud and oyster beds, a sweet aroma to Reuchmaire's nose. Oysters on the half shell and seafood chowder would be nice for lunch.

Harry called out, "Heya, Hannah, how de body?"

Two heads turned together. The woman pushed back a strand of gray hair and squinted. Her wrinkled face split into a grin dominated by a gold tooth.

She came forth with melodic dialect that startled Reuchmaire. He could follow the meaning but not all of the words.

"Ah tell Gawd t'enk ya. Yousef, Chief Harry? Oona ain gwuine cum cause me an me mon trouble? We ain done no wrong. Nun tall!" Laughing, she climbed down and propped her pole against the railing. The two came to where Harry had pulled off the highway. She further startled Reuchmaire when she pulled Harry's big head down and kissed him on the cheek. The old man's eyes were warm with the recognition of a friend. He took Harry's hand with his right and clasped his wrist with the left.

"Mr. Harry," he asked, "how oona da pretty gal oona pekins dem? Dey done get beig, eny?"

"Wife and children fine, Idrissa, just fine."

An exchange of pleasantries began between the couple and Harry. One moment their exchange seemed almost English, the next foreign, and, to Reuchmaire's even further amazement, Harry was as fluent as they.

"Ah gladee fuh meet you, Doctah Mon," Hannah said, when Harry introduced him in English. "De day pretty, eny? Much better den e bin."

Hannah was his mother, Harry said.

At Reuchmaire's raised eyebrows she laughed and clapped her hands.

"No, no, Mistah Doctah Mon. Not e real mama. E ain dun my child." She lay a skinny black hand next to Harry's meaty white one. "Eh! Dat be way big trick fuh Hannah. I ain duh no witch woman. I ain got no juju."

Ah! Gullah, Reuchmaire remembered. Part African dialect, part English, it was a Lowcountry language.

In some cases local names came to be completely changed. There was the case of Daufuskie Island, over beyond Hilton Head.

In Colonial days the British, who settled the Carolina barrier islands with plantations of cotton, rice and indigo, called those islands keys, and what is now Daufuskie was "the first key" north of Georgia. From the Lowcountry Black people on the plantations came the phonetic pronunciation "da fus' key," which evolved onto maps as Daufuskie. Their language became known as Krio and was later returned to Sierra Leone, a West African departure point for many slaves, by repatriates returning home. Further Anglicization of Krio in the Lowcountry became known as Gullah, as were the people who speak it. An oral language that has endured for over two hundred years, he had heard it among some of his patients. As he listened to the conversation, his neck hairs prickled each time he heard the name Goldfield.

Hannah turned to him. "Oona cum fuh look-see de Goldfield mon, eny, Mistah Doctah Mon?" She laughed at Reuchmaire's surprise, then fixed him with a stare, one eye nearly closed and the other wide, as though about to cast a spell. "Sho, Hannah know you Doctah ROCK-mo! Oona treat de head win e bin twiss up wid de bad spirits. Oona use juju kill dem. I know what oona do. Gullah dem kno mo den de buckra folks tink." She tapped his chest with a long bony finger. "Hannah know wey oona cum look fuh Mistah Goldfield. Oona wan fo know way e dun run at. But e ain run."

"How do you know that, Hannah?"

She slapped the car sharply with an open palm. "We kno! Gullah dem know dese tings." She leaned close and whispered, "Witch might done spirit ahm way. But oona ain yeddy da frum me. Oona need fo tak wid de Mammy Queen, oba een Frogmore. E got de juju and e know way de body dey."

"*Mammy* Queen?" Reuchmaire said as they drove away. "Isn't that—?"

Harry shook his head. "Offensive? Not among Gullah. It's a term of great respect, a tribute to Sea Island queens and mammies. And her name is Queen. *E de mama dese islands. Becumyas kno fuh gib respect fuh e power, mudda wit, life, an de spirits wha dun gon on da dey een she.* It means, "She is the mother of these islands. Even newcomers know to pay homage to her power, wisdom, life and ancestral essence."

"Well, then," said Reuchmaire, briskly tapping the umbrella, "we should indeed meet her."

* * *

A dirt road wound among bushes and moss-draped live oaks to the edge of a marsh where a faded blue house with dark blue shutters nestled. In each window hung a charm, swinging gently in the breeze off the marsh. Some were small bags bulging with unknown items, others were herbs tied together in a small bunch.

"Used to scare off witches." Harry pulled into the dirt yard, scattering a few chickens.

An old hound slept under the raised porch. The dog moved its head enough to cast a sleepy gaze, emitted a long sigh, closed its eyes again. Perched on a window sill, a black cat regarded them with intense yellow eyes.

An old black woman, hair as white as Hannah's and pulled into a bun beneath the wide brim of a sagging straw hat, sat in a rocker on the front porch smoking a corncob pipe. She was as large as Idrissa had been thin. Aged eyes, alert and confident, squinted at their approach. In her plump but dexterous fingers a cordgrass basket was taking shape. She was adorned with all manner of baubles — sand dollars, coquinas, cockles, angel wings, crab claws, shark's teeth — made into bracelets, rings, earrings, and necklaces. They tinkled and jangled with her every move.

Reuchmaire recognized the basket as identical to those he had seen in Beaufort in the summer, sold on the streets by Gullah women in bright dresses and head scarves.

Harry doffed his Stetson. "How de body, Miss Mammy Queen?"

"I tell God tanke ya." She nodded, with a tinkle of shells, the pipe clamped in a wide grin.

There followed an inquiry into the health of families, at least through parents, siblings, and children. On the way over Harry had explained the ritual, the same they encountered with Hannah. It was *de rigueur* for any meeting between Gullahs. Depending, he said, upon how steeped in tradition a particular Gullah was, failure to do so would render him anything from mildly offended to mute as a post.

The patter went on with neither Harry nor the Mammy Queen in any particular hurry. Reuchmaire waited with hands tight on the umbrella handle, pointedly not tapping it in his usual manner for fear that he might seem impatient. Which he was. He was so taken by what Hannah told them, he thought the Mammy Queen would simply announce where Goldfield was or where they would find his body. That, obviously, would make things much easier and he was anxious to find out even though he hadn't a clue how she might know. Harry said she had "the sight," sort of like a fortuneteller. Reuchmaire half expected her to produce a crystal ball.

"So, why oona come Mammy Queen?" the old woman asked, recharging her pipe and getting down to cases. She waved Reuchmaire and Harry to a sofa that had seen better days. Without waiting for a reply she carefully set the basket to one side and pointed with her pipe. "Oona cum see Mammy Queen bout de rich mon, Mistah Goldfield. I kno oona bin cumin."

Harry nodded, unsurprised. "Hannah sent us to ask you. She say you know where Mr. Goldfield is."

The old eyes glittered with amusement. "Hannah de smart gyal. E duh me sistah child, you kno. E hab lebben brudders an sistahs scatta all oba dis countee. Me hab shree sistahs an one brudda still libin. Dey lib yuh long de coast an on deese Sea Islands. We dey all up and down dis tidewater fuh two hundred years, maybe mo. I meself bin born on de Litchfield place een Georgetown, near Pawley's. We lib in de swamps; we work pun de water; we ebrywey." The Mammy Queen took a moment to suck on the pipe, exhaling a strong but not unpleasant cloud. "Hannah tell oona how I kno dese tings?"

"You have the juju, Mammy Queen," Harry said. "You can tell things we buckra — white folks — can't. You know these swamps, you know these rivers, you know what happens here even when no one sees."

Mammy Queen grinned, shifting in the chair with a soft jangle. "Oona right, Chief Harry. Oona kno we know, cuz oona duh we. Hannah oona mother." She slapped her knee and laughed. "And oona, doctah mon, Doctah ROCKmo, oona hep de peeple wit de head sickness. Oona good doctah mon, me feel it. Me kno peeple oona dun hep an dey speak bout ya. An oona hep Chief Harry sumtime solve de case, eny?"

Startled, Reuchmaire managed a reverent, "Why, yes. Yes I do."

The old woman nodded in satisfaction. "Course ya do."

"And what about Goldfield, Mammy Queen?" Harry asked, "Where is he?"

"E dead."

"Dead?" Reuchmaire blurted. "How?"

"Oona find de body. Ahm tell you."

"Do you know, Miss Mammy Queen?" Reuchmaire asked. "Do you know where the body is?"

She took the pipe from her mouth and glared at him with the same spell-casting look he had received from Hannah. "Course I do! Oona look Nort de river by Beaufort. E dey."

"We've looked there," Harry said. "We can't find it."

"Look some mo. Maybe wey oona ain tink sey e should be. Now, das all I know." She got up and started inside. "Me gwine tend some collards."

Collards! Reuchmaire loved collards, cooked slow with a salty slab of fatback, and some pork chops and mashed potatoes and pan gravy to go along. And a big pan of buttered cornbread. He looked quickly around as if Edwin might leap from behind a bush. He almost summoned the courage to ask — it would have been terribly impolite — if the greens were done. But Harry was heading for the car.

Harry waved. "We'll look some more, Mammy Queen. Good day to you."

Reuchmaire tipped his hat and went to the car, his stomach growling objection.

"Hey," the Mammy Queen called through the screen door that had slapped closed behind her. The afternoon sun glittered on her baubles. "Maybe oona should talk mo wid Wilson."

Harry squinted. "Mrs. Goldfield's butler?"

"Da right. Good day tuh ya Chief Harry and doctah mon ROCKmo."

Harry and Reuchmaire exchanged puzzled looks and got in the car.

"For a moment there I thought she was going to tell us right where to look," Reuchmaire said.

"She did." Harry maneuvered through the chickens. "All we have to do is figure it out."

Chapter 13

"This is very strange." Annabelle held a box sieve for Edwin to shovel dirt into. "I met you this morning, made love to you this afternoon, and now here I am helping you find something that may hang me. An unusual day even for me."

Edwin leaned on the shovel and used the back of an arm to wipe sweat from his forehead. "I hope you attribute it to my winning personality."

On her knees in work shirt and shorts with knee protectors and hiking shoes, she gave the box a vigorous shaking. "I do indeed, you charming man. Not many could talk me into this."

She dumped the detritus of stones and fragmented sea shells aside and waited for another load.

"You volunteered." He scooped earth into the box.

"So I did. I must be losing my mind."

He leaned on the shovel and watched as she began sifting. How sexy she looked in her mixed costume, her body shaking with the effort, and a sheen of sweat on her face. And how much more, how incredibly much more, relaxed she seemed.

"Don't you want me to sift a while? It's hard work."

"Soon. The effort's good for me."

"Why did you offer to help?"

"Well, it could be to get me off the hook."

"What?"

"If we don't find it, that would implicate this other person, this Nickie. Isn't that so?"

"Oh, well, yeah." He had become so certain, no, determined, that they would find the ball he hadn't considered the possibility. He was a bit disappointed, thinking her reasons were altruistic, a desire to see justice done and all that, even though it might jeopardize her own story. At the same time he could hardly fault her motive. It very well could get her off the hook.

Fact of the matter, the real question was why he was bothering to look for the ball, now that he knew she had shot Goldfield. Or said she had. Because Jimbo said to, he reminded himself. But there was another reason. Down inside he just could not believe that Andy could do such a thing. He was digging, he realized, to prove her innocence, because there seemed to him to be a preponderance of evidence that Nickie had in fact done it and he wanted very badly for her not to have.

She finished sifting and put the box aside.

"Ready for me to take over?" he asked.

She shook her head and sighed, and looked up at the late sun filtering through the tops of a stand of pines outside the estate.

"What then?"

"We'll have a beautiful sunset. We always do. Lowcountry perk." She shivered. "It's cooling off. It'll be in the fifties, maybe the forties tonight, back to almost seventy tomorrow."

"Something's bothering you, and it's not the weather."

She tried to smile through a pained expression. Fishing in a pocket of her shorts she held up a round metal ball. "I guess this is what we're looking for. I found it an hour ago."

He sat down heavily on the edge of the excavation and stared at the ball, then at her.

She folded her hands in her lap and said, "I'm sorry. I couldn't think of what to do. But I can't let an innocent person be convicted of something I did. I couldn't live with that." With a crooked smile, she added, "Guess I'm just going to have to take my medicine."

He took the ball from her and tried to think of something encouraging to say. "Well — well, this proves Nickie didn't do it. But — well, that doesn't mean you did."

She came over and sat beside him, their thighs touching, and placed a warm arm between his knees. "Ah, Edwin, you gallant man. Thank you for your comfort, for your support. Just telling you about it has been such a lift. You have no idea —" She leaned over and kissed him hard on the lips.

He put his arm around her, an uncertain dread filling him. He had never become so fond of someone so quickly, and he was afraid for her. It was partly the circumstances, all this happening so sudden and so fast. But there was her aura, her personality, her *elan*, unlike anyone he had known, that drew him like a magnet. There was also the intriguing twist that he had never known a billionairess before.

"Will you come visit me in prison?" She cocked her head over with that playful grin he had come to love in such a short time. Her eyes had a mischievous twinkle, as though this was all some game, as though someone would suddenly yell, 'King's X,' and everything would revert to normal.

"Andy," he said, sharper than he meant to, "you are not going to prison."

"Hah! That's all you know."

"Dammit, Andy, this is serious."

She screwed her mouth up and stared earnestly into his eyes. Placing a finger against his lips, she said, "I know. Forgive my frivolity. It's the only way I can face it." She got up and pulled him to his feet. Taking the ball, she tossed it into the air, caught it, and handed it back. "Now that we've found the damned thing, what do we do?"

"I'll take it to Jimbo — to Harry."

"Don't be so glum." She hooked her arm in his and started for the house. "I'm not in jail yet."

"Uh, we need to clean up." He indicated the excavation.

"Later. I've got something better in mind."

"Insatiable wench."

She laughed and grabbed his butt. "I may not have much time to enjoy you." Soberly, she added, "It's been a long, long time since I felt someone cared for me. And since I cared for someone. I like it."

Chapter 14

Heading back into Beaufort, Harry pulled up to the line of cars collected at the bridge and shut off the engine.

"No point in wasting gas." He lit a cigar.

"We could go back to 802 and through Port Royal," Reuchmaire said.

A tug pushing a barge in the Intracoastal Waterway was coming up from Port Royal Sound. It was followed by three tall-masted sailboats. A high broken cloud deck sprinkled sunlight across a channel rippled by a brisk wind. The detour would take longer than the wait at the bridge, but there would be the feeling of progress, of getting somewhere. Which they did not seem to be doing with the case.

Harry ignored the suggestion and leaned back, eyes half closed, and puffed on the cigar. "Sure wish I could figure out what Mammy Queen meant."

Reuchmaire resigned himself to the wait. "I didn't know you knew Gullah." He said it to fill the time with conversation. Smug over his recent victory, he did not yet want to start another game at which he felt he would not fare as well. It was unlikely he would ever catch Harry off guard again.

"Oh, yeah," said Harry. "I lived with Hannah for a while when I was a kid. Back in 1956, when I was just ten, my Ma and I lived up north of Georgetown, next to Pawley's Island down near the water. My dad was killed in Korea and we were living on survivor's benefits, such as we could. Ma waitressed, too, so we got by. Hannah was a cook where Ma worked, so they got to be friends. Hannah and her family lived only a mile or so away, and I'd go over there and play. Didn't set too well with a lot of people, a white woman befriending a black, me playing with black kids, but Ma didn't care, and neither did I. End of that summer,

Ma mentioned to Miz Hannah — they called one another Miz — that our house needed painting. I'll never forget Hannah's words. She said, 'Lawd, Miz Greta, no use paint dis house. De Gray Man done walked on de watah.'"

Harry paused to relight his cigar. Goosebumps prickled Reuchmaire's skin as he remembered the legend of the Gray Man. The Gullah said it was the ghost of a Confederate soldier who returned to warn of impending disaster. Others dated the legend to Colonial days and a Revolutionary soldier. Either way, if the Gray Man walked on the beach, there would be a bad storm. But if he walked on the water, the storm would be catastrophic. That legend, first heard as a teen up on Pawleys, was his initiation to the mysterious Gullahs. His years away dimmed it, but now he recalled how he and Edwin longed to see the ghost, often maintaining long vigils on the beach day or night. But they never did. Among the Gullah a sighting would be known almost instantaneously up and down the coast, as though by witchcraft.

"So," Harry continued, "that was the summer of Hurricane Hazel, in September. Devastated Pawley's. Maybe Ma didn't really believe Hannah, 'cause we stayed. Our place was so far off the beaten track, I guess the evacuation missed us. Or maybe Ma refused, headstrong as she was." Harry sighed a long sigh of remembrance and folded his arms over the steering wheel.

"I was never so scared in my life. Could hardly see through the rain. The whole world was a churning mass of huge waves that the wind, howling like the end of creation, shoved around like toys, first one direction, then the other. Every one was nearly high as our house. Soon as one would roar by, here would come another from a different direction and hit us with a big boom that rattled the rafters. I don't know how the house held together as long as it did. We were up in the attic, praying our hearts out, when the whole thing just came apart. Ma was swept one way, me another. I never saw her again. I wound up on a mattress, hanging on for all I was worth like it was a roller coaster. Couldn't see ten feet with the rain and wind and water flying all around. Got hit with all kinds of stuff — boards, tree limbs, bottles, cans — some washed over me, some blown. I was black and blue for a month.

"Don't know how long I was adrift, seemed like forever. I got blown inland and wound up in Hannah's yard, half drowned and cold as I've ever been. Her house was barely above water, but it held while the storm blew itself out. She nursed me back to health, and I just stayed on there. She asked around about Ma, to please me, I think. She seemed to know beforehand it was no use. Never did find her. Never knew what happened to her. Hannah told me to stay on with them, which seemed sensible since I had no relatives I knew of. I just went to school and came home to Hannah and her kids. Finally the authorities figured it out and put an end to it. That was the fifties, you know." Harry took the cigar out of his mouth and smirked sadly. "Couldn't have a white boy living with blacks.

"Turns out I had a great aunt down in Monk's Corner, above Charleston, and I got sent off to her. We hadn't been close 'cause she was fairly well to do and I think it embarrassed Ma. But every chance I got I went back to see Hannah. She taught me Gullah, which I already knew pretty well from when I stayed there.

"When I told my aunt about how I escaped the storm, she said I was a regular Harry Houdini. She started calling me Harry, and it stuck."

"Quite a tale," said Reuchmaire.

Harry laughed. "Yeah, well, the thing I remember most, other than just being plain scared, was how cold I was. There it was, still summer — I think it was in the nineties the day before — and I was freezing. From the wind and water, I guess, and fear. But I remember thinking that if I only had a wet suit, like frogmen wear, I wouldn't be so cold. I had just seen a picture in a magazine, and I guess it stuck. Like you said, the subconscious does strange things."

"You know, Harry, I keep thinking of the morning we first saw Ms. Hawthorne. Do you remember how she looked? Not really unkempt, but just not as polished as I would have expected her to be. After all, she had customers to impress."

Harry thought for a moment. "Can't say as I do. She had a scarf on her head, but it was cold."

"It keeps bothering me. I think I have seen her somewhere before, except her hair was different somehow."

The line of cars began to accordion across the bridge and Harry followed. "Well, only her hairdresser knows for sure."

"What?"

"You know, that commercial from the fifties. Or was it the sixties?"

The umbrella popped emphatically on the floor. "Harry, you're a genius. Let's go see Big Gail."

"The hairdresser? What for?"

"Just a notion."

"Can't. I've got to give the mayor a report on our so-called progress. He's not a happy camper. It won't make him any happier that I'm late. But I can say — truthfully, this time — that the bridge was open. I'll drop you at your place, unless you'd like to come along and listen to hizzonor chew my tail."

* * *

Big Gail's was just off Bay Street. The name over the door stated simply, Gail's Coiffeurs, as it was known in Beaufort. Her female customers called her simply Gail and considered her the best hairdresser in town. Chauvinistic males added Big.

Reuchmaire, after a struggling to push the door that needed to be pulled, bowed and held it open for a freshly coifed customer who had finally corrected his error from within with hand signals.

Gail, impeccably attired in blouse, slacks, and low leather heels, blonde hair swept into an avant-garde do somewhat on the cutting edge for Beaufort, was in the rear of the salon. She was not actually big, heightwise, and only put a slight fill to her clothes, which brought her about to the pleasingly plump category. But she was endowed with a bosom that turned heads, lasciviously among Beaufort men, and in envy, amazement or admiration among women, depending upon point of view. Reuchmaire, striving to maintain a professional attitude, tried hard to think of her not as Big Gail, but just Gail. However the Big seemed to creep back in of its own volition.

As he passed in review before female faces peering from under dryers or seated in chairs, Reuchmaire felt like a dog at a cat show.

There was not one set of approving eyes in the lot, although some were no more than curious.

Gail was chatting pleasantly while she teased old Mrs. du Pont's frazzle of silver hair. She smiled warmly at Reuchmaire. "Why, Dr. Reuchmaire, how nice to see you. What brings you to this ladies den?"

Reuchmaire turned his hat in his hands, still tingling from the exposed march down the aisle. "Could I, um, have a word with you — privately?" He could fairly see ears prick up, and Mrs. du Pont turned around for a look.

"Of course, Doctor. Mary, come tend to Mrs. du Pont." She patted the elderly lady's shoulder. "Now, don't you fret, Margaret. I'll be right back."

Gail led Reuchmaire to the back of the shop, as far back as was possible but he still felt uncomfortably close to the nearest customers. Every eye in the place was on them.

She laid a hand on his arm. "And how's Marla? I don't guess you've decided to give up on her? You know I've had my eye on you for a long time."

He started at the touch and laughed nervously. He wondered, as always, if she was teasing. There is some intent in the most innocent jest, and hers were often much more pointed. "No, No, I haven't." He moved his arm away. "She's just fine."

"Oh, darn, I guess I'll just have to wait."

Among the sharp salon odors of treatments, rinse, and cigarettes there came a subtle, sensuous whiff of her perfume, a bouquet he found alluring. Only his good judgment had once stopped him from suggesting that Marla buy the same. He found himself wondering if there was substance to the rumor of Big Gail's hot towel massages, given secretly — extremely secretly! — to certain of Beaufort's gentlemen. Some of whom were husbands of those women who frequented this very shop. With a sad thought about the vagaries of human nature and a reminder to himself about rumors in Beaufort, he explained his quest.

"Ms. Hawthorne? The artiste? Why sure. She comes in regularly. Funny thing, you know, I did her a permanent Monday and she came back in Wednesday for another. That's right, it was the morning after the storm. Said she got caught out in the rain, but seemed like it had been through more than that to me — excuse me. Napha, honey, you've been sweeping that same spot for five minutes. Go up front where Nancy just finished trimming Mrs. Cuthbert."

The slender young girl, dark red pouty lips in a face dark as charcoal, left with apparent reluctance, slowly sweeping, an ear trained in their direction.

"Yes," said Gail, "it was Wednesday morning she called and wanted to get in that day. Kind of nervy, 'cause I have a strict policy. But she's a good customer and tips big, so I squeezed her in. She called just before Mrs. Goldfield."

"Mrs. Goldfield? What did she want?"

"Rinse, style and set. Said she'd been down in the Sound all night and her hair was a mess."

"In Port Royal Sound?"

"That's right. She wanted to get in Wednesday, too. Can you imagine, two of my biggest customers on the same day? I just couldn't, but I told her I could take her Thursday and she didn't mind at all. You know, she's a real nice lady. I don't know how she and Bull — um, Mr. Goldfield — got together." She leaned in confidentially. "He's, well, he was somewhat of a pain in the butt, you know — Napha, we really don't need the broom back here just now. Up front, honey, up front."

Napha rolled her eyes and started working back toward the front with deliberate slowness as though drawn by an invisible force toward the rear of the room.

"'Course that's none of my business. I make it a point not to talk about customers or their husbands. Well," she winked, "not all of 'em. Like Ms. Hawthorne. Now she was in here last June —"

"June? I thought she came here last September, or thereabouts."

"Well, that's when she moved here. But she was here in June. Used a different name, said she was just passing through. I think she was around a few days."

"What name did she use?"

"Oh, Bradley or Brinkly, something like that."

"Then how —"

"How did I know it was her? Well, I never forget a face. But I particularly remembered her because she was blonde in June and brunette in September. That's when she came to stay. Had changed her style, too. But, you know, you work with hair a long time you get to recognize it, like a fingerprint. I think I would have known it was her in the dark. She has a sort of funny face, snooty looking, but sort of cute, and she walks a certain way, holds her hands just so, like she's trying to be elegant. Women notice those things."

"Yes, so you do. And it has been quite helpful. Thank you." He turned and braced himself for the return up the gauntlet. So, Ms. Hawthorne had been in Beaufort before. Perhaps he had seen her then, when she was casing the town in preparation for opening her shop. Or, that is, in preparation for her other more clandestine operations.

"Anytime, Doctor, and let me know if Marla loses interest in you." She winked and returned to Mrs. du Pont.

Reuchmaire paused outside the salon. Sunlight poured from a cloudless sky and transformed the storefronts along Bay Street into a pastel scene worthy of a portrait. No doubt the temperature would reach the sixties today and be quite pleasant if the wind stayed light. He started off to the umbrella's light cadence, reviewing all that he knew and didn't know about Goldfield's disappearance.

When he reached the spot where he had first seen Isadora and Nickie, the scene of the purse snatching, he stopped. It was just down the street from her gallery. Head down, mind churning, he was mindless of pedestrians detouring around him. Whenever he thought of Nickie and Isadora, the little butterfly would flit through his mind. There was something there. Something too obscure, that happened too far in the past, to come to the surface. Most irritating! But it would sooner or later emerge — he hoped. Sometimes those things did, sometimes not. Ah, the mind, the mind. What a labyrinth of intrigue. He looked up the street to the gallery again, thinking it was no coincidence that Nickie picked Isadora's purse to snatch.

Chapter 15

"Erwin Rotweiller!" Reuchmaire gleefully rubbed his hands together as he circled the chair in which his cousin sat slumped. "You told her you were Erwin Rotweiller?"

"It's all I could think of."

"And then —?"

Edwin squirmed slightly and an embarrassed grimace crossed his face. "Well, we went inside, talked, danced, and, well — you know. We didn't plan it, it just happened."

"Oh, Edwin, that is rich! I send you to find the errant ball and discover you have been fraternizing with the, ah — with the suspects."

"It's not funny."

"I said no such thing." Reuchmaire patted his cousin's shoulder. "This is actually quite beneficial, and I was not making light of your feelings toward Annabelle."

"Andy."

"Eh?"

"She likes to be called Andy."

"Ah, to the nickname stage already. Edwin, my loveable cousin, I recognize that look in your eye, that tone in your voice, that sweat in your palms. I've seen it a thousand times from patients on the couch, er, well, usually in a chair. They rarely lie on a couch. That's a myth. Although, I did have one patient, a senator, and a rather good speaker, who was only comfortable if he stood with one hand on a lapel and the other raised in emphasis. But I've seen it, my boy, I've seen it. You're in love!"

"Oh, Jimbo, be serious. And my palms are not sweaty." Edwin went to the kitchen to make coffee.

"Figure of speech." Reuchmaire followed and scooped up his

umbrella to thrust playfully at an imaginary foe. "Would you settle for in lust?"

"Jimbo!"

"Sorry. I am being indelicate. But it does seem obvious that you have developed a certain, shall we say, warm feeling towards Annabelle."

Edwin stirred skim milk into his coffee and stared out of Reuchmaire's window at the river beyond a stand of live oak. "She really is a sensitive person. And very nice to be around. I don't understand how she ever got hooked up with Goldfield."

"*C'est la vie. C'est l'amour.*" Reuchmaire tossed his hands in a very French gesture. "Who ever understands these things? But it makes psychiatrists necessary — or at least rich." He set the umbrella aside and poured himself a cup of coffee. "But if we may digress a moment from your, ah, relationship with Mrs. Goldfield — did you find it?"

Edwin scowled into his cup. "I wish you would get some decent coffee. You know, grounds, like Marla has."

"Never mind the coffee. Did you find the ball?"

"Oh, yeah." He dug in a pocket and dropped the metal ball into Reuchmaire's hand. "Andy found it. She helped me sift the plot. That's got to be the one Nickie fired. Look how new it looks. Not a trace of corrosion."

Reuchmaire gaped at the ball. "Why — why this is wonderful. It really does exonerate Nickie. He fired and missed. And Andy — Annabelle — Mrs. Goldfield, helped you? Extraordinary. You are a charmer."

"Why so surprised? Didn't you think I would find it?"

"Well, yes. That is, I certainly hoped you would. Oh, it's just that calculations and such leave me confused. It all seems so theoretical until proven. And you proved it, my boy. Well done!"

"There's something else."

Reuchmaire happily rolled the ball in his hand. "This convinces me that I know who — eh, what else?"

"Andy confessed. She said she killed Goldfield."

The ball fell to the floor with a loud thunk.

"What?"

"She said she snuck into the mansion through a secret tunnel and shot her husband."

Reuchmaire's hands circled helplessly in the air. "But, that cannot be. She's not the one I thought —"

Edwin shrugged. "That's what she told me."

"She just came right out and said she did it? She wasn't coerced? You didn't ask?"

"It was in a rather delicate, well, intimate moment." Edwin blushed. "In bed. We were talking, after — well, *after*. She volunteered it. I think she told the truth. It seemed a great relief for her to say it."

"I see." Reuchmaire sat down on the sofa, awakening Captain Semmes curled in his favorite place at one end and General Stuart at the other. The cat stretched, scratched briefly at his half ear, and came over to be rubbed. The General, handsomely groomed and nails trimmed, yawned and returned to his nap. "Then it probably was the truth. This is astounding."

"She gave me this." Edwin handed over a key.

Reuchmaire weighed it thoughtfully. "I've seen this before."

"It's a copy she had made of the one Goldfield carries. Identical except for a proof mark. Those two are the only keys to the tunnel."

Reuchmaire got up and began pacing around the room with slow deliberate steps, head down with the key clasped behind him. How could this key have gotten into Ms. Hawthorne's purse? Is it possible that she and Annabelle are co-conspirators? And what of Nickie? Are they all in it together? He was so certain that Ms. Hawthorne was the killer, but now.... For the hundredth time since Harry had gotten him involved, he cursed himself for thinking he was a sleuth, cursed himself for expecting to find a quick solution, and cursed his incompetence. Self-doubt welled up. He fought it down. Trust your instincts, he told himself. "So, how did she dispose of the body? Is it in the tunnel? In the river?"

Edwin looked puzzled. "I never thought to ask."

"*Somebody* got rid of it."

"She told me when she saw him fall she just ran. Went back through the tunnel to her boat and back to her yacht."

Reuchmaire stared at the key. "Well, let's go have a look at the tunnel. Maybe the body is in it."

* * *

"Will that be all, suh?"

"Yes, thank you, Wilson, please return to your duties." Wilson nodded and left Reuchmaire, with General Stuart on leash, and Edwin in the foyer.

Edwin felt along the paneled wall beneath the main staircase. "All Andy said was that she was by this newel post, then turned and went back into the tunnel. But she didn't say how. There must be an entrance here somewhere."

Reuchmaire moved down the hall tapping panels with the umbrella handle and listening for a hollow sound. "The key must fit something," he said, "but all these panels are unmarred. But here's a rather odd cabinet, isn't it? Tall, as though for china or linens, but much too shallow to hold anything substantial." He stopped before a structure protruding about six inches from the wall into which it was built. Made of the same dark wood as the panels that formed one side of the main staircase, it could be taken for a linen closet. "And, it has a keyhole."

The key worked, and the front of the cabinet creaked open. A set of steps led down into darkness. Wilson was summoned with a flashlight. The butler seemed astonished at the discovery. He said he had heard there was a tunnel but hadn't known its location. The old linen cabinet was never used, he said, the key lost in some past time.

Reuchmaire was skeptical. Something in Wilson's actions, in his speech, was not sincere. Reuchmaire secured the General's leash to the newel post with a stern admonishment to stay, and nodded at Edwin. He and Edwin entered the passageway, and the door swung closed behind them with a soft click. Reuchmaire thought of the possibility of spiders or other undesirable inhabitants, perhaps one of those animals without shoulders common to the Lowcountry. He shivered at the thought. At the base of the stairs their feet touched bare shale. The slope of the narrow tunnel decreased a short way from the stairs but his senses told him that there was a continuous downward incline. It was cut through the bluff on which the mansion stood and had bracing beams every few yards.

They moved cautiously ahead. Reuchmaire searched the floor with the umbrella tip for an excavation which might contain a body. Edwin looked for ledges or panels or such which might serve the same purpose. They finally arrived at a solid wooden door which Edwin calculated was approximately a hundred and fifty paces from the stairs. The key fit the latch. The door swung open easily to reveal the river only a few feet lower than the exit.

They emerged onto a small stone platform sloped into the water.

"This could be a boat landing," said Reuchmaire.

Edwin nodded. "Likely is, and well hidden by that marsh grass. Nearly invisible from the river."

"Well, nowhere in there to hide a body. Let's see where we are."

Scrambling up a faint, weed-choked path to the top of the bluff, they found themselves to the northeast side of the mansion a short distance from Pigeon Point.

Reuchmaire plucked a briar from his trousers. "Anyone with a key could use this route to and from the mansion."

Edwin turned and started back down the path. "Andy said there were only two keys. Goldfield has — had — one, which he always kept with him. She had the other made when she, um, planned to do him in."

"Then how did she manage to get the original from Goldfield?"

"Didn't need to. Had a locksmith come out to the house when he was away."

"Of course. One only needs a lock." Reuchmaire used his umbrella to help negotiate the steep descent back to the landing. "Then she premeditated it. I'm afraid it doesn't look good for her."

Edwin let go a long sigh, started back up the tunnel.

Reuchmaire said, "Well, I guess I had best tell Harry."

Chapter 16

Reuchmaire paced back and forth in Harry's office. Every second step the tip of the umbrella hit the floor with a sharp rap. Harry, in his swivel chair with his feet propped on his desk, turned Annabelle's key in his fingers. He looked up when Reuchmaire burst out, "I know it was not Nickie. I just know it. But Annabelle? No! I cannot accept that either."

Harry shrugged. "She confessed."

"Not officially. Only to Edwin."

Harry studied his cigar stub. His bulky frame overflowed the scarred chair that groaned with every shift of weight. "That's the only reason I haven't arrested her. I don't have enough evidence. Right now, what evidence I do have still points to Nickie."

Reuchmaire stopped pacing. "Harry, would you let Nickie take the rap for this?"

Harry gave an irritated grunt. "My meeting with the mayor was not all that friendly. Need I remind you that he is yelling for results. Need I remind you that his niece is married to the governor's son who lives on Hilton Head and has been looking around for a public office, preferably in law enforcement, to enhance his career. The mayor and the governor are what you might call 'close.' It would do me well not to make the mayor any angrier than he already is." Harry swung his size 13 boots off the desk and got up to pour a cup of coffee.

"Harry —"

"No, Doc, I'm not going to railroad Nickie. Like your grandpa says, 'When you like your job too much, you're no longer an effective administrator.' I won't cave in to pressure. Fact is, I can't hold Nickie any longer. Ms. Hawthorne wouldn't file charges so I can't hold him for robbery. Edwin found the missing ball which lets the air out of a murder charge. There's not enough to convict. Not without a body. I guess we could get him for discharging a firearm in the house, of which we do have a film, but he didn't do any damage. We could hold him for burglary, but of what? He didn't take anything. About all that's left is trespassing, and that's iffy. And not worth the effort, anyway."

"Well, you can hold him for assault."

"Come again?"

"He pulled a knife on me. Remember?"

"Doc, that's thin. Anyway, didn't you say Annabelle is going to come in and sign a confession?"

"She wants to. I asked her to wait."

The cup stopped enroute to Harry's mouth. "Are you crazy? That's — that's, well, tampering, or abetting. *Something* that isn't legal."

"It was merely a suggestion."

"Well, why'd you do it?"

"I need time. Time to devise a plan to trap the real killer."

Harry's eyebrows went up and he pushed the Stetson back on his head. "Ohhh, I see. The real killer, eh? Who is not Nickie?"

Reuchmaire shook his head.

"And not Annabelle?"

Another brief shake of the head.

"Reuben?"

"No."

"Then, for the love of Christ, who?"

Reuchmaire opened his mouth, then closed it. He wished he felt the conviction of his suspicion. "Isadora."

Harry gave a skeptical smirk. "Doc, if she was the one upstairs with Goldfield — and I'm not sure we can prove it — why would she shoot him? You know, if she was diddling him? It doesn't make sense."

"Lover's quarrel?" Reuchmaire offered, realizing how unconvincing he sounded.

Harry sat down and chewed his cigar, looking at Reuchmaire through narrowed eyes. "Hell of a quarrel."

Reuchmaire shrugged in exasperation and ran a hand through his hair, pulled it quickly away when he felt the thinness. He wondered if this case was causing him to lose more.

Harry held up three large fingers. "That would mean three people — three! — fired shots that night. It's a regular firing squad."

"It *is* possible."

"So where are the bullets?"

"We found one — the ball that missed. There is likely another in the body. And," he paused to fish in a pocket, "there is this."

Harry turned the lead slug in his fingers. "Thirty-two caliber. Where'd you get this?"

"Edwin gave it to me this morning. He found it embedded in the wall behind a painting in the upper hall."

"Doesn't do us much good without a gun to match it to. Anyway, it might have been there for years."

"Possibly, but it looks new."

Harry studied the bullet. "So it does."

Reuchmaire paced, an expectant light in his eyes instead of the earlier gloom. "Look at what we have, Harry. Annabelle says she shot at Goldfield and fled down the tunnel. She doesn't know if she hit him."

"You think she missed?"

"Yes. And that bullet in your hand is the one she fired."

Harry put his chin on his doubled fists and stared at Reuchmaire. "So how did she get back to her yacht down in Port Royal Sound? How'd she get up *from* the yacht? It's a hell of a swim, even if for an Olympian, even in good weather. Anyway, the du Ponts said she was there all night."

Reuchmaire held up a triumphant finger. "They said her *boat* was there. They don't know if she was."

Harry frowned. "So how does she get back and forth?"

The finger came down. "Well, I haven't exactly figured that out. There's bound to be a way. Ah! I'll bet there's a life raft on her boat. She could have rowed —"

"Doc, she's fifty-five years old. You think she rowed three miles upriver and three back in the middle of a storm?"

Reuchmaire looked about the room, as though expecting the answer to suddenly emerge from hiding. "Well, maybe she took all night. You know, rested along the way."

Harry shook his head, studied his cigar stub, and stood up. "Doc, we better think about this. How 'bout some lunch? Let's go to Plum's. Your turn to buy."

"It is?"

"Trust me."

* * *

Reuchmaire's heart fell when the waitress said they were out of she-crab bisque.

"It's awfully popular," she apologized, giving them a youthful grin. "Y'all should have been in sooner."

Harry tamped out his cigar in an ashtray and smiled genially. "You're prettier than ever today, Tracy. I'll have the usual."

Tracy blushed, hid a giggle behind her order pad. "The seafood gumbo? Yes, sir, Chief Harry. It's really good, Dr. Reuchmaire, if you'd like to try it."

Reuchmaire propped his umbrella in a chair. "And the shrimp salad, too, please."

"Good idea, Doc. Same for me, Tracy."

She wrote it down, scurried off to place the order. "How's that gyreen husband of yours?" Harry asked, when she returned. "'Bout finished the course?"

Tracy did a skillful waitress's dip to unload water and bread from a tray. "Next week, Chief Harry."

"You know, I went through Parris Island. Some years back, of course. I remember slogging through the swamps on maneuvers. How's Brandon like it?"

She laughed. "He says he hates it. But I think he loves it. He's so macho. But he says the drill instructors are crazy. Why, the other night when the big storm came down they had them out on the river on an exercise." She enclosed the empty tray with her arms and leaned close. "I probably shouldn't tell, but he said the funniest thing happened. He and his squad were paddling across the river in the middle of this heavy rain when someone in a skiff drove right through them. Whoever it was was head down under a tarp and never looked up. Just kept motoring on down river toward the Sound."

Reuchmaire stopped buttering his roll. "Was it a man or a woman?"

"He didn't say — oops, got a customer. Excuse me."

"Harry," Reuchmaire hissed, "it could be."

Harry pulled at his ear. "Doc, it could have been anyone."

A voice from the next table said, "I'll tell you who it was."

Reuchmaire and Harry turned.

Old Mr. du Pont leaned over. The elder gentleman was fit for his years, and his eyes contained a youthful glint. His lined features were creased with a frown.

"Hello Harry, Dr. Reuchmaire." He drained his coffee cup and deposited his napkin on the table. "It was vandals. They've been at it again."

"How's that, Mr. du Pont?"

"Down in the Sound the other night. The night of the storm, like Tracy said. Someone used up half the gas in my skiff."

Harry pulled out a pad and pencil. "That a fact?"

"Yes, sir. Snuck it off from right under our noses. Got to be kids. What they do is untie it and paddle off a distance before starting up and then take it off for a joy ride. Same thing happened last year, and the year before."

"And what time did it happen, Mr. du Pont?"

The old gentleman scratched his chin. "Had to be after dark. Margaret and I turn in early."

"After dark? During the storm?"

"Maybe. You know how crazy kids are. Might have been midnight for all I know. I sleep sound. Anyway, this time they were thoughtful enough to bring it back. I wouldn't have noticed except I just had the tank filled."

Harry stopped writing and looked at Reuchmaire whose eyes had gotten very big. "Thanks, Mr. du Pont," Harry said, "I'll look into it."

Mr. du Pont nodded. He collected his tab, left a tip, and shuffled out.

"See." Reuchmaire wriggled with delight. "See."

Harry crossed his arms and nodded. “Okay, could be. She motors up, shoots, and motors back. But Nickie said the same thing. He shot and ran.”

“That’s why I want to try something with Nickie.”

“Yeah? What?”

“I want to hypnotize him.”

Harry took the cigar out of his mouth and stared as though Reuchmaire had suggested a seance. Tracy arrived with the salads and he waited until she left. With a disbelieving shake of his head he began eating.

Reuchmaire ignored his food in his excitement. “I want to try regression hypnosis. I think Nickie is blanking what happened after he shot the gun. It’s called retrograde amnesia. The subconscious does that to protect the conscious from things it can’t bear. I want to remove the block and let Nickie tell us what happened in those crucial moments after he shot and before he left the mansion.”

“If that don’t beat all,” Harry said through a mouthful. “I’ve heard of clairvoyants being used, but hypnosis? Will it stand up in court?”

“Probably not. But that’s not important. What Nickie can tell us may reveal the killer.”

“What the hell, why not? I’m not getting anywhere.”

Reuchmaire speared a shrimp, and said, “Harry, I’m not overstepping my bounds, am I? You’re the law officer, and it’s your case.”

Harry swallowed a large mouthful and reloaded his fork with several deliberate jabs. “Hey, Doc, I’ll let you know. I’d as soon go out and put a line in the water while you do the work, ‘cept it’s bad for the image. You keep going, and I’ll step in when — if — I need to.”

* * *

“You want to do what?” Sitting in the chair at Harry’s desk, Nickie’s astonished face swung from the sheriff to Reuchmaire.

“Hypnotize you, Nickie,” Reuchmaire said, pulling up a chair of his own. “We know you didn’t shoot Mr. Goldfield, but I think you can help us find out who did."

Nickie gripped the chair arms and nervously licked his lips. "I don't know, Doc. It sounds screwy. How can that help?"

"I think you're blanking something that happened after you shot the gun, the pistol we found with your fingerprints on it."

Harry took the cigar out of his mouth and said, "Do this for us and you're free to go. No charges."

"Yeah?" Nickie brightened. "No strings? I mean, what if I say something incriminating — not that I will! But, I mean, what if I did?"

"Doesn't matter, Nickie," Reuchmaire said, moving closer. "We can't use it in court. We're just looking for information."

Nickie's small eyes shot back and forth from Reuchmaire to the sheriff, then worked the floor for several moments. "Well, okay, I guess so — remember now, no charges."

"That's a promise," Harry said.

"So, what do I do?"

"Nothing," Reuchmaire said. "Just relax and listen to my voice..." Reuchmaire began speaking in a soft monologue, impelling Nickie to relax, to let his body go, to let his muscles relax. "Begin with your toes," he said. "Relax...relax...relax." He worked slowly up his body, relaxing muscle by muscle, joint by joint, sinew by sinew. Nickie's shoulders and arms drooped slowly. His head followed, and soon his breathing was slow and deep.

"Now, Nickie, I am going to count backwards from three. When I reach one, you will go to sleep. You will stay asleep until I tell you to waken."

Nickie said nothing.

Reuchmaire made the count. "Can you hear me, Nickie?"

"Yeah, Doc."

"Good. Now I want you to think back, just take your time, but think back to the night of the storm. Do you remember where you were?"

"Yeah, Doc. In the mansion, Goldfield's place."

"Would you like to tell me what happened?"

"Yeah, okay." Nickie's face worked briefly, as though to get everything straight. "I went in the back door, through the kitchen — it was an easy lock. Then I was in the, uh, the hall — the place with all the guns."

"In the foyer?"

"Yeah, the foyer."

"What were you doing there?"

"The safe. I was going for the safe in the den. It was behind the portrait of an old guy in uniform."

"How did you know where it was?"

Nickie started to speak, frowned, and again hesitated. "What's wrong, Nickie?"

"I — I can't remember how I knew. She — somebody told me, I think…."

"Fine, Nickie. We won't worry about that. Did you get to the safe?"

"Nah. The storm cut loose and there was lots of lightning. I was holding one of those two guns, the old pistols, when I heard voices. From upstairs. And I saw a guy up there. I figured it was Goldfield, and he was coming my way. So I turned and shot." He stopped and worked his hands nervously. "Just to scare him. I wasn't shooting at him."

"That's fine. I understand. Now, tell me what happened next."

There was such a long pause Reuchmaire thought Nickie was not going to go on. At last he said, "He fell."

"The man? Goldfield?"

"Yeah. I couldn't believe it. He just dropped." Nickie ran his tongue over his lips. "I — well, I went up the stairs, and — he was dead."

"Dead? How did you know?"

"She said —" Nickie squirmed so hard Reuchmaire thought surely he would come out of it. "She said —"

Reuchmaire waited. Nickie remained silent.

"She said what, Nickie?"

"She said he was dead. Told me to get out, she'd take care of it." Nickie laughed nervously. "I mean I was so scared I didn't argue. I scrammed."

"Who was she, Nickie? Who told you to leave?"

"I — I can't remember. That was it. She told me to get out and I did."

"Was she the same one who told you where the safe was?"

Nickie's head nodded in agreement and his mouth opened, worked briefly and closed. Beads of sweat appeared on his forehead.

Reuchmaire paused. Should he push it? Nickie was obviously having trouble with who it was. Likely it was too deep for him to release, or he was too scared. If pressed, it was likely Nickie would simply awaken, not able to face what he was withholding. He decided not to try. They had at least found out there was someone else there, and it was a woman.

"Okay, Nickie, that's fine. Now I want you to start to awaken. Move your fingers and hands. Good. Wiggle your toes. Now, when I count to three, you will awaken. One…two…three."

Nickie blinked and looked around. "So, how'd I do?"

"You did fine, Nickie." Reuchmaire got up and stretched. "You were very helpful."

"And I can go now? I'm free?"

Harry said, "That's right. I'll get your stuff."

"Nickie," said Reuchmaire, "there is a favor I'd like to ask.

"Sure, Doc, you name it."

"Hang around a few days. And let me know where you'll be."

"Well, okay, if it's important. I got nowhere to go."

"Good. I think it will be very important."

Chapter 17

"Well, ain't this something." Fast Nickie gunned his Harley over the bridge and out along US 21. "Free as a bird, and the Doc asking me for help. 'Stick around,' he says, like I can do something for him. Guess I handled that pretty good. And them about to hang a murder rap on me." He liked to talk to himself when riding. It helped pass the long hours on the road, like he had somebody to talk to. He leaned back on the chopper with his hands lightly on the handles, feet propped high and his hair blowing back over his jacket collar as he surveyed the world through silvered sunglasses.

This really was pretty country down here. He could see why the Doc liked it so much. Flat, but wide open with a feeling of freedom and distance, so different from the tight, barred enclosures he spent so much time in. He particularly liked to look out over the wide marshes, a sea of some kind of long grass cut with twisty channels and sometimes an island of pines and oaks rising like a castle. Once he had gone out to the beach, miles and miles of wide flat sand with the waves just coming and coming with a low soothing sound, all kinds of birds scattering in front of his bike, rising and wheeling back around to go back to whatever they were doing before he came along. Sure was different from the dark and trashy East River where he grew up.

He throttled back to fifty-five, the posted speed limit. He didn't understand what a *prima facie* speed limit was, but it was what they had here in South Carolina. Somebody told him it meant you could go faster than fifty-five if the conditions were okay, but he wasn't taking any chances. The sign said fifty-five, so he would go fifty-five. No sense taking a chance on winding up back in jail, and he wasn't in a rush. There was nowhere he had to be. Just now he was heading out to Hunting Island. He'd hang out for a while, eat the burger and fries he bought first thing out of jail, then head over to Bluffton and wait for Isadora to call. If she was going to call.

The whole operation had gotten real screwy, what with the botched attempt in the mansion — what had happened to Goldfield? — and then the botched handoff of the key the next morning. That was two strikes on this job, and it didn't feel good. They ought to forget this one.

What *had* happened to Goldfield? Mostly he tried not to think about it. When he did he got confused. He remembered shooting the gun. He saw Goldfield drop…then he was running out of the mansion to his bike and heading back to Bluffton. That was the way the scene played over and over in his mind when he let it get started. Well, it must be okay, 'cause the Doc seemed satisfied, and the chief had let him go.

So what if he and Isadora didn't get the money? Best thing now was to forget this operation and head out. Let things cool off for a while, then find another pigeon.

He was so busy thinking he was only half aware of the black Cadillac that followed him out of Beaufort and hung back about a quarter mile. Now it came easing up and past. It jarred him out of his reverie to see Isadora at the wheel motioning him to follow.

He tried to act casual, but his throat had suddenly gone dry. What was she doing, taking a chance on them being seen together? This wasn't good. Maybe she was pissed about him showing up early and had just been covering it. His mind churned with possibilities, none of them good. He even thought of pretending he didn't see her and hauling ass. But he meekly followed her car as it slowed and raised dust on the bare ground fronting a deserted church. She drove around to the back of the white frame building and parked out of sight of the highway among some trees. As he killed the engine and swung off his bike he was startled to see her emerge from the Cadillac with a big smile on her face.

"Nickie!" she said, in her sharp New York accent, "so glad to see you out. I knew they couldn't hold you if I didn't press charges. I was driving down Bay Street and saw you go by and I thought to myself that this would be a good time to talk, to get things straightened out." She startled him even further when she hooked an arm in his and lead him to a set of worn steps. The white board sides of the church begged for paint, and here or there a nail was needed. The interior was dark and quiet, and plain windows stared mutely at their presence. "Sit here with me, Nickie, and let's catch up on things. We got interrupted, didn't we?"

He wasn't sure if she meant the night in the mansion or the morning after when the purse snatch went awry. A breeze kicked up and a swirl of dust from the bare churchyard swept over them.

"Yeah, guess we did," he said, taking off his glasses to rub his eyes.

"Kind of chilly when the wind blows, isn't it?" She pulled her jacket closed and moved close until her thigh pressed against his. The slit in her skirt revealed a length of leg above the knee.

He felt the stirring he often felt around her, thinking again how sexy her face was and what a well built body she had. If she was someone else, some dame in a bar, he would make suggestions, feel out how far she would go. But this was Isadora Hawthorne and she had class. He could not bring himself to make a play for her even though his mind began to flash fantasies about them doing it right here on the steps, or maybe in the car, or maybe in the church — wouldn't that be something. Wouldn't it be something if she suggested it? He visualized her laying naked on a pew bench, her arms reaching for him…

"Nickie," she said, and bored her eyes seriously into his, "I've got a plan. We can still get the money."

The vision evaporated. "What money?"

"Nickie," she laughed, as though he was kidding, "in Goldfield's safe. The hundred grand he keeps there. And the $10,000 check I returned to him for the painting."

"Goldfield's safe," he repeated, fishing for his cigarettes.

"Right." She took the pack from him and tapped out two cigarettes. Tamping them tight she gave him one and took the other for herself. She lit them both with a gold lighter taken from her jacket pocket and blew a long stream of smoke that carried away on the breeze. "I've still got the key to the tunnel. You hit the safe and get out, just like we planned before Reuchmaire interfered."

"Go back in? That's crazy!" He hadn't meant to speak so sharply, but it just came out. It was a crazy idea, but he remembered he had to be careful with Isadora. He didn't want to see that killer look in her eyes. She had an edge, and when she went over it anything could happen. But she surprised him by laughing pleasantly, as though he just hadn't got the point yet.

"No, baby, not crazy. The cops aren't watching the place anymore. Even if they were, the tunnel gets you right past them."

Wow, he thought, she called me 'baby,' affectionate like. She'd never done that before. And her arm had tightened on his. This is really something. He felt Ol' MacHenry stir.

"You know," she went on, blowing another stream of smoke with her head tilted back and a necklace on her smooth throat peeking at him, "I've been thinking. I've got a place up in New York, in the Catskills, a nice house, four bedrooms. You know, lots of space. Why don't we go there and spend some time together. Let the heat blow over for a while. After we finish here."

His head swam like he was drunk. She was really offering him a shack-up, really coming on to him. He saw what she was doing. After all, he wasn't stupid. But he didn't care. It was a trade-off. He goes back in, she lets him in, so to speak. He smiled at his own humor, while his mind refilled with visions of her without clothes. She was conning him, all right, and he just didn't give a fuck. He would take it if he could get it. After all, she was a classy dame and he had never done it to someone with class.

"If anyone can do it, cops or no cops, it's you, Nickie," he heard her say as brightly enameled fingernails caressed the back of his hand. But he was already sold.

"Yeah, maybe you're right," he said. "Hundred grand's worth the risk."

"Hey, I'm telling you, there's no risk. It'll be a cinch."

"Okay, when?"

"Great, Nickie." She gave his arm a squeeze. "I knew you'd do it. You just wait until I give you the word, probably tomorrow night or the next. Let me figure when the best time is."

"Sure, just let me know," he said, through the thrill he felt, still thinking of how it would be with her. Jesus Christ, what luck. She didn't realize he would have done it for the money alone, but he guessed his reaction had really spooked her into making a better offer. He congratulated himself on how well he had carried it off. Acting like it was dangerous, crazy. Guess he had thought so himself for a moment. But she was right; if anyone could do it, he could. It'd be fun if the cops were there. He'd slip right past 'em, he would. Then wouldn't she be impressed?

"Well, I guess we better get going." She led him toward his bike.

* * *

From behind the wheel of the Cadillac, Isadora watched Nickie wheel out of the churchyard in a cloud of dust. Showing off, he had gunned it on the loose dirt and got into a fishtail, saved from losing it only by the hard surface of the highway. She laughed at his childishness, amused that he wanted to impress her.

It had gone easier than she had expected. She thought she might have to resort to sex to get him to agree. Funny how easy men get when you let them have a little. The thought of doing it with Nickie raised a mixture of amusement and arousal. He was such a comical little thing, strutting around like a bantie rooster, trying to be bigger than he was. Mr. Cool, with his shades and jacket and big chopper. He wasn't exactly ugly, and his mousy face had a certain cuteness. She took a deep drag and exhaled with a laugh as she imagined him on top of her, hammering away for all he was worth, trying to show her he could measure up.

Measure up? A grimace crossed her face. The only man who could really measure up was Bull. What a damned shame that didn't work out! He may have been a bastard but he knew how to handle women, really knew how to ring her bell. She shivered with a pang of remembrance. God, he was great in bed. Something akin to remorse briefly touched her, but as quickly vanished.

"Well, too bad." She flung the cigarette out the window and started the car. "Bull's dead, and that's that."

She headed back to Beaufort, wondering if she would really let Nickie come to the Catskills with her. It would be easy enough to stall him, make an excuse he'd buy. On the other hand, the little twerp would be so grateful she could get anything out of him after that. Maybe he did deserve a chance to try to measure up. And, who knows, he might be fun.

* * *

Reuchmaire sat quietly before the window in his office waiting on Annabelle. Strange that she would call and ask to meet him here. She had said she needed to talk, but, no, she was not requesting an appointment for treatment. She just needed to talk to him about the case, as she called it, and thought it was important.

He looked at his watch. How long should he wait? It was almost seven and she said she would be here at six. The sun had set but there was a faint afterglow over the tall pines between his office and the highway. Either that or lights from the strip mall. Christmas decorations were up throughout town, and he remembered he still had his shopping to do. Marla would admonish him again for waiting until the last minute. No doubt hers was complete and presents wrapped. There were times when her efficiency was unbearable. Or perhaps that was what attracted him to her. That, and her other more obvious, should he say, physical, attributes, he thought, feeling the tingle he got when he mentally replayed one of their uninhibited love-making sessions. Last night on the couch, for instance....

Beyond the pines, traffic moved along U.S. 21, the main drag through Beaufort, people heading home from work, to dinner, to the evening's activities. His stomach signaled its impatience with a low growl. A neon dragon winked at him through a break in the trees and set him to wondering if Chinese was on Edwin's acceptable list. The world was rushing around out there, getting ready for evening. Maybe Harry was finding the clue that would solve the case while here he was waiting on someone he wished to talk with while dreading the prospect. He felt sure Annabelle was coming to confess, as she had to Edwin.

Trying to clear her conscience, no doubt. What was he to do if she did?

He still could not convince himself of her guilt. He knew who had done it. He was certain, but he lacked proof. He saw now what Harry meant by not looking for an easy answer. He checked his watch again. She must have thought better of it. Turning out the light he gathered his coat and umbrella and went out through the waiting room.

He opened the outer door and almost collided with Annabelle.

"Mrs. Goldfield, you startled me."

"Dr. Reuchmaire, I'm so sorry. The bridge...."

"Of course, please come in. Would you like coffee?" He turned on the light, propped his umbrella by the door, and deposited his coat in a chair. Hers was Alpaca. Lovely material, he thought, as he hung it carefully by the door. Maybe he could get Marla to buy him one.

She declined coffee, sat down and crossed her legs, nervously meshing her fingers with an embarrassed apologetic look. She was dressed smartly in a two-piece navy blue suit and white blouse, patent leather pumps and a modest but expensive looking necklace. He remembered her as a quietly elegant dresser. "I don't know where to begin," she said.

She seemed to have shrunk in stature, not the tall, poised centerpiece of the gala functions which were her forté. At those she was bright and cheery, but in a controlled and dignified way, a swan moving among geese, aristocratic but not condescending, appreciating and enjoying the element to which she was bred. Now her defenses were down and she merely looked pursued.

He had met her at social gatherings, but only briefly when introduced by a mutual friend. Marla had a taste for those things, fortunately not an obsession such as his former wife had (a major schism in their parting), and her broker's connections brought invitations. Enough to be interesting for the occasional afternoon or evening of "hobnobbing with the Blues," as he called it, always with a delightful assortment of *hors d'oeuvres* which made a more than ample dinner.

It suddenly struck him as odd that he should be so strongly convinced of Annabelle's innocence when he really didn't know her.

He assumed a relaxed pose. “What did you want to talk to me about?”

“I — I probably shouldn’t take your time. You can charge me for a visit, if you like.”

He smiled and clasped his hands behind his neck. “Why don’t we just talk.”

She smiled back with an uncertain twitch of her lips. “I have to confess I had trouble summoning the courage to come here. My family, you see, thought that only crazy people went to psychiatrists. Do you think I’m crazy?”

It startled him so, he laughed, but in a friendly way. “I have no reason to think so. Why do you ask?”

She relaxed some. “Well, for one thing, I’m here talking to you.”

“My dear, crazy people do not come to psychiatrists.”

“Thank you, that helps. Come to think of it, if I had come to you earlier I might not be here now.”

“What do you mean?”

There was a long pause while she seemed to gather for a hurdle. “I shot my husband.”

“Yes, I know. Edwin told me.”

For a moment she seemed taken aback. “Of course. I should have known he would. You and he are very close, aren’t you?”

Reuchmaire smiled. “Quite.”

She looked wistfully out the window. “How nice to feel so close to someone. To be able to share your thoughts and fears. When I told Edwin, it was such an immense relief, even though I didn’t really know him. There was so much pressure, keeping it hidden.”

“I expect there was.” He waited while she continued to stare out at the night.

“I don’t know why I came here,” she said, turning to him. “I guess I felt like I needed to talk to someone — professionally. I wanted to ask you what I should do.”

Reuchmaire tapped his fingers together before his face and tried to decide which role he was playing here, policeman or psychiatrist. There was a question of ethics. And there was the conviction he had that Annabelle was innocent. “Let me be certain I understand what you want. Are you asking me as a doctor, or as an assistant to Chief Doyle?"

After a lengthy pause, she said, "I think, as a friend. We've met before at parties and I remember you as warm and open, someone who would be easy to be friends with."

"Well," he smiled, "thank you. I do try to be. Then the answer is simple. As a friend I advise you to do nothing. Let the case work to its own conclusion without assistance. Please be assured I would not say this if I was not convinced of your innocence."

She laughed, a short unhappy burst. "My innocence? Dr. Reuchmaire, I know I killed my husband. How can I be innocent?"

"What did you do with the body?"

"What did I —? Nothing."

"You didn't hide it? You didn't dump it in the river?"

"No. I didn't go near it."

"You did not examine it?"

"Well, no."

"Then you can only assume you killed him."

She had been drawing herself up defensively at his string of questions, but at this statement her mouth fell open. "Why — you're right."

"But you were in the mansion the night of the, ah, incident."

"Yes."

"And you did shoot at your husband?"

"Yes."

"What made you want to do that?"

"All those years," she said, with a quiet fierceness. "All those years of him rubbing my nose in his affairs. I just got — it seems so inexcusable now, so trivial — but I just got fed up. So I shot him." She folded her hands in her lap.

"How do you feel about that?"

She took a deep breath and let it out. "That's why I'm here, I guess. At the time, it seemed so logical. At least until I pulled the trigger. Then I couldn't believe what I had done. I haven't been able to get it off my mind. It keeps coming back again and again, like some huge, pointing finger thrusting into my thoughts at every moment. I even have dreams

—" She smiled wistfully. "I'm really not a killer, Dr. Reuchmaire."

"No, I don't think you are."

"But I did shoot. I can't deny that."

"And then?"

"I ran. I thought I heard something, thought that someone else was there."

"Ran where?"

"Back down the tunnel. Back to my boat and back to my yacht, down in Port Royal sound."

"And it was that trip in the storm that ruined your hair, prompting you to have it redone the next day."

She started at this revelation. "My, you *are* the detective, aren't you."

He bowed an acknowledgment. "It's not hard to find things out in Beaufort. Is there anything else you want to talk about — strictly as a friend?"

She took a moment, frowning at her exquisitely polished nails. "No. You've been very helpful."

Reuchmaire felt a great sense of relief. His theory was proving out. There was just the tricky part about her being in the mansion, and that she fired a shot but did not kill her husband. But he thought he had the explanation to that.

He quickly stood as she rose to leave.

"Oh, yes, I almost forgot. I found this in Bull's safe." She opened her purse and handed him a piece of paper Reuchmaire recognized as a check.

"A check for $10,000 made out to Isadora Hawthorne," Reuchmaire read, noting Bull Goldfield's illegible, grandiose scrawl on the signature line. The butterfly in his mind began to flutter madly. "*Sacre Bleu*," he whispered, remembering fast Nickie's Freudian slip in the jail and the painting in the window of the gallery, a forgery that should never cost $10,000.

"I thought it might be helpful. I don't know what it was doing there."

"In the safe?" Reuchmaire said, tapping the check briskly against his fingers.

"Yes, I — well, I looked in there yesterday," she said apologetically, as though it may have been improper. "Bull didn't know I found out where he recorded the combination. He was so paranoid he changed it every few months. Guess I was just curious. The estate would be coming up for probate — I thought he was dead, you see — and I wondered what else he might be hiding from me."

"Change the combination — " Reuchmaire muttered to himself, handing the check back.

"Shouldn't you give that to Chief Doyle?"

"No. No, that's quite all right. I would like for you to return it to the safe."

"Return it?"

"Yes. And tell no one. Absolutely no one."

Chapter 18

Reuchmaire looked out over the tidal marsh encompassing the entire northern boundary of Dataw Island. He sat with his back against a live oak, a huge grandfather of a tree resting one large twisted arm on the ground. In his cupped hands a cup of coffee warded off the morning chill. Around his body the greatcoat was buttoned tightly, his head adorned with the fur cap. Dataw was an island only by virtue of tidal creeks and marshes and in reality lay as part of the larger Lady's Island. At low tide it was not an island at all, if one accepted an empty tidal creek bed as solid ground. But anyone who has ever left shoes behind in the sucking gooey mud knew it wasn't. Still, like so much land around Beaufort it was known as an island and on it blossomed the exclusive development in which he lived known as Dataw Country Estates. He wondered what around Beaufort *wasn't* "country," and what new development wasn't an "estate."

The tree had sold him on the house. In nice weather he would climb to a perch high in the leafy castle to sweep the marsh with binoculars. Herons, egrets, ibises, ducks, cormorants, and an endless variety of other marsh birds winged and waded before his eyes. A pair of ospreys had nested the year before on a lightning-blasted loblolly pine a short distance away and he hoped to see nestlings in the spring. While not a serious birder, he found marsh life fascinating. Raccoons and possums stopped by regularly looking for scraps or for the corn he put out for deer. He had not as yet devised a method to keep these clever nocturnal thieves and the equally adroit daytime squirrels from pilfering it. Admittedly, he did not try hard, enjoying those creatures along with the rest. He even saw an occasional otter. A few times deer, almost near enough to reach down and touch, passed beneath his perch unaware of or unconcerned by his presence.

The house, even without the tree, was quite nice. "Opulent," his senses had cringed when Marla insisted that he buy it. It amazed him that Marla could talk him into such an extravagant place. There seemed no limit on what she could talk him into — he admitted it, he was putty in her hands. But when he saw the tree, and the serpentine arm of the Morgan River beyond the marsh, his resistance, such as it was, vanished. After an appropriate show of resistance, he accepted Marla's plan to get him, and eventually them, into what she referred to as a really nice place and out of the small, stereotypical, and cheap (frugal, he insisted) condo in which he lived when they began dating.

Tree and marsh symbolized the Lowcountry. The beaches were nice, and he enjoyed strolling the sandy expanses, particularly late of a summer's day with drink in hand and Marla at his side with the mesmerizing rote of the surf in his ears and breeze enough to keep the mosquitos and no-see-ums away. But he preferred to sit by this sea of spartina, sun-bronzed in the early light, cut by serpentine tidal channels out to where the river met Lucy Point Creek, and think.

Eastward beyond creek and river lay Coosa and Lady's Islands whose hazy tree lines of pine and oak defined the horizon. The sun, just over the tips of the trees and muted into a dull red by fog and haze, brought to mind the sailor's old aphorism, *Red in the morning, sailor take warning.* The temperature overnight had dropped into the fifties and he was roughing it with the cap's earflaps up even though his ears were beginning to tingle a bit. A heron knee-deep in water a short distance off came up with a minnow. Edwin had promised shrimp and oyster gumbo for tonight. Wonderful seafood was another Lowcountry asset, and he had not yet found a dish or preparation he did not like. Edwin, when he was here, and Marla when he wasn't, kept him away from the creamy preparations he loved, but, he had to admit, there were other equally appealing ways to fix the Lowcountry delicacies. And much healthier, Edwin never failed to remind him.

He came out this morning to ponder the case. He needed to sort out all that had happened and all that he and Harry thought had happened, or thought might have happened. As interesting as this whole thing was, and a refreshing divergence, it was far more complex than he expected. So now, he said to himself, we seem to have eliminated Nickie and implicated Annabelle. She has even confessed and has a motive.

He sighed. That was not at all how he wanted it to end. Not at all how it should end. He was absolutely convinced it had to be Isadora. Since that first night in the mansion when Wilson handed him the hankie, he was sure of it. But how to prove it? How to keep Annabelle from being convicted? It would be horrible for her to go to prison for something she did not do and, worse, for something that detestable Yankee, Isadora Hawthorne, did. Worry, worry, worry. How to figure all this out. There had to be a way.

He took a long swig of coffee, felt the warmth flow all the way down, and wondered whether birds and animals had the same psychological nuances that plagued humans. Were those flutters, mutters, head bobs, grins, chirps and wing flicks only primitive instinct or did they signal a deeper subconscious purpose that one creature might have and another not? Pecking orders, Grandfather Reuchmaire (and a number of others, some published) once observed, were not reserved for birds. When Reuchmaire tried these thoughts on Marla, usually while sipping a drink and waxing philosophical up in the tree (they fit nicely together in a high crotch), she invariably gave him a raised eyebrow, half-smile, and a skeptical, "No doubt."

Animals, he reflected, do not plot murder.

Captain Semmes, followed by General Stuart, emerged through the pet door from their breakfast inside the house. The Captain stepped delicately through the dewy grass, stopping every so often to flip moisture from a paw and utter a mild complaint. The General sniffed the crisp air, gave a small disapproving yip, and withdrew inside no doubt to curl up by the fire.

Captain Semmes completed the journey to Reuchmaire's lap and settled in to groom his damp fur. Finished with his toilette, he gazed at Reuchmaire with his why-aren't-you-scratching-my-ear look, and dissolved into one of his goofy expressions of pleasure when his request was answered.

Reuchmaire had just drained his mug and was contemplating a

second, pitting desire against the inconvenience of a trip inside, when he saw the boat.

It was a punt with a lone figure oaring up a tidal fork that ended almost at Reuchmaire's property. The spring-fed channel was deep enough to allow light boats access to his property. He planned to build a pier for crabbing, as soon as he found someone who would meet his price. Astounding what carpenters wanted! Even with back turned and a corduroy jacket over the shoulders, the silhouette and crew cut of Reuben Conner was obvious.

Reuben had an open invitation to visit whenever he liked, Reuchmaire's way of keeping the lines of communication open if Reuben's turbulent past came back to the surface. It would save him the expense of appointments, and in return Reuben tended Reuchmaire's lawn and garden for free. A fair bargain.

Reuben had said he felt awkward driving his battered pickup full of mowers, rakes, blowers, gasoline cans and other implements of his trade into Dataw Estates if not there on business. So he used the "back entrance," as he called the waterway on the rare occasions he showed up. When he did, it meant something big was on his mind.

Today, Reuchmaire knew what it was.

The tide was nearly full, allowing the boat within a few yards of firm ground at which point Reuben hopped out onto the mud flat and dragged it clear of the water, moving expertly on his artificial legs. Reuchmaire, as always, was astonished at his dexterity.

Reuchmaire waved good morning.

"Mornin', Doc," Reuben said, working up the bank. He leaned against the huge grounded branch and blew on his cupped hands. "Chilly, eh?"

"Care for coffee?"

"That'd be fine, if it's no trouble."

Reuchmaire set Captain Semmes aside and got up. "None at all. How do you like it?"

"Black."

"Care to come in?"

"No, thanks. Here's fine. I like the marsh in the morning." His breath made a faint mist as he spoke.

"So do I. Back in a moment."

The Captain gave an irritated twitch of his kinked tail and went over to accept a head scratch from this unexpected but convenient visitor.

Reuchmaire returned with two steaming mugs and handed one to Reuben.

They finished half their mugs in silence while watching the sun rise higher in the hazy sky. Reuchmaire unbuttoned his coat in the rising warmth. "So, what brings you out here?"

Reuben held his mug up with both hands and stared into it, as though the answer lay within. He swallowed a mouthful and looked out over the marsh. "Doc," he finally asked, "you think I could kill someone?"

Reuchmaire used his own coffee to delay while he thought over his answer. "I know you once thought you wanted to kill someone."

Reuben nodded. "Yeah, Hildy."

Reuchmaire waited through a long silence before venturing, "What's on your mind?"

"Goldfield. I really want to kill that bastard."

Who doesn't? thought Reuchmaire, relieved. One of the suspects had been eliminated. With the confident little smile that appeared before he asked questions to which he knew the answer, Reuchmaire said, "Do you really?"

"Well, no, not really. I just mean…well, you know how I mean it."

Reuchmaire nodded.

"That's all behind me. Hildy, and all that." Reuben began to talk, about things in general at first but working into the encounter between him and Goldfield over Cissy. He covered the event in detail and took a while to get through it, even repeating certain parts to articulate how he was handling it all internally. Then he stared out over the marsh, and said, "He's a bastard. A real bastard."

Reuchmaire said nothing, but was pleased that Reuben had delivered this catharsis.

"I guess he's still missing."

Reuchmaire nodded. "It seems so."

Reuben drained his mug and stared at it. He stood up and handed the empty mug to Reuchmaire. "Guess I'll be going. Thanks for the coffee."

Reuchmaire walked with him down to the edge of the marsh. The tide had completed its rise and was under the punt making it easy for Reuben to float it and hop in. His foot slipped in the shallow water but he caught himself and laughed. "I better be careful, I sure can't walk on water." As he rowed away, he called, "Thanks, again, Doc. Thanks for everything."

Reuchmaire watched the boat ease around a bend in the creek and head toward the river. Only three suspects remained. But really, only one. The little butterfly began to flutter in his brain. Something Reuben said set it off, and made him think of Marla, and the Mammy Queen, something each had said. He looked out to where Reuben's boat was just entering the channel. 'Can't walk on water,' he said. ON water, no, but someone could — *Sacre!* He knew where the body was!

He dashed into the house to get his car keys. As he burst into the kitchen the phone rang.

"Doc, it's Nickie."

"Yes, Nickie," Reuchmaire panted, impatient to get away. But Nickie would not have called just to pass the time of day.

"Doc, you did me a real favor, getting me out. So I figure I owe you one. There's something I think you should know."

Reuchmaire sat down to quiet his pounding heart. Nickie confessed to the art scam he and Isadora ran. He described their operation just as Reuchmaire had suspected but could not actually prove. Then Nickie said something that brought him to his feet.

"She's planning for me to go back in and hit the safe. She wants the check and the money, then we're clearing out, probably tonight or tomorrow night. That's all, Doc. Like I said, I owe you. Now we're even."

"Nickie —"

"I'm thinking I'll just beat it. I tell ya, Doc, she scares me."

Reuchmaire tried to piece together a plan before the whole thing slipped through his fingers. "Nickie, that's a real favor. I can't tell you how much help it is."

"Yeah, well, like I said —"

"Nickie, there is one more thing you could do for me."

"Doc, we're even. I think I better go."

"Well, if you need to, then you should." Reuchmaire crossed his fingers. Would Nickie hang up?

"Yeah, well —"

"By the way Nickie, I talked to Warden White yesterday. Guess who's in Allendale? Greasy Malone."

"Greasy! He's the asshole — sorry, Doc — he's the one who…"

"Who turned you in, in Columbia?"

"Yeah, well, I think so."

"Not according to him. He said it was Isadora."

"What?"

"I'm afraid so."

There was a long silence in which Reuchmaire only heard heavy breath in the receiver.

"Okay, listen, Doc. I appreciate you telling me."

"Would it be worth a favor?"

"Damn right! That double-crossing sleaze bitch — sorry, Doc."

"Thanks, Nickie. Tell you what, just stay put until you hear from me."

"Yeah, Doc. I'll do it."

Reuchmaire breathed a great sigh of relief. There was not a moment to lose. After a frantic ten-minute search for his car keys, aided by an excited General Stuart ululating at his heels, he discovered them in his pants pocket and rushed off to Marla's office.

Chapter 19

"Jimsy, I'm sorry. Really I am, but I just can't get away now."

"But, but — I know where the body is," he pleaded as the umbrella beat a tattoo on the floor.

Marla calmly continued to work her keyboard and smiled sympathetically. "Well, then get Harry and —"

"He's over on Hilton Head talking to the governor." Harry had been worried enough about the mayor — if Harry ever worried about anything — now the governor had called and requested that he "drop by" and fill him in on the case. Reuchmaire realized that it was he, himself, that feared for Harry's job. He would miss their chess if Harry had to relocate.

She came around the desk to give him a hug. "Jimsy, you know I'd do just anything for you, but I really, really can't right now. I've got three big-money customers who want to sell, four bmc's who want to buy, and another half dozen who want to know whether to buy or sell. It's just not a good day."

"But I can't swim. I need someone who can swim."

"Oh, pooh, you can too swim." She grinned and tickled his ear with a finger. "Don't you remember last summer, our midnight rendezvous in Repository Cove. Just like *From Here to Eternity*. I bet we melted some sand."

"I can't swim well enough." He brushed irritably at her hand. "I need a strong swimmer who's comfortable underwater."

"You're so cute when you're angry. Look, I'll work real hard and maybe by three or four —"

"I need to go this morning! Now!"

"Jimsy, are you absolutely certain you know where Goldfield is?"

"Yes! Well — almost certain."

"Um, hum."

"Enough to know where to look. Approximately."

"Ah, ha." She returned to her typing.

His shoulders sagged and he moaned, "But I need someone… someone who…"

"Patty can swim," she said.

* * *

Reuchmaire steered the dinghy downriver toward the Goldfield estate. Stowed beneath the seats were towels, blankets, a length of rope, a knife, a wooden stake and a mallet. He had dredged a pea jacket and knit sailor's cap from his old Navy gear (the cap still fit), and sat holding the not quite buttonable jacket closed against the morning chill. He soon discovered that he had overestimated the cold. The sun was pleasantly warm and there was no wind. Shortly cap and coat joined the other supplies in the bilge.

In the bow, trim and fetching in a wet suit, with that irritating youthful disdain for cold, Patty was eagerly pulling on her flippers.

"Patricia, are you sure you'll be warm enough? I don't want you catching pneumonia."

"Oh, sure, Dr. R. I could do it without a wet suit. The water hasn't gotten really cold yet. The other night was the first hard freeze this year."

"Feels cold to me." He shook water off his fingers.

"Well, without the suit I couldn't stay down as long."

She tucked a last blonde lock under the headpiece. "This is so cool, Dr. Reuchmaire. Looking for a body. Do you really think we'll find it?"

"Quite certain, Patricia, but I must warn you. It may not be a pretty sight."

"Dr. ROCKmore," she admonished, "I've worked weekend night shift at the Savannah hospital for two years. I've seen a dead person."

"This one," he warned, "has been in the water several days."

"Ohh, cool."

"Patricia — oh, never mind." He steered the boat close to shore to stay away from the channel. Out there was the Intracoastal Waterway and the possibility of large craft. The small, battered engine struggled against the flow of tide and gasped uncertainly from time to time. Reuchmaire worried that they might be too late. Then he worried that they would not get there at all. Then he worried just to worry.

He convinced himself again that he knew the location of Goldfield's body — at least to within a matter of yards. But what was keeping it there? How had Isadora Hawthorne, nee Grundel Schmidt, secured the body to prevent the tide from taking it away? Haste was essential, before some fickle current caused the body to be lost. With it would go any hope of solving the case and of saving Annabelle. Not to mention Harry's job.

Eventually the boundary fence of the estate crept past. He headed for where he remembered the tunnel entrance to be. He found the concrete ledge and nosed the boat against it. Just as he did the engine quit. It restarted reluctantly and continued a low muttering.

"It was the only one I could find — at an acceptable price," he said to Patty's frown.

"Hold it here with the engine." He picked up mallet and stake and almost fell in as he struggled from the boat onto the ledge.

Patty flopped to the tiller, with comically high flippered steps over the seats, herself almost tumbling overboard. "What are you going to do?"

"Measure," he called from the top of the bluff. He stepped off one hundred meters. There he drove the stake into the ground where it could be seen from the boat. If Ms. Hawthorne had indeed carried the body underwater she could have made it no further. A body is much bulkier than a pair of bar bells. He returned to the boat and puttered back to the stake.

"It should be right around here," he said.

Patty's eyes glittered excitedly. She slipped on a mask and went over the side.

A minute and a half later, she emerged with a head shake. "Nothing." She hyperventilated briefly and dove again. On the fourth return she hung onto the boat, breathing heavily. "Dr. Reuchmaire, I could do a lot better with tanks."

"I know, Patricia, but it would have taken quite some time to get them, and speed is of the essence." A frown creased his brow. "I had thought you would find it right away. I was just so sure it was here."

"Um, Dr. Reuchmaire, why do you think it should be right here?"

She listened in round-eyed astonishment to his theory. "So cool," she said. "So you think the murderess *walked* underwater with the body and placed it on the bottom weighted with shot."

"Exactly."

"But why just this far?"

He smiled patiently and explained about the Olympic pool.

"Oh." She nodded solemnly and spit in her mask and wiped the lens. "But couldn't she have come up for air?"

Reuchmaire stared blankly. "What?"

"Why was she limited to a hundred meters? She wasn't trying to win a bet. She was hiding a body."

"*Sacre!*" He slapped his forehead. "Patricia, you're a genius." His face clouded. "But then — *sacre bleu*, it could be anywhere."

"Well, I know where I'd put a body if it was me."

"You do?"

"Up there where the old dock used to be."

"Old dock?"

"Yeah, about another fifty yards." She let go of the boat and stayed afloat easily treading water with the fins. "An old wooden dock. It was falling down, but we used to come dive off it when I was a kid. Had to sneak around the fence. One day Goldfield came out and shot at us."

"SHOT at you?"

"Yeah, with a shotgun. He was a long way off, but Randy Carter got a couple of pellets in his butt and screamed his head off. Just lightweight birdshot. Don't know why he yelled so. Mostly scared, I think. Goldfield would have got in big trouble, but he gave Randy's parents a bunch of money and promised not to do it again. So they didn't do anything. But we never went back. About five years ago a hurricane knocked the dock down. Same one that put the tree over there in Repository Cove. But the pilings are still there, all jumbled up.

Sometimes at extreme low tide one or two of them break water. Anyway, that's where I'd hide a body. Stick it under the pilings and tie it down."

* * *

"Got it!" Patricia surfaced several yards from the idling boat. She held aloft the end of the rope Reuchmaire had brought along. It was drawn taut against the weight of something heavy still underwater.

Reuchmaire leapt up and almost fell overboard. His theory was proven and in moments they would have the prize.

"It's all wrapped in plastic," she called and stroked for the boat with her free hand. "I can barely drag it."

"Patricia," Reuchmaire shouted, "wait there. I'll come to you. The bottom drops rapidly to the channel."

She slid under with a startled yelp. A moment later she surfaced paddling furiously and barely able to keep her head above water. Again she went under. She came back sputtering. "It's sliding deeper."

"Let it go, Patricia. Let it go!" He tried to get the balky boat to respond.

"Can't. Rope's around my wrist."

Reuchmaire gunned the engine. It gave one loud belch and quit. He began to drift away with the tide, tugging furiously at the lanyard amid a fusillade of French expletives. The engine refused to start. Patty slid under once more. Out of the possibilities racing through his mind an impulse seized him. He ripped his shoes and trousers off. Dousing the pants in the water he quickly tied off each leg at the cuff. Knife clamped in his teeth, pants gripped in one hand and the other pinching his nose, he leapt overboard.

The sudden shock of cold took his breath away. He fought down panic and forced his mind to recall his Navy training. With the waist held open like a grocery sack he slapped the pants down into the water. The legs filled with trapped air and he snugged the belt tight. With the bloated pants serving as a makeshift float, he set out for Patty. The sight of only Patty's nose above water and her free hand thrashing desperately, set him to a furious effort. The gap narrowed with fearful slowness. Just as she vanished beneath the surface his hand closed on hers. He guided it to the improvised water wings.

Her face surfaced, sucking air. The pants were barely enough to offset the drag of the body. But they would not last. Even now he could hear air seeping out.

"Can you undo the rope?" he asked.

"Too tight," she gasped. "The weight's too much." He drew a deep breath, prepared to dive.

"Don't cut it," she said. "We'll lose it."

He stared for one unbelieving moment, and it flashed through his mind how indefatigable youth was. "Patricia — oh, never mind."

He slid under and sawed through the rope. As the body slid toward the depths he hung on briefly, the weight now being pulled by the tide. Was there no way to save it? Finally he released the rope and struck for the surface.

It took a while to overtake their drifting boat. Patty's flippers helped and when the pants had deflated into a useless mass she pulled an exhausted Reuchmaire the last few yards. They clambered aboard and collapsed into the scuppers.

"Thanks for saving me, Dr. Reuchmaire. I don't think I would have come up again."

"I'm glad you're safe, Patricia," he wheezed.

She giggled. "Dr. Reuchmaire, you've got cute little roosters on your C.K.'s."

A blushing Reuchmaire quickly wrapped himself in the blanket intended for Goldfield's corpse. "Gamecocks, Patricia. They're *gamecocks*."

She and removed her flippers and tossed them aside. "We almost had it. Now it's gone."

Reuchmaire feared she was right. The tide was running out. By the time this obstinate engine could get them to the marina and they came back with dredgers there was no telling where it might be. *Sacre.*

"AHOY!"

They turned at the hail. A shrimper bore down on them. "Do you need some help?" came a call from the bridge.

Reuchmaire's heart soared. "Look, Patricia, a shrimper. A lovely, lovely shrimper with those lovely, lovely draglines festooning the yards."

* * *

Harry looked up from paperwork when a rejuvenated Reuchmaire walked in.

"That was really great work, Doc. The mayor is a lot happier, although the governor didn't seem as pleased. I think he was ready to replace me."

Reuchmaire bowed with a flourish. "Not bad for a mere psychiatrist, eh? Although, Patricia did help a bit."

Harry smiled. "No, not bad at all. So we were looking the wrong way — downriver."

"Rote procedure, just as our programmed minds did with Gibaud vs Lazako. Bodies float downstream, eh? Isn't the power of the subconscious interesting? Mammy Queen was right, we just needed to look in the right place." Reuchmaire sat down and laid his chin on the umbrella's handle. "How did she know?"

"She has de juju."

Reuchmaire frowned. "Someone must have told her. Perhaps one of her many kinfolk witnessed the event but was reluctant to come forward."

"Maybe," Harry shrugged, "or maybe she has the sight, can see things we can't. The Gullah have quite a network. It's helped me more than once over the years, but I tell you, there's something creepy about it. At times it seems to move faster than talk, faster than telephones. I never could decide if it was word of mouth, or — juju."

"I think it's all up here." Reuchmaire tapped his head. "The mind conceives things that are or aren't depending upon what the subconscious dictates."

Harry chewed a cigar stub, an amused glint in his eye. "I think it's juju. By the way, the morgue called."

"And?"

"That plastic sheet Goldfield was wrapped in came from the patio construction on the side of the house. Whoever killed him stuffed his pockets with shot from the gun room, and wrapped a bunch of lead ingots with him. Enough to keep him on the bottom." Harry took the stub out of his mouth with a solemn stare at his friend.

"Yes, go on."

"Well, Doc, we were both wrong. Goldfield's got a big hole in him. Only could have been done by one of those dueling pistols. Looks like Nickie did it after all."

The umbrella slipped from Reuchmaire's grasp and fell to the floor. "Whaaat? I don't believe it."

"Can't argue with the evidence. And something else." He opened a drawer and brought out a gun. "Goldfield had this .32 automatic in his pocket. It had been fired once. Same caliber as the bullet —"

"Edwin found in the portrait," Reuchmaire completed, and threw his hands in the air. "Every time I think we are where we should be, something else comes up."

"That's crime work, Doc. That's how this business is. You keep trying theories until one fits." Harry made quotation marks with his fingers, and said, "When you've eliminated all that's impossible, whatever remains, no matter how improbable, is the truth."

"Indubitably," Reuchmaire muttered. How could he have been so wrong? Well, at least Annabelle was off the hook.

"So," Harry went on, "I'm thinking Nickie shot at Goldfield from the foyer. We got that on tape. Goldfield retreated to his bedroom, got his own gun, came back out and shot at Nickie. Then he got shot by Nickie."

"And put his gun in his pocket as he fell?"

After a prolonged silence, Harry said, "Yeah, I guess that doesn't make sense. Maybe Nickie put it there."

Reuchmaire went over to where the impounded dueling pistols were stored. "Two pistols," he murmured. "One with Nickie's fingerprints, the other with none. Both fired."

"We could only tell that the fingerprinted one was fired. The other was too clean," Harry said.

Reuchmaire turned. "Both empty?"

"That's right."

"But Goldfield always kept all his guns..."

Harry chuckled. "Come to think of it, maybe we should arrest you. Your prints were on the gun with Nickie's."

"Well, of course they were. I was out there the day before trying to buy — *Sacre!* Harry, let's run the tape again."

An hour later Harry sipped another cup of stale coffee, grimaced at it, and set it aside. He sat down with a huge sigh. Rubbing his eyes, he said, "Doc, we've watched that thing two dozen times, at least. Nickie fires, creeps up the stairs out of the picture, a minute later runs back down the stairs and is gone."

Reuchmaire hit his umbrella hard against the floor, and snapped, "There's something there we're missing. I know it! Why can't I see it?" He rewound the tape and got up to get coffee.

"I got to run a patrol," Harry headed for the door. "Want to go along? Start another game? You look like you could use a break."

Reuchmaire shook his head and restarted the tape. "Go ahead."

"Glutton for punishment." Harry closed the door.

It was on the third rerun that Reuchmaire at last saw it. "*Sacre Bleu!*" he cried, and fell back in the chair. It was so impossibly simple they had overlooked it. He reran the tape and stopped it with an empty-handed Nickie in full stride about to exit screen left. Beyond him on the display shelf lay the ornate case holding the other pistol.

"So," he said to himself, "This will clear Nickie. Now we can clear Annabelle with Mammy Queen's help."

Chapter 20

Wilson's polite but slightly haughty expression, with which he greeted callers at Riverbriar, faded into surprise with an undertone of concern when he opened the door to face Reuchmaire, Edwin and General Stuart.

"Good morning, Wilson." Reuchmaire entered without waiting to be admitted and handed his hat to the startled butler. "Cooling off a bit, eh? The warm spell didn't last long. They never do this time of year. I prefer summer myself in spite of the heat." He shrugged out of his coat, handed it to Wilson, and strolled into the parlor. The General tagged along and settled beside the sofa.

Wilson hurried back in after hanging the coats. "Dr. Reuchmaire, suh, Mrs. Goldfield is out. I don' know when to spect her."

"Not a problem, Wilson. Actually it is you we came to see."

"Me, suh?"

"Indeed. I think you can help us solve the disappearance of Mr. Goldfield." He guided the butler to a chair.

Wilson brought out a handkerchief and dabbed his brow. "Dr. Reuchmaire, I tol' you all I know. I don't see —"

"Tut, tut, Wilson, let me ask the questions and I think you'll begin to understand." He furrowed his brow and paced, the umbrella tip keeping time lightly on the wooden floor. "It concerns the day you discovered Mr. Goldfield missing. The day after the night of the storm."

"Yes, suh, but —" Reuchmaire raised a hand and the butler fell silent.

Reuchmaire sat next to Wilson and leaned close. "Now, Wilson, have you told us everything you feel is of importance?"

Wilson worked the handkerchief in his hands and refused to meet

Reuchmaire's eyes. "Yes, suh."

"No, Wilson," Reuchmaire said patiently, "I think there is something very important you have not told us."

Wilson stood with an angry thrust of arms, an avoidance ploy Reuchmaire had expected.

"Dr. Reuchmaire, I have told you —"

The doorbell interrupted him. Before he could move, the door opened and Harry entered with the Mammy Queen. She flowed into the room, her large frame rolling and strolling, tapping time to her cadence with a gnarled thick walking stick, her eyes sharp and fiery, looking for juju, looking for trouble. She had come to woik someone. Cocinas and clams, sand dollars and crab claws, beads and stones, in necklaces, bracelets, rings and earrings swung and jangled with the rhythm of her walk. About her shoulders was a shawl over a bright print dress. She stopped, swept the room with stern eyes, and rapped the floor with her stick, as though a judge with a gavel.

To the shrinking butler she said, "Wilson, wha dis I ya? Oona ain tell de doctah man wha ya kno. Oona ain tell Chief Harry. Oona wan becum witch? Oona duh mi blood an I ain gwine hab duh story. Oona hafa tell. If oona ain gwine tell I ga mek oona witch an ya ga dead. Mi hab de juju. I kin do um."

Wilson began to tremble. His eyes rolled in search of escape. "I dun tell de doctah eberyting I kno," he pleaded. "I swey."

Mammy Queen looked at him without pity. "Speak, Wilson. Tell wi wha oona kno."

He hung his head and gave it a brief shake.

A slow sigh escaped Mammy Queen. Her head tilted back, riveting the butler with a baleful stare. Only the soft tinkling of baubles could be heard in the room. Although a foot shorter, she seemed to glare down at him from a throne. From her waist she took a pouch and with two thick fingers reached in and brought forth a small pale lozenge to hold before him.

He fell to his knees, trembling even harder. "Queen, I ain kno no mo! I dun tell ebryting!"

"Hush!" She thrust the lozenge in his face. "Swallow dis. Ef hunnah tell de trut, nutin ga happen. Ef hunnah don, hunnah gwine tun eentuh a witch an die."

Wilson clasped his hands before him as though praying and began to sway from side to side. "I can't, I can't."

"Hunnah must! Hunnah da Gullah. We da fambly. Tek it!"

Reuchmaire was transfixed. The butler's terror seemed to fill the room. A vision formed of dark forms around a large fire, flame patterns on black sweaty bodies swaying to the beat of drums, and an ornately-masked figure towering over a helpless victim. He caught a whiff of almonds. It seemed to come from the pouch Mammy Queen held. *Sacre Bleu!* She is threatening him with strychnine. What if he swallows it? This must stop!

Harry's large hand closed on his shoulder. He silenced Reuchmaire with a quick headshake.

"Wait!"

Everyone turned. Annabelle entered the room and went to Wilson.

"It's all right," she soothed, helping him stand. "Tell them."

"Miz Annabelle —"

She put an arm around his shoulders. "Tell them what happened."

Mammy Queen drew back with a satisfied nod, and said, "Now lissen tuh Miz Annabelle. E kno wha hunnah hafa do." She dropped the lozenge back into the pouch and returned the pouch to her belt.

Wilson nodded meekly. "Dr. Reuchmaire," he said, returning to English in his slow drawl, "the night you came to the mansion I told you Mrs. Goldfield had been on her boat down in the Sound all day. She, had, except for once when she came by the mansion before going back."

The umbrella tapped rapidly on the floor. "Yes, just as I thought. And she entered the mansion from the river...dressed as her husband."

Wilson nodded.

"And why did she come back?"

"To return this." Wilson went to a display case and reached for one of Goldfield's guns.

"Don't touch it!" Harry went to the case and collected the gun with a handkerchief. Inserting a pencil in the barrel, he held it up for inspection. "This it? This is the gun Mrs. Goldfield put in the case?"

"Yes, suh. But it won't have her fingerprints on it. It won't have nobody's fingerprints on it, 'cause I wiped dem off."

Annabelle said softly, "Thank you, Wilson, for trying to protect me."

"Twenty-five automatic." Harry looked at Reuchmaire.

The tapping ceased. Reuchmaire turned to Annabelle. "You are absolutely sure that is the gun?"

"Yes, that's it. I took it with me when I went to the anchorage in the Sound, before the storm. The next day, I brought it back and returned to the Sound. I dressed like Bull, flew his pennant, to establish an alibi."

"It can't be. You missed —"

"Jimbo." Edwin pulled his cousin's sleeve. "Come out in the hall."

At the newel post in the foyer, Edwin pointed at the portrait of Goldfield peering ominously over the right bannister at the top of the stairs. "You can only see him from the face up. The bullet I found — which remember was .32 caliber — was lodged further down, in his stomach. Well, I mean in the painting's stomach. Anyway, the night it all happened Bull was over there to the left of the stairs, way off line."

"*Sacre.* Then she must have hit him."

"That's how it looks. Otherwise, there would be a broken pane in the atrium."

A dazed Reuchmaire returned to the parlor. He had been convinced Annabelle had not killed her husband, but now — "Wilson," he asked, "is there anything else? You must tell us everything you know." Things looked black. He had gotten to like Annabelle more and more as this mess unraveled. She had, as Edwin said, a *Frenchness* about her, an *elan*, an *esprit* that elevated her above her boorish husband. He welcomed the pleasure on her features when she was with Edwin. And he was happy for his cousin, too. But he was afraid he had delivered the death blow. It did seem she was guilty. How could he have been so wrong?

"I was trying to protect Miz Annabelle," the butler said sadly. "I knew she did it, that night when I saw her drag the body into the tunnel —"

Annabelle jerked, blinked. "What do you mean?"

Wilson looked trapped. "I'm sorry, Miz Annabelle. I'm really sorry. I won't say any more."

"No," she said, "you must. Tell everything you saw."

He glanced at Mammy Queen and received a firm nod. "I came up from quarters during the storm. I thought I had heard something, faint, but like a gunshot. The lights were out, but by the lightning I saw the open window up in the atrium. I went up to close it and something below scraped, down in the lower hall where the tunnel door is. I looked over the bannister and I could see by the lightning —"

"See what?"

"You, Miz Annabelle. You bent over dragging something, something big, like a man, into the tunnel." His face contorted as though with pain. "I knew what you had done, but I didn't want to know. I went back to quarters and stayed there."

Annabelle put her hands to her face. She looked at Edwin and shook her head violently. "I didn't! After I shot him I just ran."

Wilson continued as though mesmerized, lapsing into Gullah, "Nex day, I taught maybe I bin duh dream, mayb e ain so. Den wen de maid find de blood, I start lookin an I fin de shell from de gun down dey een de hall. E had git unneat de granddaddy clock, but e been dey. Den I bin kno fuh true."

Reuchmaire sat down heavily. "*Merde*," he whispered. That had just about done it. Annabelle was guilty.

Harry came back from the kitchen with the gun in a plastic bag. "I'll take this down and have it checked."

Reuchmaire felt deflated. All his work, all Harry's, had led to *this*. Some sleuth he was!

"Mrs. Goldfield," said Harry, "I guess you'd better come with me."

Annabelle looked bemused. "But — the body. What happened to Bull's — body? I thought you took it."

Harry fingered his Stetson. "No, ma'am."

She shrugged, gave a soft, ironic laugh. "Well, what's the difference? Get my coat, please, Wilson." She kissed Edwin quickly and squeezed his hand. "There's no need for you to leave. Stay awhile. You, too, Dr. Reuchmaire. Wilson will see to you."

"I'll go with you," Edwin said.

"No, don't, please. I'll be fine."

Wilson seemed rooted to the floor. His eyes had moved from one to the other of the speakers, his shoulders drooping with each new revelation, and now he sagged like a whipped dog.

Mammy Queen moved to him, smiling like a teacher approving of a favorite student's recital, and patted his arm. "Hunnah do fuh right, Wilson. Ain dun de wey e look. Now, hunnah fuh git Miz Annabelle e coat, den cum dribe me home. Don worry. De doctah an e cousin ken tek cyare deysefs." With a jangle of beads and shells, she adjusted her shawl and led Wilson from the room to the slow thump of her walking stick.

At the door she turned and fixed Reuchmaire with a stare that prickled his hair. "Dr. ROCKmo an e cuzin ya be all right ya. De doctah mon don tink Miz Annabelle guilty. Dey ain finish look fuh tings. Maybe I should mek um a witch so e'll kno whey tuh look." She leaned back merrily with a long cackle and stuck her pipe in her mouth. "Dey ken leave when dey ready. Now cum."

Edwin flopped into a chair. "I wonder what she meant by that."

Reuchmaire let out a long breath and wondered when he had felt so down. Perhaps a refreshment would help. "I wonder if there is any of that superb coffee."

Edwin got up. "I'll check."

Reuchmaire wandered out into the foyer. He stopped at the newel post and looked up to where Goldfield had stood that fateful night. Edwin was right, it was nowhere near the line to the portrait. Bull's face, haughty as ever, mocked him over the bannister.

He went to the gun case, where Nickie had stood, and tried to recreate the scene. What really happened? Was there any way to know? He plodded up the stairs. General Stuart followed behind. They wandered up to the atrium where Reuchmaire stared up at Goldfield's portrait and the small bullet hole. He could just reach high enough to insert a pen into the hole. The pen pointed straight across the hall, to the door of Goldfield's bedroom. The butterfly danced through Reuchmaire's mind.

On the way to the bedroom he propped his umbrella against the bannister, the tip on the polished floor where remnants of the bloodstain remained. He went to the doorway and aimed at the pen still stuck in the portrait. Why would Goldfield shoot from here? Who was he shooting at? The line of sight was directly over the point where the umbrella tip rested on the floor, exactly where the bloodstains were. And the bloodstains were where the body had fallen.

Beside the bed he opened the control panel for the night vision camera, flipped it on and off, and closed it. He moved among the opulent furniture, appreciated the quality with his fingers but shuddered at the cost. At one of the French windows, he gripped a drape and stared long and hard at the river.

Suddenly, the butterfly alit. He whirled and went to the burned spot in the rug. It was not a small hole a careless ash would make. It was a long scar, where a cigar had fallen and been left. Even a careless man would not do something like that. But a terrified man might.

Reuchmaire darted to the doorway and stared at the portrait on the far wall. The path of the bullet was clear. To the top of the stairs he went and looked down to the gun case where Nickie had stood, and turning, looked up at the atrium to where the window had been open. At the opposite railing he looked down at the night vision camera, the one that had filmed Nickie and only Nickie. Only Nickie! Now he realized what was on that tape. Finally, he went back to where Goldfield had fallen and looked down at the newel post picturing in his mind Annabelle standing there aiming upward. All at once the whole incredible thing jelled in his mind. There were not three guns involved. There were four!

Sacre, Sacre, Sacre! What a terrible, barbaric thing to contemplate. And yet, it had to be. There was just one thing missing, one last key that would pull it together and identify Isadora as the murderer. He sat down heavily on the top stair and leaned his chin on the handle of the umbrella. The General sat close to offer condolences, requesting a scratch with a nudge of his nose.

Edwin, bearing coffee, found them there.

Reuchmaire sipped and thought aloud. "Annabelle was telling the truth. Nickie was telling the truth. Isadora Hawthorne nee Grundel Schmidt was lying."

"But Annabelle is in jail," Edwin said.

The umbrella tip began a staccato on the stair. "We must devise a plan to trap Ms. Hawthorne. We lack one last piece of evidence."

Edwin took a long slow swig, savoring the flavor. "Sure is good coffee. Speaking of evidence," he said, setting down his cup to fish in a pocket, "Harry said to give you this."

Reuchmaire turned the key over in his fingers. "Annabelle's key to the tunnel."

"Yeah. Harry said he got a powerful itch whenever he thought about it."

Reuchmaire stared at the key. Then he stared at the spot where the bloodstain had been. He set the cup and saucer down hard enough to spill coffee and make Edwin flinch.

"Careful," Edwin said, "that's good china..."

But Reuchmaire, General Stuart yipping behind him, had plunged downstairs toward the tunnel door. "Come on," he called to his surprised cousin. "Bring a flashlight." He stopped only long enough to secure the fidgeting General to the newel post. At the far end of the tunnel the door swung open with a moan, admitting a rush of cool river air and light into the narrow entrance. Reuchmaire inhaled the brackish, fishy, marsh smell of the breeze, Lowcountry attar. With it flashed childhood remembrances of muddy, breathless adventures.

"Search backward toward the mansion with the flashlight," he instructed Edwin. "Look in every nook and cranny, floor, ceiling, walls, anywhere a ball might have found its way. I'll search down here as far in as the light will reach."

On hands and knees, he worked along the floor until light faded to shadow then back into the light along the opposite side. Marla would give him a scolding for what he was doing to the knees of his pants. Too bad. As Grandfather Reuchmaire used to tell him, "You're a big boy; you can take a talking to." A search of walls and ceiling revealed only that the tunnel was basically undisturbed after two hundred years. There was nowhere to hide an errant musket ball. Dejected, grimy, he leaned against the doorway. The river flowed placidly by, unconcerned with guilt or innocence, while the breeze stirred the sedge guarding the entrance.

Edwin's light came back down the tunnel. He had found nothing.

"I guess that's that. We're back to square one." Reuchmaire heard General Stuart barking impatiently up in the house. He closed the outer door and followed Edwin and the light back up the tunnel into the hall.

Amidst a cacophony of remonstrating barks from the General, he removed the leash from the post. The General dashed for the tunnel, yanking the leash from Reuchmaire's grasp, and shot through the door an instant before it closed.

What had got into the General? Reuchmaire waited. He expected yelps of remorse to come from behind the door, along with the sound of tiny feet scratching on the wood. None came.

"What are you doing?" Edwin asked.

"Teaching the General a lesson."

"Down there?"

"Yes."

"In the dark?"

"Yes."

Edwin leaned on one hand against the wall. "I presume we shall disregard the General's several hundred years of inherited DNA that predispose him to hunt rats in dark burrows."

Suddenly from the depths of the tunnel came the unmistakable sound of the Rebel Yell.

Reuchmaire fumbled for the key lost somewhere in his clothes. He threw open the door and grabbed the flashlight from Edwin. "Come on!" He plunged down the steps into the tunnel barely avoiding a tumble in his haste.

General Stuart, head high, yodeled between pauses to scratch furiously at the floor of the tunnel just feet from the river door.

It took both hands for Reuchmaire to drag the General from what he was doing. "*Sacre*, Edwin, look!"

In the coarse dust of the floor, detritus from two hundred years of use, and penetrated by the General's wee paws, the flashlight reflected a metallic gleam. Reuchmaire brushed away more of the thin layer. Someone had smoothed it near the door, and for some distance inward. As he cleared away the dust the flat surface of a small round piece of metal emerged. It was embedded in the rock and the rock itself stained darkly around it.

"*Voila!* Edwin, give me your pocket knife."

A few moments prying brought out a pistol ball flattened by impact. It encompassed a smaller circular protrusion in its center.

"Odd looking thing," said Edwin. "What do you suppose that smaller thing is? A different color, apparently a different metal."

Reuchmaire felt his pulse quicken as he pictured the event he believed had taken place here. "Astounding! More than I bargained for, but I believe I know. The police lab will confirm it." He looked at the ball with sadness in his heart. "I am sorry to say it, but this is both good news and bad."

"What?"

"It appears that both Annabelle and Ms. Hawthorne shot Mr. Goldfield. It may convict Annabelle, but fortunately, it will hang Ms. Hawthorne. However, we need her cooperation."

"Oh, right. Just how do you propose to do that?"

"With your help, my boy. You're going art shopping."

Edwin grimaced. "I hate it when you have things for me to do. You probably want me to tell some more lies."

"Tut, tut, my boy, only embellish the truth. Remember what grandfather Reuchmaire says. 'Being honest consists of always telling the truth, but not necessarily all of the truth.' Now, come along and I'll tell you some innocent remarks I want you to let drop to Ms. Hawthorne. And we need to stop by the store and buy a filet mignon for General Stuart. He has solved the case."

Edwin stopped in his tracks. "A filet? You? For the General?"

"Well," Reuchmaire said, chucking the happily panting Yorkie under the chin, "perhaps hamburger. I think the General likes it just as well."

After Edwin departed, Reuchmaire called Nickie and arranged a meeting time. Next he called Marla, to give her instructions. Next

Harry, to ask his cooperation. His final call was to a locksmith. Then, feeling quite pleased with himself, he got coffee and waited for Wilson to return while General Stuart gnawed a bourbon ball and took a nap.

* * *

Isadora excused herself from the customer to whom she was showing paintings and went to answer the phone. She started in spite of herself when she heard Nickie's voice.

"Ni — ah, Mr., ah, Nichols. How are you?" She wanted to scream at him for calling her here. "Ah, yes, Mr. Nichols, I can be free by eleven. Meet you? At the usual place. Of course, I'll be delighted."

She replaced the receiver and took a moment to compose herself. "I am sorry, Mr. ah…?"

"Rottweiler. Erwin Rottweiler."

"Yes, Mr. Rottweiler. And you were saying?"

"Oh, about the Goldfield estate. I hear it's going into probate."

Isadora forced calm on herself. "Yes, well, I suppose that's the usual procedure." She and Nickie had better get in quick before the safe was opened.

She tried not to appear rushed as she showed the rest of the works. It was obvious that Mr. Rottweiler knew little about art and was not rich enough to be a scam prospect. She got rid of him quickly. Fuming, she drove to the small church and waited for Nickie.

Moments later he roared up on his bike.

She was out of her car as soon as he rolled into the church yard. He could see she was pissed. Easy does it, he told himself, she won't do anything here. She wants the money too bad.

"Yeah, I know," he nodded, when she started in on him about the call. He hoped he didn't look as nervous as he felt. This had to be played cool, like a movie role, like Bogie. "But I heard something you ought to know, about the probate of Goldfield's estate."

"What?"

He relaxed some. Now he had her going. He had saved their bacon before with some item he had picked up on the street, and she knew it.

"The safe's going to be opened for probate tomorrow. If we're going to get the money, we better do it tonight."

Isadora smiled and offered him a cigarette. "O.K., sorry I blew up. You were right to call."

He took a deep drag and let the smoke out slowly. "Look, I been thinking. It ain't too smart for the two of us to go back in."

"Oh? Why not?"

"I think I got a tail on me. I think the police are still checking me out. Best thing for me to do is beat it, clear town."

"But I need you to open the safe."

Nickie shook his head and ground out the cigarette under his boot. He handed her a piece of paper, pleased that his fingers were steady. He was doing O.K. He fancied he even talked a little like Cagney. "That's the combo to the safe. You don't need me."

She looked at the numbers. "How —"

"The other night. I had just got the safe cracked when I heard the commotion upstairs. Didn't have time to get anything, but that's the combination."

"Ohh, Nickie," she cooed, looking really pleased, "this is great. Yes, it's probably better that only one of us go. Less chance of discovery."

"Yeah, that's what I thought, too."

"Good. Look, why don't you head on out and we'll meet next Saturday in Norfolk, where we agreed."

He paused for effect, just like De Niro or Nolte would play it. "Yeah, O.K. Sure you can do it?"

"No problem." She squeezed his arm. "See you Saturday."

"You bet." He grinned, and started the bike.

Before heading back to Beaufort, she smoked a cigarette to let Nickie get on ahead. Yeah, she thought, this will work out better. Get Nickie out of town and the cops will quiet down. And it will give me time to decide about the Catskills. Maybe I'll call Nickie. Or maybe I'll just disappear. By this time tomorrow I'll be long gone from this burg.

Chapter 21

Isadora gripped the key, an ear to the tunnel door. The hall clock struck midnight. With a small flashlight she found the lock and inserted the key. Careful to make no noise, she began cracking the door inch by inch while she surveyed the empty lower hall. Key and flashlight went into her purse. She insured the .32 automatic purchased that afternoon from a Savannah pawn shop was in its secret pocket. She moved into the hallway to the newel post at the base of the stairs. The house was quiet and only a lone low light shone from across the foyer in the study, her destination. Upstairs through open atrium drapes moonlight flooded hall and stairs with a pale and ghostly hue. Hugging the left bannister she crept up the stairs and turned left into Bull's bedroom. She turned off the night vision camera, then returned to the lower hall to pass unnoticed across the camera's inert field. Just an added precaution, although it didn't really matter what the video showed. She would be long gone before anyone saw it. But she was always thorough. In the study she went quickly to the portrait of Bull's grandfather and lifted the painting from the wall to expose the safe.

"Good evening, Ms. Hawthorne."

Isadora whirled. Reuchmaire stood in the doorway, General Stuart cradled in one arm. He flipped on the overhead lights and stepped into the room, followed by Edwin and Annabelle.

Reuchmaire came forward and blocked Isadora's path with his umbrella. "And what brings you here this night, may I ask? Rather a late hour to come calling, although, as always, we find you dressed most fashionably. Perhaps for a trip, eh?"

Isadora's initial shock changed to cold calculation. Her eyes flicked from one to the other of the group as though weighing the possibility of escape. Edwin blocked the doorway. Annabelle eased into a chair and stared icicles at Isadora.

"I came for my check." Isadora casually opened her purse and extracted a cigarette.

"Your check? Indeed?" Reuchmaire set General Stuart on the floor. "And where might that be?"

The Yorkie, after giving Isadora a suspicious sniff and dodging a roughly thrust foot, retired to watch the proceedings from near the window.

Isadora blew a cloud of smoke and motioned to the safe. "In there."

"I see. And how did you plan to open it? Fast Nickie isn't here." Even though she tried not to show it, he saw he had hit home.

"I don't know what you mean. Who is Fast Nickie?"

With exaggerated aplomb, Reuchmaire offered her a seat. "Fast Nickie is the person from whom you got the combination to the safe, is he not? Your accomplice in the art scam you've been running."

"You're insane. Bull gave me the combination."

"Did he?"

"Yes, there is a great deal about Bull and I you are unaware of." She flicked a superior glance at Annabelle. "Indeed?" said Reuchmaire.

"We were going to be married. After he divorced — her."

Annabelle slowly shook her head. "You poor fool."

"But, Ms. Hawthorne," Reuchmaire said, "that does not explain your presence here tonight. This is a rather unusual hour to come calling."

"I, ah, heard today that the safe was to be emptied tomorrow and the contents impounded for probate. The check in there is for an art purchase Bull made that turned out to be a forgery. I had him hold the check while I obtained the original, which is now in my gallery. I wanted the check — ten thousand dollars is a lot of money — and did not want to have to wait out the probate process."

"Not to mention the hundred grand Bull kept in there," Annabelle added.

Isadora ignored her and crushed the unfinished cigarette out in an ashtray. "I simply came for what is mine."

How delightful, Reuchmaire, thought, it is exactly as Nickie described. Now to open the gambit. He stepped aside and bowed, "Then by all means take it and leave."

Isadora narrowed her eyes at him. "You mean, open the safe and go?"

The doorbell rang and Reuchmaire paused. A moment later Wilson passed down the hall towards the front door and Reuchmaire, satisfied, resumed. "Absolutely. If the check is yours, I agree that to submit it to litigation, which could last months, if not years, is unnecessary. None will be the wiser. You will be gone and Beaufort will be free of another unscrupulous Yankee."

Isadora seemed about to make a retort but apparently thought better of it. Taking a slip of paper from her purse she stepped to the safe.

"And what is that you have?" asked Reuchmaire.

"The combination Bull gave me," she said, glancing at the paper as she turned the dial. "He wrote it down for me."

"Then it must be correct."

"Of course it is! I told you he gave it to me. We were very close, and he trusted me. There, see." She opened the safe with a flourish. "And here is my check."

Reuchmaire bowed with a greater flourish, and said, "You, madam, are a liar. Bull Goldfield could not have given you that combination unless he did it this afternoon, and we both know that to be impossible."

Isadora wheeled, fists clenched, color rising. "How dare you call me a liar, you — you two-bit country shrink."

"Ah, Ms. Hawthorne, 'what a tangled web we weave'... You are not Isadora Hawthorne, you are Grundel Schmidt, of New York, of various small towns from California to Maine, originally from right here in li'l ol' Beaufort. You have cultivated your false accent well. And this is your accomplice, Fast Nickie Machetto." Harry escorted Nickie into the room.

Reuchmaire was delighted to see Isadora — Grundel — turn pale. For once, she was speechless.

"Bull could not have given you that combination, Ms. Schmidt," he said, "because this afternoon I had a locksmith install it, replacing the old one which is on file at the police station. What you have in your hand I instructed Nickie to give to you with the story that the night of the murder he had learned that combination when he opened the safe. Actually he never got to the safe and did not know the combination. You have just used a combination that has been in the safe for only a few hours. Isn't that so, Nickie?"

"Yeah, Doc. Just like you said. I never got to the safe. That slip she's got are the new numbers you gave me."

"You stupid little *bastard*!" Isadora started for Nickie. Harry stepped forward and Nickie scooted behind him. Reuchmaire halted her with the umbrella tip to her stomach.

"Tut, tut, Ms. Schmidt. Let's not lose our temper."

She flung the check in his face. "All right. I conned Bull for the price of the painting. But that was all. It was just an art scam. After he proposed, I told him everything."

"Tch, tch, tch, Ms. Hawthorne. Such a propensity to prevaricate." Reuchmaire lowered the umbrella and motioned to her to be seated. He was thoroughly enjoying himself. This was better than a game with Harry. This was better than their Gibaud vs Lazako match, because now each move was his own, not a replay from memory. And she was falling for each one so beautifully. "But let us leave for the moment that crime, to which you have just confessed, and deal with the more serious one, the murder of Bull Goldfield."

"You're not going to pin that on me." She reached into the open purse and extracted another cigarette.

"Oh, but I am, Ms. Hawthorne." Before she could stop him Reuchmaire reached into her purse and withdrew the key. He held it before her and said, "With this."

"Bull gave me that." She laughed, and gestured casually at Annabelle. "I used it to come and go through the tunnel when she was away. Do you have such a hard time realizing Bull and I were having an affair? You can't seem to understand that we were going to be married. I had no reason to kill him."

"Only passion, Ms. Hawthorne, only passion."

The flash of comprehension that shot across her face told him he had delivered a body blow. Although having heard the wildest ploys from patients who wished to evade issues, he was none the less intrigued. Isadora Hawthorne nee Grundel Schmidt moved coolly from one lie to another as easily as a mechanic discards an inappropriate tool for a more functional one. He clasped his hands behind his back and tapped the umbrella lightly on the carpet, contemplating her with a sad, almost sympathetic, smile. At last, he thought, we come to the end of it. Now, for checkmate.

"I fully believe you," he said, drawing a surprised look. "I believe you were in love with Bull, or thought you were. That night he told you he was breaking it off, that the affair was over, just as he had done with countless other women. I can just imagine the plans you had for a life as a billionaire's wife, perhaps even abandoning the art scam to bask in luxury. The rejection was too much for you and you threatened to shoot him, bringing from your purse a pistol we mistakenly thought was his but is in fact registered to one Grundel Schmidt of New York. He was so startled, so afraid, he dropped his cigar on the rug upstairs where it lay and smoldered, leaving a long, ugly scar. He fled. Something a man like Bull Goldfield would not do unless he felt extremely threatened.

"He reached the top of the stairs, and at that moment, amidst storm and confusion, a most extraordinary coincidence occurred. The three of you — yourself, Nickie, and Annabelle — all fired at the same time."

Ms. Hawthorne slowly sank back in the chair and listened impassively. She drummed her fingers on the arm of the chair. "What an absurd notion. You can't prove it."

"Oh, but Ms. Hawthorne, I can. This," he held up a pistol ball, "is from the gun Nickie fired and was found outside the mansion by my cousin Edwin and Annabelle. This," he brought an object from a pocket, "a bullet from your gun struck — ironically — Mr. Goldfield's portrait in the upper hall, but not Mr. Goldfield, at whom you were shooting. Ballistics will confirm it came from your gun. And, finally this." He brought out the flattened ball he had dug out of the floor of the tunnel. "This is the most horrible, the most incriminating evidence of all.

"It is the ball fired by you, point blank into Goldfield's chest, where, after dragging him to the mouth of the tunnel, you carefully placed the muzzle of the second dueling pistol to obliterate the wound made by the bullet already in his body. A bullet that was there from the gun fired by his wife, Annabelle. It is her bullet that dropped Goldfield at the top of the stairs but did not kill him."

Annabelle jerked upright. "I — I didn't kill him?"

"No, my dear, you did not."

"Thank God," she sighed, and buried her face in her hands. Edwin placed a comforting hand on her shoulder.

"I'd like to know how you think you can prove that," Isadora said angrily.

"The blood, Ms. Hawthorne. The bloodstain at the top of the stairs was too small for the gaping wound created by your shot in the tunnel. The floor of the tunnel held a greater stain than the one in the house. And this misshapen mass," he paused to show the flattened pistol ball, "is Annabelle's bullet mashed into the pistol ball by the impact with the floor of the tunnel. A mass imbedded so firmly in the shale you were unable to remove it, so you hid it by smoothing the detritus of the floor over it."

Reuchmaire glanced at Harry, who stood hands in pockets in the back of the room with his eyes nearly closed and his lined face set with an expression of approval. He gave Reuchmaire a reassuring nod.

Reuchmaire continued to recount events. Isadora paled and her lips formed into a thin crease. Her eyes, riveted on him as he paced about the room like a lawyer before a jury, smoldered. He stopped before her.

"Your aim," he said, holding up the ball and bullet mashed together, "was perfect. So perfect that it will hang you."

"You can't prove I fired that gun. It was Fast Nickie."

"Ah, there is more, Ms. Hawthorne, much more." He reached inside his jacket and brought out a linen hanky. "This, I believe, is yours, found by Wilson in the hall the morning after the murder." Isadora attempted a casual glance at the hanky but her countenance seemed to slip just a bit, as though she felt her position slowly eroding, an island being eaten away by a tide of evidence.

At Reuchmaire's signal Harry opened a cabinet, turned on the TV inside and inserted a tape in the accompanying VCR. Isadora watched the scene in stony silence: Nickie fired the gun, crept up the stairs then, moments later, ran back down and out of the picture.

"So what?" she said. "That just proves it was Nickie."

"No, Ms. Hawthorne." He nodded at Harry to replay the tape. "See, Ms. Hawthorne, there is Nickie shooting the gun. Then, see how he moves slowly upstairs in a pose of disbelief. Were it not for his mask you would see the astonishment on his face. And, most importantly, look at his right hand. It still holds the pistol. Now here, moments later, he runs down the stairs — there, Harry, stop it."

The frozen frame showed Nickie about to exit to picture left. "See his hands, Ms. Hawthorne, they are both empty. He left the gun at the top of the stairs. At the top of the stairs where you, realizing Goldfield was not dead, told Nickie to leave and you would take care of things. Nickie, panic stricken, fled. It was after he left that you went to the bedroom and turned off the camera then drug the semiconscious Goldfield into the tunnel and killed him. You weighted his body, using a plastic sheet from the patio construction to contain the weights, ingots and shot you got from the gun room with the same key used for the tunnel. You then hid the body in the river."

"That's absurd." Isadora lit yet another cigarette. Her hand shook just perceptibly. "How could I have gotten his body upstream against the current?"

Reuchmaire raised his eyebrows. "Oh? And how did you know where the body was?"

She blinked. "I — I read it in the newspaper."

Reuchmaire laughed lightly. "Well, perhaps you did —"

"Or maybe you used our old high school trick, Grundel." Marla stepped into the room, delighted at the expression frozen on Isadora's face. "Just walked it along underwater. You couldn't swim with that weight, but you could walk. And should a late barge happen down the channel, no one would see."

Isadora shifted sullenly in her chair. "And most importantly, look at the screen," Reuchmaire went on. Beyond Nickie's fleeing figure there is the other pistol still in its case on the display shelf, as yet unused. That is the pistol you used to kill Goldfield and then cleaned to remove all traces of its being fired, as well as any fingerprints. Particularly your fingerprints. It should have had *some* fingerprints on it, Ms. Hawthorne. It should have had *my* fingerprints on it from the day before when I was here to inspect those pistols for the purchase Goldfield refused. Afterwards, you returned both pistols to their case carefully leaving Nickie's prints, and unknowingly mine, on the gun he fired where they were found by Chief Doyle.

"And this," said Reuchmaire, holding up the key he had taken from Isadora's purse, "is the clincher. The literal key."

"Bull gave me that key," she insisted.

"Oh, no, Ms. Hawthorne. This is the key with which he let you into the mansion the night of your *liaison.* Entering through the tunnel where no one would see. This key never left Mr. Goldfield's person, did it, Wilson?"

"No, suh. He kept that key with him always."

"Always, Ms. Hawthorne," said Reuchmaire, "as anyone who lives in Beaufort will tell you. He was never seen at social functions without its chain draped most conspicuously across that, ah, hideous orange vest he wore, or twirling it casually with his hand. It is even in the portrait of him in the upstairs hall. Isn't that so, Annabelle?"

"Yes." Annabelle stared serenely at Isadora, enjoying the progress of events. "The only other key is a copy I had made. I used it the day of — the murder."

"Further proof, Ms. Hawthorne. See this mark." Reuchmaire held the key for her inspection. "It is the locksmith's proof mark made over two hundred years ago when the tunnel was built and it is only on Bull Goldfield's key. You could have a hundred copies made and not one would have that mark stamped on it.

"You took that key from his body after you killed him because you needed it to get back into the house. The door into the house, designed to automatically swing closed, has a spring latch that must be held open with the key. You needed to get back into the house to get into the gunroom. That key not only opens the tunnel doors, it also opens the gunroom where you obtained weight for the body and where you cleaned the pistol you used. And in cleaning the pistol, got gun solvent on your gloves and on the handkerchief you inadvertently left behind. The one with your real initials, GS, embroidered in the pattern.

"It was that solvent I smelled on your gloves the morning we met on Bay Street where you and Nickie performed your *modus operandi*, a fake purse snatching, for departing a town you had worked, and, in this case, to get the key to Nickie for another try at the safe. It was then that I saw that very same key in your purse, the morning after you killed Bull Goldfield."

Reuchmaire leaned forward with both hands on his umbrella handle. "There is just so much evidence, Ms. Hawthorne. So terribly, terribly much." He turned away in contempt, as a matador scorning a bull. "Harry," he said, and jerked a thumb toward the glaring woman.

Harry reached for his cuffs.

Isadora slid a hand into her purse and withdrew the pistol. "Let's not be hasty."

Reuchmaire turned at the collective gasp. Harry stopped. Fast Nickie scrunched his slight frame close behind Harry. Edwin put an arm around Annabelle, moving her aside, and General Stuart retreated to a more strategic position beneath a table draped with an ornate brocade cloth.

"Easy does it, everyone." Isadora moved toward the window which she unlocked and raised with one hand while pointing the gun with the other. "I'll be out of your way shortly."

General Stuart's withdrawal beneath the table was not as complete as he would have wished. The tip of his tiny tail protruded from beneath the cloth, only an inch or so, but sufficient for Isadora, as she positioned herself for a step through the window, to unknowingly place a spike heel directly upon it.

The General, attacked from the rear, leapt from cover emitting his shrillest Rebel Yell. Isadora shrieked, wheeled, and fired blindly. The yell ceased.

A pang of fear surged through Reuchmaire. "*Sacre Bleu! La scelerat!*" He leapt for the gun.

General Stuart was quicker. Narrowly missed, deafened, and outgunned, he shot past Isadora. His trailing leash snapped like a whip around her ankles. She tipped over, out the window.

Reuchmaire and Harry reached the window together. Isadora lay entangled in one of the large azaleas bordering the house. Just coming around the corner of the house was Buster, gun drawn and ready for action.

"Read her her rights, Buster," said Harry. "Wait for me in the car. You won't need the gun. She's disarmed."

Marla took Harry's place at the window. "By the way, Grundel, you still owe me fifty bucks."

Harry tipped his hat to Annabelle. "Mrs. Goldfield, it'll be best if you'll come in and let's talk about your status. I'm afraid I'll have to charge you."

Annabelle looked startled. "Oh, yes, of course. Will the morning be all right?"

Harry grimaced and shuffled his feet. "Well, Ma'am, that's not really procedural —"

"Please." She placed a hand on his arm. "I promise to be there."

"Well — sure, that'll be fine." He touched his hat brim and left.

Annabelle turned to Edwin. "Please stay with me tonight."

Edwin squeezed her hand. "You bet. Let's go have a drink in the cupola."

Marla stifled a yawn and headed for the door. "Jimsy, my love. Gotta be at work early tomorrow. Let's have dinner tomorrow night at your place. Edwin can fix."

Reuchmaire, after tracking down General Stuart's new headquarters beneath the kitchen table, agreed to drive Nickie back to the police station where he left his bike. They pulled out of the mansion's drive, the General snoring in Reuchmaire's lap.

"Doc, it just hit me."

"What, Nickie?"

"What happened on the stairs that night."

"Tell me about it."

"I went up the stairs and she was there over Goldfield's body. He was lying there face down, not moving. 'He's dead,' she said. 'You shot him.' Jeeze, I was scared. I didn't know what to do. Then she told me not to worry, she'd take care of it. Told me just to get out and go back to Bluffton and wait for her to call."

"And you did."

"Sure I did. I was really scared. Then she must have done just what you said, just the way you said."

"I think so."

"But, how did you know?"

"It seemed logical. I just didn't think you did it."

"Just like you knew about our art scam. How did you figure that out?"

"Well, Nickie, it seemed quite a coincidence that of all the women in Beaufort, you should pick Isadora's purse to grab."

Nickie was silent for a moment, frowning as though trying to put it all together. "Yeah, I guess it is pretty logical."

Reuchmaire waited until Nickie finished his cathartic revelation of the art scam, including his declaration that Isadora was with Goldfield that night. "You know, Nickie, I finally remembered where I had seen Ms. Hawthorne — Isadora — before, when she was blonde, not brunette. It was the day you got out of Allendale last summer. I was there, remember?"

"Oh, yeah. You wished me luck."

"She was the one who picked you up, was she not?"

"Jeeze, Doc. You're a genius."

"Thank you, Nickie. Now, let's talk about how you can help out even more."

Chapter 22

"How nice." Reuchmaire, seated at the dining table read for the third time the account of the Goldfield case in the *Beaufort Times*. "They spelled my name correctly. Perhaps it will be on the evening news."

"Your fifteen minutes," said Marla. On the other side of the table she was busy writing onto a small orange ticket stub.

Reuchmaire looked at her over the top of his glasses. "What *are* you doing, my dear?"

"Getting Cissy a bike." Marla dropped a completed stub into a large-mouthed gallon jar half-filled with other stubs.

"How?"

She patted the jar. "With these. Church raffle." Reuchmaire set the paper aside. "How can you be sure…"

"She'll win? Easy. I bought all the tickets but one and put her name on all of them."

"I see. What if by remote chance that one is drawn?"

"No problem. I sold that one to her."

"That strikes me as — well, illegal."

Marla shrugged. "The church gets the money, and since I'm running the raffle Mrs. Taliaferro will be none the wiser."

Reuchmaire scowled and shook his head. "Illegal."

"Jimsy, look at it this way, suppose you are selling raffle tickets and the first person you approach says, 'sure, I'll buy 'em all.' Is that illegal?"

"I'm sure it is," he said, giving his beard a thoughtful scratch, "I just can't think of how."

"Nonsense! I'm that first person, that's all.

He threw up his hands in surrender. "Edwin! What's for dinner?"

"A quickie," his cousin called from the kitchen. "Grits and salmon, succotash on the side."

"With butter?"

"Jimbo!"

"Just asking." Reuchmaire strolled into the kitchen to observe.

"Only a dash of olive oil in the grits," Edwin said. He stirred the drained contents of the last of three cans of salmon in spring water into grits simmering on the stove. A tablespoon of dill weed and two tablespoons of Teriyaki sauce followed, stirred thoroughly, and the mixture was set aside to cool.

"Looks gross," said Reuchmaire.

"Oh, Jimsy," said Marla, "you scarf it down every time Edwin fixes it." She removed Captain Semmes from her lap and got up. "I'll get the salad. Sit down and enjoy a drink, Edwin."

"Comfort food," said Edwin accepting Marla's offer.

Captain Semmes relocated to Edwin's lap and gave him a hopeful look. Edwin began massaging the good ear, drawing a contented look and a loud purr. "Be brave, Jimbo, tomorrow I'll fix hamburgers."

"Hamburgers? Red meat?"

"Nothing wrong with lean red meat. Has no more cholesterol than fish or chicken. It's not so much what you eat as how much of what you eat. No more than a quarter of a pound a day."

"Just one hamburger? I'll starve."

"We'll have roasted potatoes with it — basted with olive oil, vegetable seasoning and pepper. They'll fill you up. Fruit for dessert."

"We'll see." Reuchmaire hated to admit it, but the food was good. Hardly traditional, but good (once you got used to it), and he had already begun to lose weight in the short time since Edwin's arrival.

Edwin leaned back in his chair and sipped a drink from a frosty glass. "What I don't understand is how you knew what happened between Bull Goldfield and Isadora — Grundel — up in the bedroom."

A coy smile edged Reuchmaire's lips. "Well, it seemed logical."

"You guessed."

"It was an educated guess."

"What about the second pistol?" Marla called from the kitchen. "How did you know Goldfield wasn't dead? How did you know

Annabelle's bullet didn't kill him?"

Reuchmaire tapped his head with a finger. "I hab de sight. I got de juju."

"You got de luck," Edwin said.

"What is that you're drinking?"

"My newest creation, in honor of your solving the Goldfield case. Double Beefeater's on cracked ice, a splash of tonic and a wedge of lime, stirred seven times. I call it a double-oh-seven."

"Well, quite flattering, my boy, but I'm afraid you're a bit presumptive. Double-oh-seven was an international counterspy. Fictional, at that."

"Ah, Jimbo, this is just the beginning. Who knows where it may lead."

"It had better lead me back to my patients whom I have badly neglected."

Edwin slid the glass across the table. "The secret is keeping the gin in the freezer, the tonic and lime in the 'fridge, and use cracked ice. Small cubes for optimum chill. The Queen Mother's drink, I'm told, although I'm don't know which Queen Mother."

"If you drink it, it must be healthy."

"Well, it's my one vice. Limited to one — or maybe two, it isn't UN-healthy. Try it."

"Ahh, that is nice. Will you fix me one?"

"Sure." Edwin dismissed Captain Semmes and went to the kitchen.

Marla brought tossed salad and bread to the table. "Jimsy, I think you did it to protect Annabelle."

"Eh, did what?"

"Said that Annabelle didn't kill her husband. Now she can't be tried for murder."

"Perhaps attempted murder, perhaps not tried at all."

Edwin called above the sound of the icemaker crushing ice. "Not at all?"

Reuchmaire joined his hands behind his head and leaned back, basking in the attention, the company, a good drink, and food (possibly good). What more could one ask? He had turned out to be an effective sleuth after all. "There is only one witness to Annabelle's presence in the mansion that night."

Edwin and Marla chimed, "Who?"

"Annabelle. And she does not have to testify against herself."

"What of the footprint?" asked Edwin, handing Reuchmaire the drink and reclaiming his own.

"It was faint. Anyway, Annabelle and Isadora share the same shoe size."

"Her bullet?"

"Not found in the body, and too misshapen to be matched to the gun."

Edwin thought a moment. "What of the other flash we saw on the tape, the small one to the side when Nickie fried?"

A puckish twitch played at Reuchmaire's mouth. "Probably lightning."

Edwin smiled, sipped his drink, and shrugged. "Okay by me."

"Jimsy, you're a genius," said Marla.

"Thank you, my dear. Edwin this double-oh-seven is superb. The gin packs a nice icy punch enhanced by sweet tartness of tonic and lime."

"Lemmie try," said Marla, sweeping Reuchmaire's glass from his hand. "Whoosh! That'll curl the lace on your drawers! Make me one, Edwin."

"Sure. Back shortly."

Reuchmaire knew that after dinner Marla would leave to go to Savannah for another performance at the Lion. He didn't care. The case had left him ebullient, as success so often does, and self-satisfaction fosters tolerance.

The house was packed. A sea of faces was riveted to the velvet curtains closed across the stage. The expectant murmur filling the hall fell silent as a spotlight flashed upon the curtains. From the orchestra came a provocative overture. At stage center, front row table, Reuchmaire sipped his brandy and nodded at the appreciative smile flashed by the Hollywood producer, Mr. Goldwyn (it was the only Hollywood name he could think of). A fanfare parted the curtains and there in the spotlight behind gently waving coral-pink fans was Magnificent Marla, the Vamp of Savannah - his Marla. She flowed into her routine and the crowd sighed. Every eye followed her across the stage and back, across and back, every mouth scarcely drew breath. Goldwyn leaned over and whispered, "We must discuss a contract. I'm prepared to offer —"

Reuchmaire cut him off with a gesture. "I'm afraid not. She is retiring after this performance. To marry me."

"Impossible!"

"No, it is true. In any case, she is the one you should discuss it with, not I."

Goldwyn sat back, dumbfounded. "You are an unusual man, Reuchmaire." Turning again to the stage, he added, "And a very, very fortunate one."

Edwin brought in Marla's drink. She kissed at him and accepted the glass with both hands. Elbows on table she smiled dreamily at Reuchmaire. "What about Isadora? Do you think she'll be convicted?"

"Two bits says not," Edwin said.

Reuchmaire blinked away Goldwyn. "What? Oh, yes, of the art scam, certainly. We have the doctored painting, and Nickie has agreed to go state's evidence and describe their partnership. I convinced him of the wisdom of it. Of murder?" He waggled a hand. "That's a bit iffy. Everything's circumstantial. We still can't positively place Isadora in the mansion the night of the murder."

"But what about Nickie's testimony?"

"His word against hers. Maybe a jury will believe it, maybe not. No one except Nickie, and of course Goldfield, saw her there. Wilson saw her from above and behind, not a positive identification at all."

* * *

It was one of those rare days in the Lowcountry, but not uncommon in spring, when the temperature was warm, but not uncomfortably so, and the humidity low, before the wet, wilting heat of summer arrived. A drive with the windows down was a pleasure. Reuchmaire took a swing through the narrow quiet streets of the Point, among stately old homes afire with pink and red and white clouds of azalea and dogwood. Edwin was flying Annabelle to the Bahamas to retrieve her yacht, the big one. Harry was fishing, but had invited Reuchmaire over later for a game. Marla, working as usual, insisted she would not be late, and had promised to fix him Edwin's recipe for shrimp Creole.

Such a glorious day it was that Reuchmaire found himself not the least perturbed over a lengthy wait at the bridge. He simply called up Chessmaster on his new laptop to plan his next move. The computer was an early birthday present from Marla in celebration of the conclusion of the Goldfield Case (as they now referred to it). Even though his heart fluttered when he discovered what these little machines cost, he was able to assuage his unease when he found that with its assistance he was able to hold his own with Harry, or nearly so. And that was a considerable improvement. Happiness has its price, he sighed, and fortunately Marla is willing to supply it. He must get her something really nice as a wedding gift, perhaps a new purse. She frequently complained about the age of the old one, about the size of a small backpack and containing enough paraphernalia to sustain a squad of marines for a week (or so he was convinced). He made a mental note to check for sales.

A soft breeze rippled the Inland Waterway and the sun turned the sweep of the river into a sequined gown. The last tall mast of the parade of boats passed through and the swing bridge ground and clanked slowly around to release the line of cars. Out toward Frogmore, he hummed a passage from *The Rite of Spring*, while all around flowers budded, trees displayed a fuzzy rebirth of leaves, and acres and acres of marsh grass shone with a pale green hue. Fish leapt in the tidal creeks and herons, egrets, ospreys and pelicans were about their business in the wide prairies. He left the highway onto the rutted weedy track of a road to Mammy Queen's.

She was on the porch, overflowing her chair as usual, clad in one of her flowered dresses. Her shrewd eyes watched his approach from beneath the brim of her straw hat as she popped snap beans and dropped them into a pot. The unlit corcob pipe was clamped in a corner of her mouth. Her shell baubles glittered and danced with the swift sure motion of her hands, she not even watching the beans as they popped and fell into the pot.

"Mammy Queen, how de body?" he called as he got out of the car.

"I tell Gawd t'enk ya," she grinned. "Mi gout ain so bad, an mi lumbago tolerable. Ya kno I hab new great-granchile, a nex one fuh me to fuss ober. Cum ya, Dr. ROCKmo'." She removed the pipe from her mouth and patted the sofa. "Sit wit me an tell me how oona do."

He sat in the old couch, relocated once off an adventuresome spring, and declined an offer of tobacco as Mammy Queen stoked up her corncob. A fragrant cloud soon enveloped her. The chickens in the dirt yard eyed him curiously and went back to their business. Reuchmaire heard the old dog beneath the porch emit a lazy exhale.

"Wan tea? I jus made it." She filled two glasses on a low wooden table. "I se Chief Harry de oda day. E look good. E say e wife an churn oba de flu. E speak bout oona, too. E say how oona hep him so wid de Goldfield ting. E a shame da rich man hab tuh die. Shame fuh anybody to dead. But e ain bin da good mon. Wilson tell me. E tell me how bad e treat Miz Annabelle. Miz Annabelle always bin good to Wilson."

The tea was cold and sweet and went down well in the warmth of the day. He listened to Mammy Queen talk for a while about her family, about the Lowcountry, about the islands and Beaufort and the many people she had seen come and go. Her voice was a melodious accompaniment to the birds and crickets in the trees around the house and off in the marsh all punctuated by the soft snap, snap, snap of beans being popped and dropped into the pot.

"Were you expecting someone?" He was thinking of the two glasses she had set out.

"Well," she said, "oona neba kno win somebody might cum by. Maybe I bin duh expect ya." At his raised eyebrows she cackled among a jolly rattle of baubles and blew a cloud of smoke. "So, wha oona cum out ya fuh see Mammy Queen fuh?"

"I came to thank you, Mammy Queen. To thank you for helping me figure out Goldfield's murder."

She shrugged, set the beans aside. "I ain dun much."

"But you did. You told us where to look."

"Oona looked whey oona wanted tuh."

Reuchmaire tapped the umbrella lightly on the floor. "Well, maybe so. But oona tink you hep."

"Doctah Rockmo'! Oona speak Gullah!"

He laughed, realizing he actually had.

Her eyes filled with mischief. "I shoulda made oona a witch. Den e wouldn't a taken oona so long. But den oona would hafa bin a witch, an da wouldn't be a good ting."

"Definitely not." He tried to imagine what it would be like.

"But I coulda cured oona. I use de juju and dribe de witch from ya body. Jus as oona dribe de spirits from peepol head."

"Well, it's not quite the same."

"Ohh, yes, Mr. Doctah Mon, e de same ting! E all up ya." She tapped her gray hair with the pipe. "Sumtime peepol believe wha real. Sumtime dey believe wha ain real. Ef dey believe de juju, den e work. Ef dey believe de si-ky-a-tree, den dat work. Ain da true?"

Reuchmaire replaced his empty glass on the table and got up to leave. "Maybe you're right, Mammy Queen. Maybe you're right. But thank you, anyway, for all you taught me. I will use it in my, ah, medicine. My si-ky-a-tree."

Mammy Queen extended a plump hand adorned with rings. "Oona a good mon, Dr. Rockmo. A good mon." She pulled a small pouch from her waist and extracted a lozenge. "Cyare fuh a candy?"

Reuchmaire caught the faint smell of almonds and drew back in spite of himself. "Why, ah, no. No, thank you." He patted his waist. "I, ah, I've been trying to lose weight. I'm avoiding sweets."

With an enormous grin, Mammy Queen popped the lozenge into her mouth. All the way up the road to the highway he was sure he could still hear her laughing.

The End

Printed in the United States
108392LV00004B/408/A

9 781413 736151